IF YOU WANT A JOB DONE RIGHT . . .

"It's my wagon."

The worker stopped, then turned toward him. "What?"

"This wagon," Parker replied. "It belongs to me. And the purchase contract says that it will be fit for travel. The way you are packing the wheel hubs, it ain't fit."

"Get out of here, kid. Go bother someone else." The worker turned back to the wheel.

"No, sir, I'm not going anywhere. I'm going to make sure you do that right," Parker insisted.

The worker had just scooped out a paddleful of grease. This time though, instead of putting it around the wheel hub, he turned quickly and wiped it across Parker's shirt.

"Hey!" Parker shouted in surprise and anger.

The big man laughed. "Now get out of here, kid, and let a man do his work. *Your* wagon," he said, laughing again. "That's a good one."

Parker walked over to a drum of coal oil, wet a cloth, and used it to clean the grease from the front of his shirt. That accomplished, he picked up a bullwhip and returned to the wagon. . . .

Ralph Compton

Demon's Pass

A Ralph Compton Novel
by Robert Vaughn

A SIGNET BOOK

SIGNET
Published by the Penguin Group
Penguin Group (USA) LLC, 375 Hudson Street,
New York, New York 10014

USA | Canada | UK | Ireland | Australia | New Zealand | India | South Africa | China
penguin.com
A Penguin Random House Company

First published by Signet, an imprint of New American Library,
a division of Penguin Group (USA) LLC

First Printing, August 2000

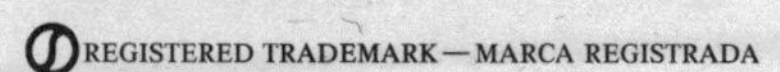

ISBN 978-0-451-19763-4

Printed in the United States of America
20 19 18 17 16 15 14 13 12 11

The Immortal Cowboy

The saga of the "American Cowboy" was sparked by the turmoil that followed the Civil War, and the passing of more than a century has by no means diminished the flame.

True, the old days and the old ways are but treasured memories, and the old trails have grown dim with the ravages of time, but the spirit of the cowboy lives on.

In my travels—which include Texas, Oklahoma, Kansas, Nebraska, Colorado, Wyoming, New Mexico, and Arizona—there's something within me that remembers. While I am walking these plains and mountains for the first time, there is this feeling that a part of me is eternal, that I have known these old trails before. I believe it is the undying spirit of the frontier calling, allowing me, through the mind's eye, to step back into time. What is the appeal of the Old West, of the American frontier?

It has been epitomized by some as a dark and bloody period in American history. Its heroes, Crockett, Bowie, Hickock, Earp, have been reviled and criticized. Yet the Old West lives on, larger than life.

It has become a symbol of freedom, when there was always another mountain to climb and another river to cross; when a dispute between two men was settled not with expensive lawyers but with fists, knives, or guns. Barbaric? Maybe. But some things never change. When the cowboy rode into the pages of American history, he left behind a legacy that lives within the hearts of us all.

—Ralph Compton

Chapter 1

North Kansas, Spring, 1868

The boy's name was Parker Stanley, and he had heard all the jokes about having a name that was backward. "Putting the horse before the cart, and so forth." Now, as he sat leaning against the broken wagon wheel, he tried to hang on to his name . . . to hang on to anything that would tell him that he was still alive.

He wasn't sure how long he had been watching the approaching rider. Heat waves shimmering up from the sun-baked earth gave the rider a surrealistic appearance, bending the light in such a way that sometimes the rider was visible and sometimes he wasn't. Parker wasn't that sure there really was a rider. If so, was he human? Or, was he an Angel of the Lord, coming to take him to join his mother and father?

Parker looked around at the burned wagon, and at the scalped bodies of his mother and father. A few of the arrows the Indians had shot at them were still protruding from their bodies.

There was very little left of the wagon's contents. The Indians had taken all the clothes, household goods, food, and water. They had taken his older sister, too. Elizabeth hadn't cried, not one whimper, and Parker remember how proud he was of her bravery.

The Indians hadn't found the little leather pouch, though. It contained all the money from the sale of the farm in Illinois, and was to have been the start of their new life. Parker saw his father hide the pouch, just before the attack began.

How long had it been since the attack? No matter how hard he tried to think, Parker couldn't come up with the answer. Was it an hour ago? This morning? Yesterday? He had been sitting right here, at this wheel, for as long as he could remember.

The rider reached the wagon, swung down from his horse, then walked toward Parker, carrying a canteen. Parker watched him, almost without interest. When he felt the cool water at his lips, though, he began to drink thirstily, gulping it down in such large quantities that he nearly choked.

"Whoa, now," the rider said gently, pulling the canteen back. "Take it easy, boy. You mustn't drink it too fast. It'll make you sick."

The rider wet his handkerchief, then began rubbing it lightly on the boy's head.

"You took a pretty good bump on the head," he said. "They must've thought you were dead. You're lucky you still have your scalp. They generally prize blond hair like yours."

The water revived Parker's awareness, and with it, the realization that both his parents had been brutally killed. He managed to hold back the sobs, but not the tears.

"Your folks?" the rider asked softly.

Parker nodded.

"Cheyenne, I expect. I'm real sorry about this, son," the rider said.

"There was a white man with them," Parker said.

"What? A white man? Are you sure?"

Parker thought of the big redheaded man who had cursed when they found no money in the wagon.

"Yes," Parker said. "I'm sure. He was a big man with red hair and red beard. I'll never forget him."

"There's nothing worse than a white man who has gone bad and thrown his lot in with the Indians." The rider looked over at the bodies of the boy's parents. "You stay here, I'll bury them for you."

"I want to help," Parker said, stirring himself to rise.

The rider smiled at him. "Good for you, lad," he said. "In the years to come it'll be a comfort to you to know that you did what you could for them." He looked toward the wagon and saw part of a shovel, the top half of the handle having been burned away. "You can use that, I've got a small spade on my saddle."

They worked quietly and efficiently for the next half hour, digging only one grave, but making it large enough for both his mother and father. They lowered Parker's parents into the hole, then shoveled the dirt back over them.

"You want me to say a few words over them?"

The boy nodded.

The rider walked back to his horse and opened a saddlebag. Parker watched as he took out a small leather-bound book and returned to the graveside. With his own survival now taken care of, and with the business of burying his parents out of the way, Parker was able to examine his benefactor closely. He saw a tall, powerfully built man, clean-shaven, with dark hair. Parker wasn't old enough to shave yet, but he knew the trouble it took to shave every morning, and he thought the rider must be a particularly vain man to go to such trouble on a daily basis, especially when on the range like this.

"What are their names?" the man asked, interrupting Parker's musing.

"What?"

"If I'm going to say a few words, I need to know their names."

"My ma's name is Emma. My pa's is Amon. Amon Stanley."

The rider cleared his throat, then began to read:

" 'I am the resurrection and the life, saith the Lord; he that believeth in me, though he were dead, yet shall he live; and whosoever liveth and believeth in me shall never die.

" 'Oh God, whose mercies cannot be numbered: Accept these prayers on behalf of thy servants Amon and Emma Stanley, and grant them an entrance into the land of light and joy, in the fellowship of thy saints; through Jesus Christ thy Son our Lord, who liveth and reigneth with thee and the Holy Spirit, one God, now and forever. Amen."

"Amen," Parker echoed quietly.

The rider closed his book and looked down at the mound of dirt for a long moment, then he looked over at the boy and smiled, and stuck out his hand.

"I'm Clay Springer," he said. "How are you called?"

"Parker. Parker Stanley. Parker is my first name."

"Parker Stanley . . . that's a fine name for a man," Clay said. "Well, climb up on back of my horse, Parker. We can ride double."

"Wait," Parker said. "Can I tell my ma and pa one more thing?"

"Of course you can, son. Take all the time you need."

Parker cleared his throat, and looked down at the pile of freshly turned dirt.

"Ma, Pa, if all your teachin' about heaven and all that is right, then I reckon you can hear me, 'cause the Lord has, for sure, taken you into his arms. So, what I want to say is . . . don't worry none about me. I aim to live the kind of life you would'a both wanted me to live. And I figure, the way things are now, why, you'll both be watchin' over me even more'n you would'a if you was still alive.

"And you can set your minds to ease about Elizabeth, too. I aim to find her. It may take a while, but I promise you, if it takes twenty years, I'll keep lookin' for her.

"I reckon this is good-bye for now, but, if you don't mind, I'll be talkin' to you from time to time. Oh, I prob'ly won't be comin' back out to this place anymore. But, then, I don't think your souls will be hangin' aroun' here anyway."

Clay stood a few feet behind Parker as he said his final words. He was glad he couldn't be seen. It wouldn't be seemly for the boy to see him wipe the tears from his own eyes.

"I reckon that's it," Parker said.

"You'll do your folks proud, Parker, I know you will," Clay said.

Parker started toward the horse, then he remembered the hidden pouch of money. It was under a loose board in the front of the wagon, a part which hadn't been damaged by the fire. He started toward it.

"What're you going after?"

Parker looked back toward Clay. The man had saved his life, helped bury his parents, and even read prayers over their graves. But a sudden cautiousness made him hesitate to tell Clay of the money. What if all the help this man had given him had only been a ruse to see if there was anything of value left? He felt almost ashamed of himself for being suspicious, but he thought it would be better to be safe than sorry.

"Just some letters," Parker said. "I want to keep them."

"All right."

Parker moved the board to one side and picked up the small leather pouch. He could feel the hefty wad of bills inside. As he had overheard his mother and father talking about it, he knew they had one thousand dollars left over after buying the wagon and supplies.

Parker slipped the pouch down inside his waistband, then walked back over to the horse. Clay was already mounted, and he offered his hand to help Parker climb up.

The air was perfumed with the smell of rabbit roasting on a spit, while Clay and Parker drank coffee. Parker hadn't been a coffee drinker before. His ma told him she'd as soon he not drink coffee until he was an adult, and that was what he told Clay when Clay offered him a cup.

"Well, Parker, some folks become adults before other folks," Clay said. "Seems to me like that time has come for you."

Clay was right, Parker thought. He was on his own, now. As far as being an adult was concerned, that sort of sped things up. He accepted the coffee. It tasted a little bitter to him, but he was determined to acquire a taste for it.

Clay sipped his own coffee through extended lips and studied Parker over the rim of his cup. "How old are you, Parker?"

"I'm sixteen," Parker said.

Clay raised one eyebrow.

"All right, fifteen . . . and a half."

"Where were you folks comin' from?"

"Illinois."

"You got any relatives back in Illinois that you want to go to?"

Parker shook his head. "No, all my ma's folks live in England and I don't even know their names. My pa had a brother, but he got killed at Antietam."

"Bloody battle, Antietam," Clay said, shaking his head. "Any close friends or neighbors?"

"None I would want to be a burden to," Parker replied. He took another drink of his coffee. It seemed to him that it went down a little easier this time. "Anyway, I don't want to go back. I've got to find my sister."

"Older sister? Or younger?"

"Older. She's eighteen."

Clay studied the boy for a long moment before he talked. "Boy, you have to face the fact that you may never find her. A group of renegades like that . . . especially if they have a white man riding with them . . . will sell her to the highest bidder."

"I'll find her," Parker insisted. "It may take me a while, but I'll find her."

Clay started to caution him against false hope, then he checked the impulse. Instead, he smiled at Parker. "I'm sure you're right," he said. "If anyone can do it, you, my stalwart young lad, can."

"What's a stalwart?" Parker asked.

Clay laughed. "It means resolute, courageous, determined," he said.

"Determined. Yes, that's what I am. I am determined."

"Well, now, the question is, what are we to do with you?"

"Do with me? Why do you have to do anything with me? Just get me back into a town somewhere and I'll be grateful."

"I can't just turn you out on your own," Clay said "You're too young."

"I thought you told me I was an adult."

Clay cleared his throat. The boy was trapping him with his own words.

"Well . . . you are, as far as I'm concerned. But there's other things to consider. Your schooling for example. You being only fifteen, you're going to need another couple of years of schooling, and I don't think you can get that on your own. Tell you what, I'm going into Independence tomorrow. Suppose we go see the judge and let him decide your case."

"What do you mean, decide my case?"

"Decide what to do with you," Clay said.

"Oh." Parker was quiet for a long moment. "Mr. Springer, will the judge put me in an orphanage?"

"He may," Clay admitted. "I believe there is an orphanage in Independence."

"I don't want to go to an orphanage."

"Why not? There will be people there to look after you. You'll be fed and clothed, and you'll go to school," Clay said, trying to paint as attractive a picture as he could.

"I don't need to be looked after. I can feed and clothe myself."

"Parker, I don't know how much money there is in that pouch you've got stuck down in your waistband, but I'd be willing to bet there isn't enough to take care of you until you are full-grown."

Parker gasped and instinctively felt for the pouch.

"You were right not to tell me about it," Clay said. "I'll give you credit for that. But this should prove something to you, I hope. If I were the type person who would rob you, I could have already done it. So even your attempt at secrecy wasn't enough. See, you'd be better off going to an orphanage." Clay pulled a blanket from his saddle roll and tossed it over to Parker. "Here," he said. "Wrap up in this and get some sleep. It's been a bad day for you, but you'll see things more clearly tomorrow."

Black thunderclouds rumbled ominously in the northwest all the next morning, but they held off long enough for Parker and Clay to reach their destination.

Independence was laid out like a giant cross, with Liberty Street forming the north-south arm, and Independence Avenue cutting across it, running east-west. Independence Avenue continued on as a wagon trail running west, out of town.

Parker looked at this town which was to be his new home. It was a very busy town. There was a lot of wagon and buggy traffic, and dozens and dozens of people walking along the plank walks which lined both sides of the streets. At intervals, there were boards stretched all the way across the dirt streets to allow people a way to cross when the roads were full of mud. This was the first town Parker had seen since his family had stopped for a few days in Sedalia, Missouri, some six weeks earlier. Despite the unhappy circumstances under which he was now seeing Independence, he found it very exciting to be in a town again.

At the intersection of Liberty and Independence, Clay stopped in front of the Morning Star Hotel.

"Why don't you take my horse on down to the livery and get a stable for him?" Clay suggested, handing Parker a coin. "Tell the hand to feed him oats and rub him down. Then come on back to the hotel. I'll be up in my room."

"Where will your room be?"

"I don't know yet. I haven't registered. You can check with the desk, they'll tell you."

"What's the desk?"

By now Clay had slipped down from the horse to allow Parker to move up into the saddle. Clay looked up at him and smiled.

"Are you serious?"

"I've . . . I've never been in a hotel before," Parker admitted.

"Believe me, from the condition of some of the ones I've been in, you haven't missed much," Clay said. He removed his saddlebags and hung them over his shoulder, then pointed through the door. "Look, when you come back, just go inside here, there will be a man behind a counter. Ask him what room number Clay Springer is registered in, and he'll tell you."

"All right," Parker said.

Parker watched Clay go into the hotel, then started riding toward the livery, which was about three blocks down on Independence. He reached down and patted the neck of the animal he was riding. His father had never owned a horse. Back in Illinois, he had farmed with mules, but he sold those when he made the decision to take the family West. He had then replaced the mules with a team of oxen.

Parker thought it would be nice to have a horse, and the freedom to go wherever a horse could take you. What if he just kept this horse? With a good mount and a thousand dollars, he could get a start somewhere.

And he wouldn't have to go to an orphanage.

But even as the thought crossed his mind, he knew he wouldn't do it. No matter how he might justify it to himself, it would still be stealing . . . and worse, he would be stealing from a man who had helped him.

By now Parker's slow ride down the street had brought him to the livery barn. Turning in, he climbed down from the saddle and handed the horse over to the attendant who met him, a boy not much older than himself.

"This your horse?" the boy asked.

"It belongs to a friend."

"Looks like a good horse."

"He sure is," Parker said, almost possessively.

"I ain't seen you around here," the livery attendant said as he took the horse's reins.

"I've never been here."

"You'n your folks gonna live here?"

"I . . . I don't have any folks."

The boy looked around in surprise. "You an orphan?"

"Yes."

"I'm only half an orphan. I got me a ma, but she sure ain't much."

Parker gasped. He had never heard anyone speak so freely of their own mother.

"You think that's evil of me, don't you?" the boy asked.

"I would never say anything like that about my ma. If she was still alive," he added.

"Yeah, well, most mas is good, I guess. But my ma is what they call a whore. She works down at the Crystal Palace 'n when she's not layin' up with some man, she's more'n likely drunk. But at least havin' a ma . . . any kind of a ma . . . means I ain't a orphan, so I don't have to go live up on The Hill. Any ma's all right if she keeps you offen The Hill."

"What's The Hill?"

"You kiddin'? You an orphan 'n you ain't never heard of The Hill? It's the orphanage. It's run by Ol' Man Slayton. Jebediah Slayton. They say he's the meanest man ever lived. He works the orphans till they're 'bout ready to drop, 'n he beats 'em when he don't think they're workin' hard enough. Just you wait. If you're a orphan like you say you are, 'n you're movin' here, you'll find out soon enough."

"Maybe I won't go to the orphanage," Parker said.

"If you stay here, you'll more'n likely have to. Seems like that's the law or somethin'." The boy looked at the sky. "It's fixin' to rain somethin' fierce. If you ain't got a place to get out of it, you can stay here for a while."

"Thanks," Parker said. "I've got a place."

"Better get to it then," the stable boy said as he disappeared into the barn.

At that moment the thunderclouds delivered on their promise, and the rain started coming down in sheets. Parker dashed across the street and up onto the wooden sidewalk. Many of the stores had roofs that overhung the sidewalk, so though Independence Avenue was already turning into a river of mud, Parker was able to return to the hotel without suffering too much from the weather. He stomped his feet just outside the door to make certain he had no mud on his shoes, then he went inside.

The hotel lobby seemed huge to him. There were a dozen or more chairs and sofas scattered about, several potted plants, mirrors on the walls, and a grand, elegant staircase rising to the second floor. Parker looked around for a moment, taking in all the images of this, his first time in a hotel. Then he saw a counter and a man behind it looking at him.

"Boy, what you doin' in here? This isn't a place you can just come in out of the rain," the man behind the counter said, gruffly.

"I'm looking for Mr. Clay Springer."

"Springer. He just check in?"

Check in wasn't a term Parker had ever heard used, but he reasoned what it must mean.

"Yes, just a few moments ago."

"Yeah, thought that was his name. He's in room 212."

"Where's that?"

"Well, if it's 212, it must be on the second floor," the man said in exasperation.

"Oh."

The man sighed, and pointed to the stairs. "Go up these stairs," he said. "It's the first room on the left."

"Thank you."

Parker climbed the stairs, then when he saw the right door, he opened it and went inside. Instantly, he heard a metallic click, and he turned to see Clay holding a cocked pistol leveled toward him. Parker gasped in surprise and took half a step back.

"Boy, don't frighten me like that," Clay said, sighing in relief. He released the hammer and lowered the pistol. "Most people knock before they come into someone's room."

"You told me to come on up," Parker said.

"So I did," Clay said.

"Well, that's just what I done."

Clay was in the midst of changing his clothes.

He had already put on another pair of trousers, but was bare from the waist up.

"I had some bathwater brought up," Clay said. "I've already taken mine, and the water is still warm, so you can take yours, now. I'll be back later this afternoon, then we can go downstairs to take our supper. I'll bet you've never eaten in a restaurant either, have you?"

"No, I haven't," Parker admitted. "But, listen, I don't need a bath. It hasn't been that long since I had one."

Clay smiled at him. "It's been long enough," he said. He pointed to the tub. "Take a bath." Clay started toward the door.

"Mr. Springer?"

"Yes?"

"Are you going to check on the orphanage?"

"Maybe."

"I already did," Parker said.

Clay stood there with his hand on the door frame. "What did you find out?"

"It's like you said. They've got one here," Parker said. He didn't say anything else about it.

Clay nodded. "That's good to know," he said. He let himself out, then closed the door behind him.

After Clay left the hotel room, Parker got undressed for his bath. He held the pouch of money for a moment, trying to decide what to do with it, then he saw the bed. Hiding the pouch under the mattress, he returned to the tub and slipped down into the still-warm water.

Don't forget to wash behind your ears, Parker, his ma's voice came back to him.

"I won't, Ma," Parker said, quietly. "I won't."

Chapter 2

Clay found Marcus Pearson exactly where he thought he would, in the Brown Dirt Cowboy Saloon on Liberty Street. Marcus was the best wagon handler Clay had ever met. He had driven wagons for Clay ever since Clay got into the business, mostly down into Texas, though he also made some trips into Nebraska. They were friends as well as employer and employee, and three years ago the two had even wintered together in the mountains of Colorado, trapping beaver.

As Marcus once said, "The only way you can get closer to a body than winterin' with 'em, is to marry 'em."

Marcus was a small man, with such weathered skin that he looked seventy, though he was actually just a little over forty. He was missing two fingers on his left hand, the result of getting his hand caught in a trap. Despite the loss of two fingers, he could handle most things as easily as if he had his entire hand, and he demonstrated that now, by deftly pouring whiskey into Clay's glass.

"Did you take a look at those three wagons down to Garland's place?" he asked.

"Yes. They're pretty good wagons."

"Can't beat 'em for the price," Marcus replied.

"I know. That's why I bought them."

"So, you are really going to do it, aren't you? You're going to sell goods to the saints out in Utah."

"I said I was, and I'm going to."

"You know, you could do two trips to Texas in the same time it's going to take you to go to Utah," Marcus said.

"I know. But if everything goes all right, I can make five times as much on this one trip as I can on two Texas trips."

"You said it. *If* everything goes all right. You could also wind up losing everything," Marcus said. "From here to Utah by wagon is no easy trip. You'll have plains, desert, rivers, and mountains to deal with, to say nothing of Indians, wild animals, and who knows what else? And then, even if you do make it through, them Mormons aren't known to be any too friendly to gentiles."

"I know it's going to be hard. But if it was easy, there wouldn't be any profit in it. I think I can do it, but I'm going to need a good man as my head driver."

When Marcus realized that Clay was referring to him, he paused and laughed, then added, "I reckon I could go with you."

"Good, I was hoping you would."

Marcus smiled, and held up his glass. "Utah, here we come," he said.

Clay touched his glass to it, and they drank a toast to the venture.

Marcus chuckled, then wiped his mouth with the back of his hand. "Don't reckon we'll be doin' much drinkin' out there. I hear-tell them Mormon fellas don't take to spirits."

"That's what they say," Clay said.

"I've always wanted to go there, though."

Clay looked at Marcus in surprise. "You've always wanted to go to Utah? Why?"

"I want to take me a swim in that Great Salt Lake they got."

"Marcus, I've known you for six years, and I've never known you to go near water."

"There's a reason for that. I can't swim," Marcus said, easily.

"If you can't swim, what's the attraction to swimming in the Great Salt Lake?"

"Because they say that even folks who can't swim won't sink in that lake. You just jump in, and next thing you know, you're floatin' around on top of it, just like a cork."

Clay chuckled. "That's a sight I'll be wanting to see. Marcus Pearson bobbing on top of the water, like a cork."

"You're goin' to see it, 'cause I aim to do it," Marcus insisted. "Now, tell me, how did your scoutin' trip go? That northern route out of here going to work out all right?"

Clay shook his head no. "Oh, it might save some time in the early spring, when the creeks and rivers are in freshet stage farther south," he said. "But, this time of year, we may as well go the regular route."

"That's sort of what I thought," Marcus said. "But you was dead set to check it out."

"Well, as you pointed out, it is going to be a long trip out there, and I'm open to any suggestion that might save a few miles." Clay was silent for a moment, then he continued, in a more somber voice. "I came across a burned-out wagon while I was out there."

"Freighter?"

Clay shook his head. "No. Immigrants. Man, wife, son, and daughter. The man and his wife were killed and scalped. Indians took the girl. I've got the boy."

Marcus had just started to take a drink, but he pulled the glass back down. "The hell you say. You've got the boy?"

"Yes."

"Where is he now?"

"Over in my hotel room."

"This here was immigrants, and they was just the one wagon, travelin' by itself?" Marcus asked.

"Yes."

"I know there's not as much Indian trouble as there once was, but, still, I don't think that was any too smart. What kind of Indians? Crow? Cheyenne?"

"More'n likely Cheyenne, though probably a bunch of renegades. The boy says there was a white man with the Indians."

"Damn, that would take some kind of particular mean son of a bitch to do something like that," Marcus said. "What are you going to do with the boy?"

"I don't know. I know there's an orphanage in town. I thought I might leave him there."

Two women came over to the table then, and looked down at the men.

"You might want to check on that orphanage before you leave the boy there," Marcus said.

"Check on it? What for?"

"I've heard a little talk about it. Seems like it's more of a jail than an orphanage. 'Course, the boy ain't your responsibility. And you sure don't owe him nothin'."

"Maybe not," Clay said. "On the other hand, I don't think I'd like the idea of leaving him in a jail."

One of the two women standing by their table cleared her throat, and Clay and Marcus looked up at them.

"Hello, darlin's," Marcus said.

"Hello, Marcus Pearson. I'm glad to see that we hadn't turned to clear glass. I swear, if I wasn't beginning to think you couldn't even see us," the older of the two women said. She was attractive, though in a garish way, with dyed-red hair that added to her gaudiness.

Marcus chuckled. "Oh, no, we can see you just fine," he said. "Sit down and join us."

The two women took their seats and, almost immediately, the bartender brought them drinks, doing so without asking. When Marcus made no effort to pay for the drinks, Clay gave the bartender some money.

"Thank you," both women said.

"Ladies, this here is Clay Springer. He's a freighter, my boss, and my friend. Clay, I don't believe you've had the privilege of meeting two of our town's loveliest citizens, have you?"

"I haven't had the pleasure," Clay admitted.

"Then allow me. The young woman to your right is Belle. Ain't she lovely?"

Belle, who was the more attractive of the two, beamed under Marcus's praise.

"Belle allows as how she is practically a virgin, since she is some particular as to who she goes to bed with," Marcus explained.

Clay laughed.

Belle was a soiled dove, but she couldn't have been in the business very long, for she hadn't yet taken on that dissipated look which was so common to women of her profession. The other woman, Clay noticed, did have that look.

"Now, Suzie, our redheaded friend, is considerably more democratic than her younger sister," Marcus said. "She will hop in bed with anyone who has the price."

"Me and Belle ain't sisters," Suzie said quickly.

"Didn't mean actual sisters," Marcus explained. "I was usin' the term in the Christian sense." Then, to Clay he added, "Suzie, you see, believes that when the Bible says, 'Love thy neighbor,' it is tellin' her to go out and love as many of her neighbors as she can. Of course, she will only love those neighbors who pay."

Suzie laughed good-naturedly. "You are really a card, you know that, Mr. Pearson?"

"Come to think of it, I'm also a neighbor, and I've got money," Marcus said. He stood up, then extended his hand. "Mayhaps you would like to relieve me of some of it."

"Why, I would be very pleased to do just that, Mr. Pearson," Suzie replied, standing to join him.

After Marcus and Suzie walked away, Belle reached across the table and put her hand on Clay's wrist. "What your friend said about me being particular is true," she said. "I will only go to bed with people I like."

"I see," Clay said.

"And I like you."

"That's good to know."

"I do indeed."

"Belle, you been in Independence long?"

"I was born here."

"Do you know anything about the orphanage in town?"

Belle got a strange look on her face. "Why are you asking about the orphanage? What have you heard about me?"

"No. It's just that recent events have left me in charge of an orphan, and I was thinking about making arrangements to leave him there. I thought that if you had been here for a while, you might be able to tell me something about it."

"Why don't you just shoot him? He'd be better off."

"What?" Clay replied, surprised by the bitterness of Belle's response.

Belle took a drink. "They call it The Hill, and I know a lot about it."

"Tell me what you know."

"You ever wonder how girls like me wind up whorin'?"

Belle's comment seemed like an abrupt change of subject and Clay paused for a second before he answered. "Well, I don't reckon I've ever given whoring that much thought," he finally said. "I figure a woman does whatever she wants to do. I'm not one to judge."

"I started whorin' when I was sixteen. That is, I started gettin' *paid* for it when I was sixteen. Mr. Slayton actually broke me in to the life when I was fourteen, but he didn't pay me for it, unless you count food and a bed."

"Who is Slayton?"

"Jebediah Slayton is the man that runs The Hill. 'Course now, with boys, it's different. He just rents them out like slaves. They work from before sunup till after sundown. He collects their wages, and they get something to eat and a place to sleep. The funny thing is, I've never been able to figure out who got the worse of it . . . the boys or the girls."

"How can he get away with something like that?" Clay asked.

"Who's going to complain? The only ones

there are the orphans, and that means they've got no one to complain for them."

"You paint a pretty gruesome picture."

"I reckon I do. But it's somethin' I think you should know about if you're thinkin' about puttin' someone there."

"I won't be putting him there," Clay said resolutely.

"You won't?"

"Not after what you've told me."

The girl smiled. "Then I've done my Christian duty for the day. So, what are you going to do with the boy?"

"Well, I don't know," Clay admitted. He stared at Belle for a moment. "I don't suppose you would be interested in taking him in for a while? He wouldn't be any trouble. He's a fine-looking, strapping boy, nearly sixteen years old."

Belle laughed. "And you want to leave him with someone like me? Don't you know that boys that age start getting pretty curious about women? And if this boy's as good-lookin' as you say . . . I might just satisfy that curiosity for him."

Clay cleared his throat. "Yeah, maybe you have a point," he said.

"So, are we going to sit down here for the rest of the day and talk? Or, would you like to come upstairs with me?"

Clay had come into the saloon to have a few drinks and to talk business with Marcus. He had no intention of consorting with a soiled dove.

But he was surprised at just how quickly Belle had been able to stimulate his sexual appetite. And he was equally surprised when he heard himself accept her offer.

"My room is at the head of the stairs, the third door down on the right. You go on up and wait for me there. I'll get us a fresh bottle."

Clay went upstairs to wait. When Belle knocked on the door a moment later, he was amused by the idea of her knocking on her own door.

"Come in, by all means, come in," he called. Belle slipped through the door, then closed it behind her. She stood in front of it and smiled self-consciously at Clay.

"Here I am," she said.

Belle held up a bottle. "I hope you like this. It is real Tennessee mash, not some local rotgut."

"I'm sure that I will like it," Clay said. He reached for the bottle, but when he saw no glasses in her room, he pulled the cork and drank right from the bottle, never taking his eyes off the girl.

Belle undid the ribbon that help up her hair, then shook her head to let it tumble down. That simple act created the amazing illusion of transforming her from a prostitute to an innocent young girl, and for a second Clay hesitated. He thought about her story of being abused by Slayton when she was fourteen years old. He had no intention of being a despoiler, but that was exactly what he felt like.

"Is something wrong?" Belle asked, noticing the expression on his face.

Clay took another drink straight from the bottle, then shook his head to clear the image. "No, just thinking, is all."

Belle moved closer, then reached out to touch him with cool, soft hands. His need for her grew stronger, and he moved his hand from her hand up to the top of her dress. Holding it there for a moment, he could feel her warm, heavy breast through the material.

"I'll get undressed," Belle said. Her voice didn't sound like that of a little girl now. On the contrary, it was deep and sultry, and she looked at him through smoky gray eyes as she began removing her clothes, pulling the dress off her shoulders and pushing it down her body.

Clay watched her undress, fascinated by the almost languid way she did so. Her studied actions had the effect of inflaming his desire to an even greater pitch.

Belle folded her clothes very carefully and placed them, one item at a time, on the chest near the water basin. Then she turned to face him once more. Her body was subtly lighted by the lantern that burned on her dresser.

"Shall we?" she invited, gesturing with her arm toward the bed. Though she was naked, and the bed beckoned, the invitation was as guileless as if she had just asked him if he wanted a cup of tea. It made the moment all the more erotic because of it.

"Yes, we shall," Clay said with thickened tongue as he, too, began to undress.

After he left the Brown Dirt Cowboy, Clay went to the various warehouses around town where he made arrangements to take delivery of the goods he would be transporting to Utah. One of the places he visited was E. G. Farben, Authorized Agent for Winchester Firearms.

"They tell me folks are willing to pay up to ten times what these rifles cost out there," Farben said as he watched Clay examine some of the rifles he had on display.

"Yes, I've heard that as well," Clay said. He raised one of the rifles to his shoulder and sighted down the barrel.

"I can let you have fifty of them at a very good price."

Clay lowered the piece, looked at its smooth lines, then shook his head. "I'd sure like to," he said. "These are beautiful guns, and I know they'd fetch a good price. But I haven't bought my mules yet and I don't know how much money I'll have left."

"Why don't you buy oxen? They're cheaper."

"And a lot slower. No, thanks, I'm going to buy mules."

"Well, you could always take on a partner," Farben suggested "If you want, I could look around and see if I can find someone who would be interested in making an investment."

"A partner?" Clay replied. "No, I don't think I would be interested in . . ." He paused, then he smiled. "Wait a minute," he said. "Yes, that's it! That's the answer! Thanks for the suggestion, Mr. Farben. Maybe I will take on a partner at that."

"So, you want the rifles?"

"Will you throw in two Sharpes fifties at no extra cost?"

Farben stroked his chin and thought about it for a long moment, then he nodded.

"All right, fifty Winchesters, and two Sharpes. "Now, do you want me to see if I can find a partner for you?" Farben asked.

"No need for that," Clay said. "Unless I miss my guess, I've already got one."

Parker was taking a nap on the bed when Clay returned to the hotel room. The opening and closing of the door awakened him, and he sat up and rubbed his eyes.

"Oh, I'm sorry," he said. "I fell asleep."

"It's just as well," Clay replied. "It took me a lot longer than I thought it would. It's nearly time for supper. That is, if you're hungry."

"I'm starving," Parker replied.

"Thought you might be. By the way, you look a little better after your bath. Smell better, too. It's too bad you don't have a change of clothes to put on."

Parker shrugged. "The Indians got everything. This is all I have left."

"Then you're going to need to spend some of that money to buy yourself some more clothes," Clay said. "Fact is, you'd better get yourself a complete trail outfit while you are at it, clothes, blanket, waterproof, a rifle. I looked at some beautiful rifles today. You'll also want a pistol, a hatchet, a rope, and a good knife. You have to have a good knife out on the trail."

"Out on the trail?"

"You aren't planning on staying here in Independence, are you?"

"I don't know. What about the orphanage?"

"Yes, well, I checked up on the orphanage, and it didn't sound all that good to me. You said you checked on it too. What did you think?"

"It didn't sound all that good to me, either."

"So, tell me what you think of this. I've found a bargain on three wagons. I bought them, as well as a thousand pounds of flour, five-hundred weight of beans, and an equal amount of coffee and sugar. I also bought twenty-five cases of matches, twenty-five cases of ammunition, fifty rifles, assorted cooking utensils, two hundred bolts of cloth, needles, thread, and buttons."

"What are you going to do with all that?" Parker asked.

Clay smiled. "Well, my young friend, as soon as I can find eighteen sound mules, I'm going to haul those goods out to Salt Lake City where I intend to sell them to the Mormons for a great profit. You ever heard of the Mormons?"

"Yes, I've heard of them. Don't know as I've ever seen any, though."

"Well, you're going to. That is, if you throw

in with me. They're out in Utah, and that's where I'm headed."

"I seem to recollect Pa tellin' me somethin' about the Mormons," Parker said. "Wasn't there a wagon train attacked out there in Utah one time? And lots of folks killed, too, I hear. All by Mormons and Indians."

Clay shook his head. "That's right. I reckon Mormons can be mighty unfriendly to us gentiles if they think we're coming to cause them harm. But that happened a long time ago." He took a letter from his pocket. "And I've got a letter here, from Colonel Alexander Doniphan. Doniphan and Brigham Young are close friends. In this letter, Doniphan introduces me to Young, and asks him to treat me kindly, and trade with me fairly. Now, tell me, Parker Stanley, how much money do you have in that poke you're carrying around?"

Parker hesitated for just a beat, before he answered.

"One thousand dollars."

"Good. I was hoping you would have about that much. You see, the thing is, I've spent everything I've got on the wagons and trade goods, and I've still got to buy the mules. That's goin' to leave me flat broke, and we're going to need money to hire a company, and for operating expenses. If you are of a mind to, Parker Stanley . . . you can throw your thousand dollars in with me, and we'll be full partners . . . fifty-fifty."

"Fifty-fifty?"

"That's what I said."

"But, you've got a lot more'n a thousand dollars invested, haven't you?"

"I've already got five thousand invested," Clay replied. "But if we're going to be partners, I figure it's best that we be equal partners. That way, we'll start our friendship out on an even keel. Now, what do you say?"

A broad smile spread across Parker's face. "What do I say? I say yes! Yes! Oh, thank you, Mr. Springer."

Clay held up his hand and smiled back at the boy. "Now, that's another thing, Parker. If we're going to be equal partners, I think you should call me Clay, don't you?"

Parker nodded enthusiastically.

"Yes, Clay, I think so too," he said.

Chapter 3

A Cheyenne Village, West of the Republican River

When they reached the encampment, the Indian who was carrying Elizabeth pushed her from his horse. By now she was so sore from the hard ride that she barely felt the fall. She was also still in considerable shock from having watched her family butchered. The bloody scalps of her mother and father now hung from a leather thong tied around the waist of one of the Indians. The last time she saw her brother, he had been struck on the head by one of the Indians, and was lying by their burned-out wagon. She was sure he was dead as well.

They had arrived at a small village, which lay alongside a stream. Here, women and children gathered around her, staring at her with eyes that were wide in curiosity and wonder.

Although Elizabeth noticed them, she didn't return their gaze. Instead, she concentrated on one of her captors, a big man with an unruly mane of red hair. She stared at him, unable to understand how one of her own kind could be a party to something like this. He noticed her staring at him.

"What are you looking at, girlie?" the man asked gruffly.

"Nothing," Elizabeth said.

"Nothing, hell. You were staring at me," the man said.

"Yes," Elizabeth replied. "As I said, I'm looking at nothing."

Elizabeth was surprised when one of the Indians laughed.

"What are *you* laughing at, Brave Eagle?" the white man demanded.

"I am laughing at what Captured Woman said," Brave Eagle replied. "She has said you are nothing." He laughed again. At the curious stares of the other Indians, the brave said a few words in his own tongue that Elizabeth couldn't understand, then many laughed, including the women and children who had gathered around.

The burly red-haired man came over to glare down at Elizabeth.

"You got a sassy mouth, missy, and you're makin' me look bad in front of my Injun friends. I don't like that."

"What's going to happen to me?" Elizabeth said.

The big man grinned. He took a tress of her blond hair in his hand and looked at it, stroking it between his thumb and forefinger. "Well, now, it depends on how good you are to me. If you got what it takes to please ole' Red Talbot, then like as not, I'll let you live."

"Talbot? That's your name?"

"That it is, missy, that it is," Talbot said, pleased with himself. "I 'spect you've heard of me, all right. I'm Satan's unholy angel. Mamas use my name to scare their children."

"No, I haven't heard of you," Elizabeth replied. The simplicity of her negative answer seemed to upset Talbot, and he smirked at her.

"Well, no matter. You'll soon know all about me." He smiled evilly. "What I like, and what I don't like," he added, suggestively.

"If pleasing you is what it takes to survive, Mr. Talbot, I would rather die. Go ahead and kill me now."

With an angry growl, Talbot grabbed the bodice of her dress. He jerked his hand down and, tearing it open, exposed her breasts. Reacting instinctively, Elizabeth raked her fingernails across Talbot's face, leaving four bloody streaks on his cheek. With a cry of pain, he jumped back from her, as she crossed her arms across her breasts, attempting to restore some sense of modesty.

"Bitch!" Talbot shouted, putting his hand up to his cheek. He looked at his bloody fingers, then glared at her with eyes narrowed in anger. He started toward her. "Maybe I'll just grant you your wish and kill you right now."

"Go ahead," Elizabeth said defiantly.

At that moment, Brave Eagle stepped in between them. He glared at Talbot. "You cannot do this," he said.

"You stay out of this, Brave Eagle," Talbot growled.

"No," the Indian said firmly. "You cannot kill her."

"This here's got nothin' to do with you. This here is between two white people."

"She is *our* prisoner."

Talbot took out a dirty handkerchief and dabbed at the blood on his cheek, then he gave another snort.

"Do whatever you want with her," he said. "This whole thing has been a waste of time, far as I'm concerned. They didn't even have one penny with them." He glared at Elizabeth. "What kind of fool was your pa, that he would start out like this with no money?"

Elizabeth knew about the money hidden in the wagon. For a moment she thought about telling Talbot, hoping to use it to buy her freedom. But she intuitively knew that it wouldn't help. He would take the money and leave her to the Indians, and it would gain her nothing. This way, she could at least deny him that.

"I knew nothing of my father's business," she said.

"Business? The old coot didn't have a business." He pulled a watch from his pocket. "Maybe he planned to sell this."

"That's my pa's watch!" Elizabeth said. She reached for it, but Talbot pulled it away with one hand while pushing her back with the other.

"It's mine now," he said. He looked at the Indians, then shook his head. "It was the only thing worth a damn in the whole wagon. You keep the girl, I'll keep this, and we'll go our own way." He started toward his horse.

"Mr. Talbot!" Elizabeth called to him. "You . . . you aren't going to leave me here with them, are you?"

Talbot swung into his saddle, then looked back at her. "Missy, you done let it be known how you feel about me," he said. "Don't guess there's much use in tryin' to change your mind on that account. So you stay here with these Injuns. They'll use you till they're tired of you, then, like as not, that blond hair of yours will wind up decoratin' some buck's lodge pole. I reckon then you'll wish you'd been a mite kinder to ole Red Talbot."

Elizabeth watched Talbot ride away with mixed emotions. On the one hand, it seemed to her that any white man, even someone like Talbot, would be preferable to being left with savages. On the other hand, he was a known evil, and she didn't know how the Indians could be worse.

One of the older Indian women brought her a gourd dripping with water. She held it up, indicating that Elizabeth should take a drink and, because her throat was burning with thirst she took it, then drank eagerly.

"Thank you," she said, though she didn't know if the woman understood her or not.

Brave Eagle came to her then. "Do you want to eat?" he asked.

Elizabeth shook her head no. She hadn't eaten

since early this morning, but she knew that she wouldn't be able to keep any food down, not now, anyway.

"What is going to happen to me?"

"That is for council to decide."

"Council? What council? When?"

"Tomorrow. Council will meet to decide your fate tomorrow." Brave Eagle then turned to the old woman who had brought her the water and said something in a language that Elizabeth couldn't understand. The old woman nodded, then reached out for Elizabeth.

"What . . . what does she want?"

"Go with her," Brave Eagle said.

The old woman led Elizabeth to one of the dozen or so teepees that made up the encampment. She pulled the flap aside and indicated that Elizabeth should go inside. Elizabeth did so and the old woman followed her in. There were skins on the ground and, at the old woman's invitation, Elizabeth sat down on one of them. The old woman sat across from her.

"Do you speak English?" Elizabeth asked.

The old woman gave no response. There wasn't the slightest flicker in her eyes, nor the barest hint of a change of expression on her face.

"What is your name?" Elizabeth asked.

The old woman remained silent.

Elizabeth pointed to herself. "Elizabeth," she said, mouthing the word slowly.

There was still no response. Finally, the woman got up and left.

Elizabeth was left alone. Now, for the first

time, she allowed herself the luxury of crying, weeping not only for the uncertainty of her own future, but for her mother, father, and brother, all of whom were lost forever to her. She cried until she could cry no more, then she sat, very still and very quiet, trying hard to drain herself of all feeling, emotional and physical.

Night came, and the old woman returned just long enough to light a pine knot lantern.

"Thank you," Elizabeth said. Again, the old woman remained silent.

Outside, a large campfire was lit and the wavering orange of the campfire's glow joined with the flickering flame from the pine knot to bathe the inside of Elizabeth's teepee in an eerie gold light. She could hear the Indians chanting a strange, discordant, yet hauntingly beautiful melody. The drums pounded incessantly and she listened to their crescendo, trying to reckon the passing of time. Time and space seemed to hang suspended now, and she was having difficulty believing she was actually here. Finally, she lay down on the skins, surprised at what a soft and comfortable bed they made.

The flap of the teepee was opened and the morning sun streamed in. It wasn't until then that Elizabeth realized she had even been asleep. It had been a terrifying night, with the pounding drums and savage sounds. Now, with the darkness gone, she felt less afraid, and when she saw that the old woman was carrying something in a bowl, she realized that she was ravenous.

"You eat?" the woman asked, speaking for the first time, holding the bowl toward her. It contained some sort of stew and it smelled very good to her.

"Thank you," Elizabeth said. Then, with a shock, she realized the woman had actually spoken. This was the same woman from whom she had been unable to get a response the day before. "You speak English!"

"Yes."

"But when I tried to talk to you yesterday, you wouldn't say anything."

"I had nothing to say," the old woman replied.

"Umm, this is good," Elizabeth said, chewing a piece of meat. "What is it?"

"Meat," the old woman said without elaboration.

Elizabeth giggled, her first laugh since being taken prisoner the day before. "Meat, yea, I'll have to remember that," she said sarcastically. "What is your name?"

"I am called Moon Cow Woman."

Elizabeth looked at Moon Cow Woman and decided that the name fit. She was short, very rotund, and rather moon-faced.

Moon Cow Woman was carrying a bundle and she opened it now to pull out a dress. It was made of soft deerskin and decorated with red and green porcupine quills. Elizabeth, who took pride in her own ability as a seamstress, was able to recognize right away the quality of workmanship in the dress.

"Oh, my, that is beautiful," Elizabeth said.

"You wear before council," Moon Cow Woman said.

"Oh, no, I can't take this," Elizabeth said, pushing it away.

Moon Cow Woman looked hurt. It was the first change of expression Elizabeth had ever seen on her face.

"You not like?"

"No, no, that's not it at all! I think it is a lovely dress," Elizabeth insisted. "But . . . I can't take it. I have nothing to give you in return."

Something in Elizabeth's demeanor and tone of voice touched Moon Cow Woman and she warmed to the young captive. "It is a gift," she said. "You do not need to give anything for it. Wear it before the council and it will move their hearts to vote in any way you wish."

A spasm of hope flared up in Elizabeth. "You mean, they might set me free?"

Moon Cow Woman realized then that she had instilled false hope in Elizabeth and, again, her eyes reflected sadness.

"No," she said. "They will not let you go. But, they will listen to you when you say who, among our men, you wish to marry."

Tears sprang quickly to Elizabeth's eyes. "But I don't want to marry anyone," she said.

"If you do not marry, you will become a slave."

"Then I will become a slave."

Moon Cow Woman shook her head. "No, you do not want that. To be a slave is very bad. You will not eat until all the people and all the animals have eaten. You will be worked until you can no longer stand. And, because any man who wants you can have you, you will be hated by all the women of the village."

"Oh," Elizabeth said softly. She let out a long sigh. "Well, that doesn't leave me much choice, does it?"

Elizabeth took off her torn dress, then put on the dress Moon Cow Woman had brought her. When she had it on, she turned toward Moon Cow Woman, as if modeling it. Moon Cow Woman smiled, and nodded in appreciation.

"Come," Moon Cow Woman said. "I will take you to the council."

When Elizabeth stepped out of the teepee she saw that several men, women, and children, were gathered around a circle of men who were sitting on the ground. The men were smoking a pipe and passing it around. Occasionally, one of them would get up and speak to the others . . . pacing back and forth as he spoke, his voice rising and falling in a strange, syncopated rhythm, his hands waving expressively . . . then he would sit down. Often there would be long moments of absolute silence, but the silence didn't indicate that the meeting had broken up, for they continued to sit in the great circle, passing around the pipe.

Brave Eagle was one of the Indians in the circle. But the Indian who made the greatest impression on Elizabeth was an older man to whom all the others seemed to defer. There was a gentleness in his face that drew Elizabeth's attention toward him.

"Who is that?" Elizabeth asked, pointing toward the old man.

"He is called Two Ponies," Moon Cow Woman answered. "He is a man of much medicine."

"Medicine? He is a medicine man? Like a doctor?"

Moon Cow Woman shook her head. "He is what the white-eyes call a chief."

"A chief," Elizabeth said. She studied Two Ponies for a moment or two longer and saw that he did seem to be in charge of the council. "All right, if I am given a choice, I will choose him for my husband," Elizabeth said.

Moon Cow Woman looked at Elizabeth in surprise.

"You will not choose Brave Eagle?"

Elizabeth looked at the Indian who had led the raid on their wagon yesterday. He was taller than most of the Indians, and, she had to admit, a fine-looking man. She had also noticed yesterday that he actually took no part in the attack, but stayed back on his horse, just watching. Still, he had been there.

"No," she finally said. "I will not choose Brave Eagle."

"But Brave Eagle is a good hunter," Moon Cow Woman insisted. "Your teepee would never be without meat if you chose Brave Eagle as your husband. He is also a young man. He would pleasure you as often as you want."

Elizabeth blushed, then thought it was worth noting that her first emotion was embarrassment, rather than fear. "I don't want to be pleasured by Brave Eagle. I don't want to be pleasured by anyone."

"You don't want to be pleasured by Two Ponies?"

"No."

"Then why do you wish Two Ponies for your husband?"

"You tell me that I must choose someone. I choose him because he looks like a kind and good man."

"Yes," Moon Cow Woman said. "He is very kind and very good. He is my husband."

Elizabeth gasped. "Two Ponies is your husband?"

"Yes."

"Oh, Moon Cow Woman, I'm sorry. Here I'm talking about wanting to choose him, and you tell me he is your husband. And . . . and you've even brought me this lovely dress to help sway the council."

"Two Ponies can have more than one wife," Moon Cow Woman said. "If you become his wife, you will be my sister. It would please me to have you as my little sister."

"Captured Woman!" Brave Eagle called out interrupting them. "Come!"

Elizabeth took a deep breath, then let it out slowly, bracing herself for the ordeal.

"Beaver Pelt will offer the pipe to you," Moon

Cow Woman said. "When he does, you must take it."

"Oh, I hope not," Elizabeth said, screwing up her face in an expression of distaste. "I don't think I could smoke it."

"You must," Moon Cow Woman said. "Beaver Pelt is the oldest and wisest of the council. He is a shaman. If you do not smoke the pipe when it is offered by a shaman, you offend the people, and the decision will go against you."

"I . . . I'll try," Elizabeth said. She walked toward the council then, and at Brave Eagle's invitation, sat down.

The council began with Beaver Pelt, the shaman Moon Cow Woman had mentioned, taking the first puff from the pipe. He took a long draw, then, as he exhaled, he waved his hands through the smoke to bring it back into his face. Afterward, just as Moon Cow Woman had predicted, he passed the pipe directly to Elizabeth.

Beaver Pelt was, perhaps, the oldest man Elizabeth had ever seen. There was scarcely one spot on his face that wasn't filled with lines, yet his eyes were bright and vibrant. Summoning all her courage, she took a puff the same way she had seen the others do, even using her hands to fan the smoke back into her face, then she passed it on. The Indians all grunted in a favorable response to her action.

"Moon Cow Woman," Two Ponies said, speaking in English. "Come. You will be the ears for Captured Woman. You will tell her what words are spoken by the council. And you will be the tongue of Captured Woman. You will tell the council what words are spoken by Captured Woman."

Because Moon Cow Woman was to have a function in the council, albeit only as a translator, she, too, was offered a smoke from the council pipe. The pipe was handed to her and she took a puff, then handed it back and took her position beside Elizabeth.

"And now, the council will hear Elk Heart," Two Ponies said, with Moon Cow Woman translating almost simultaneously to Elizabeth.

Elk Heart came before the council, and Elizabeth recognized him as one of the Indians who had participated in the raid on her father's wagon. Unlike Brave Eagle, Elk Heart had been actively engaged in the killing. He was also the one who had carried the grisly scalps of her parents across his horse.

"I was the one who claimed coups at the fight. By right, the woman belongs to me."

"No," one of the other Indians called. This was the Indian who had scooped Elizabeth up and put her on his horse to bring her back. "I, Kicking Horse, am the one who put the woman on my horse and brought her to our village. By right, she belongs to me."

Brave Eagle spoke next, speaking in his own tongue. "Elk Heart counted coups, not on warriors, but on an old man and an old woman," he said. "And Kicking Horse put Captured Woman on his horse only because he was closest to her. But, hear me, this was not a fight in which courage and bravery were counted. There were many of us and few of them. We were told by Talbot that there would be many wagons, filled with goods for trading, and guarded by armed men against whom we could test our courage. But Talbot lied. There was only one wagon and it had only a family of white-eyes going to a new land. I would have let them pass in peace, but Talbot began the attack and others followed."

Brave Eagle paused in his presentation for a moment while he studied the reaction his translated words were having.

"That is why I think Captured Woman should be given to me. It is a bad thing that her mother and father have been killed. Now I want to protect her and feed her, as her mother and father would have done."

Brave Eagle sat down.

"Who else would speak for this woman?" Two Ponies asked.

"I would speak again," Elk Heart said. "It was I who counted coups. And though she rode on the pony of Kicking Horse, it was I who captured her. By what is right she must either belong to me, or become a slave. If she does not become my woman, I will become a contraire."

"What is a contraire?" Elizabeth asked as Moon Cow Woman translated for her.

"It is a life of great sacrifice. One who is a contraire must do all things backward. He must laugh when sad, cry when happy, sleep when rested, wake when tired, be friendly to those people he would harm, and be rude to those who are his friends."

Elizabeth laughed. "That doesn't make sense. How can anyone do such a thing?"

"No one can," Moon Cow Woman said. "Those who become contraire go crazy very soon, because it is not possible to do the things they have vowed to do."

Elk Heart sat back down in the center of the circle and crossed his arms across his chest. He stared straight ahead, looking neither left nor right, and he waited for the decision of the council.

"And now, I will let the woman speak for herself," Two Ponies invited.

Elizabeth nodded, then got up to address the council.

"First, I wish to thank the council for hearing me speak. I have heard the words of those who have spoken for me, especially the words of Brave Eagle. I believe Brave Eagle to be a good man whose heart is right. But, if it is my right to choose who will be my husband, I choose"—Elizabeth paused for a moment and looked directly at Two Ponies—"Two Ponies."

As Elizabeth's words were translated, there was an immediate reaction of surprise and, Elizabeth believed, indignation, from many of the Indians.

"I am an old man," Two Ponies finally said. "I do not think I will be a good husband for you."

"You are a chief," Elizabeth said. "Do you say

that you will not be able to feed and protect me?"

"There are other things a husband must do," Two Ponies said, now speaking in English. It was obvious to Elizabeth that he was uncomfortable with the way things were going, and if her own position had not been so tenuous, she could have even found humor in the situation.

"You are the husband of Moon Cow Woman. She speaks very highly of you."

"But, Moon Cow Woman is an old woman and does not need the same things a young woman needs."

"I want you for my husband," Elizabeth said. "If not, then I choose to become a slave."

Two Ponies blinked a couple of times, then nodded. "Very well," he finally said. He turned to the council and, once again spoke in his own language, which Moon Cow Woman translated for Elizabeth. "I, Two Ponies, will take Captured Woman as my wife. And I give her a new name. From now on she will be known as . . ." He paused and looked at Elizabeth. Her blond hair was shimmering in the light of the council fire. "Sun's Light," he said.

"Sun's Light. It is a fine name," Moon Cow Woman said.

Elizabeth smiled and turned to say something to Moon Cow Woman. At that moment, Elk Heart, in a fit of rage, grabbed a spear and threw it at Elizabeth. Brave Eagle saw it from the corner of his eye and, moving instantly, shot out his hand and caught the spear as it flew by, stopping it with the broad, sharp point just inches away from piercing Elizabeth's body.

Nearly all had seen Brave Eagle's great feat and they cheered him and expressed their admiration for such a deed. Brave Eagle turned toward Elk Heart, ready to do battle with him if needs be, but Elk Heart stomped away from the circle, walking backward and smiling politely at everyone. He climbed onto his horse, facing to the animal's rear, and he rode away. His life as a contraire had begun.

Chapter 4

Independence, Missouri

Parker Stanley was busy taking a careful inventory of the outfit he had put together, using as his guidelines a chapter devoted to "clothing preparation" in the guidebook, *The Prairie Traveler:*

Two blue or red flannel overshirts, open in front with buttons.
Two woolen undershirts. Two pairs thick cotton drawers.
Four pairs woolen socks.
Two pairs cotton socks.
Four colored silk handkerchiefs.
Two pairs stout shoes.
One pair boots.
Three towels.
One gutta percha poncho.
One broad-brimmed hat of soft felt.
One comb and brush.
Two toothbrushes.
One pound hand soap.
Three pounds soap for washing clothes.

One belt knife and small whetstone.
Stout linen thread, large needles, a bit of beeswax, a few buttons, paper of pins, and a thimble, all contained in a small, buckskin or stout cloth bag.

Having assembled his outfit as prescribed by the manual that all prairie travelers followed, Parker decided to take in the sights of the city of Independence. From one of the taverns, he could hear loud singing, from another hearty laughter. At a third, two painted women stood just outside, shouting and waving at the men who passed by. Parker had never seen women painted so garishly, and he couldn't help but stare. One of them saw him looking at them.

"Hello, honey," she called. "Do you like what you see?"

"Yes, ma'am, I reckon I do," Parker replied, not quite sure how to respond.

"Oooh," the harpie squealed. "Did you hear him, Emmalou? He said yes ma'am. He's a gentleman, he is."

"He's too fine for the likes of you, Marilee," the one called Emmalou said. "Honey, how would you like to see the varmint?"

"See the varmint?" Parker replied. "What is that?"

"Lord, chile, you mean you ain't never seen the varmint?" Emmalou lifted her skirt all the way above her knees. "Well, you just come with me, I'll teach you how to pet the varmint just right."

When Parker suddenly realized what she was talking about, he blushed crimson.

"Thank you all the same, ma'am," he said. "But I reckon I'd better pass."

Seeing that they had lost their opportunity with him, the two painted women immediately turned their attention to two other men who were walking by, and Parker continued his exploration of the town.

Three decades earlier, Independence, Missouri, had been built to accommodate the great migration west. Then, there were often trains leaving Independence with anywhere from thirty to as many as three hundred wagons. But the days of the giant trains were over. In the old days they were blazing new territory and it took that many wagons, not only to provide safety in numbers, but also to carry the food and supplies they would need to sustain them for the six-month-long journey. The wagon trains were, in effect, cities on the move.

Such large trains weren't necessary today. Although the transcontinental railroad had not yet been completed, it was being built and much of the plains east of the Rockies could now be reached by rail. And as the railroad progressed west, so did civilization. Towns were now scattered all across what was once wide open territory. Because they would never be more than a couple of weeks away from the nearest settlement, those going West by wagon could now travel in much smaller groups.

Like the giant trains of the past, however,

these smaller trains of immigrants and freight wagons still used Independence as a point of departure. And while the individual trains weren't as large, the departures were much more frequent so that the total number of wagons passing through was still nearly equal. As a result, all of the town's industrial energy and commercial enterprises continued to be dedicated to that singular purpose.

Both sides of Independence Avenue were lined with stores that offered everything one needed to outfit a wagon, and many things one didn't need. Some specialized in cooking utensils, and as Parker Stanley picked his way gingerly down the foul-smelling street, he passed by piles of Dutch ovens, kettles, skillets, reflector ovens, coffee grinders, coffeepots, knives, ladles, tin tableware, butter churns, and water kegs. Another store specialized in bedding and tent supplies, yet another in weapons and ammunition, still another in tools and equipment, including complete surgical and medical kits.

"Here, boy, get the hell out of the way!" a loud, angry voice shouted, and Parker looked around to see a large wagon bearing down on him. The wagon was without bows or canvas, or any of the other accoutrements that would indicate that it was a traveling wagon. The driver popped his whip over the team, keeping them moving in a brisk trot. Parker jumped back enough to avoid the wagon but he couldn't avoid being splashed by the manure and mud which flew up from the rapidly turning wheels.

The wagon was loaded with several large items of furniture: beds, chifferobes, chairs, lounges, dressers, cabinets, and even a large, stand-up clock.

"You'd best be gettin' out of the road, boy," a friendly voice called to him. "The next scavenger might not be kind enough to give you a warning."

Parker stepped up onto the boardwalk which ran alongside the road, and joined the man who spoke to him.

"Thanks," Parker said. "What did you call that man? A scavenger?"

"A scavenger, aye, for that's what he is."

"I don't understand."

"Didn't you see the goods on his wagon? The furniture and such?"

"Yes, I saw it."

"He scavenged it. When the pilgrims start headin' west in a wagon, they are nearly always loaded down with stuff that they got no need in carryin' . . . things like dressers and tables and clocks and the like. Mostly it's fine items that folks want to hold on to. They figure if they made it this far, they can make it all the way to Oregon or California." The man chuckled. "It don't take too long 'fore they see what a damn fool thing it was to try 'n hang on, so they start throwin' things off . . . heavy things." He pointed to the wagon that had come by a moment before. "Folks like him take their wagons down the same trail a few days later just pickin' up the leavin's. They bring it all back an' sell it to the town folks, or to the next wagon that comes through. I tell you, we got some of the most grandly furnished houses in the country right here in Independence ever since the first wagon started West."

"Yes, I can see how that might be the case," Parker said. He experienced a moment of sadness then, as he remembered how his own father had been forced to set off a heavy chest a few days before their wagon was attacked. The chest was a prized piece, brought over from England by Parker's mother's family. She had cried, but Parker's father had explained that there was no way they could continue to haul it with them. Parker had no doubt but that right now, that piece was decorating the parlor of someone's home somewhere in Kansas.

Today there were six wagons drawn up on Independence Avenue. The teams had been hitched, the wagons loaded, and good-byes spoken. This was a hybrid party, consisting of three freight wagons heading West with trade goods, and three wagons of settlers. Wagon trains were generally referred to by the name of their leader, and this train was no exception. It was being called the Reynolds party, so named because Josh Reynolds had been elected as captain of the train.

The three freight wagons had petitioned Reynolds to let them join their freight wagons to his train and he had agreed to let them do so, provided they didn't slow him down. The owner of the three freight wagons was Ira Joyce.

Clay Springer and Ira Joyce had started in the freighting business at the same time, and though there had always been a healthy competition between them, it had been good-spirited. The men were good friends and had even come to each other's aid on occasions in the past.

"It's too bad you didn't get your outfit together in time to start out with us," Ira said as Clay and Parker came down to tell the Reynolds party good-bye. "You could have gone with us as far as Denver."

Clay saw Parker looking at Sue Reynolds, the pretty, fifteen-year-old daughter of the captain of the wagon train. Sue was smiling flirtatiously back at Parker.

"Ah, it's probably a good thing we weren't ready," Clay said. "Otherwise, my partner would get smitten with the young Reynolds girl, and I wouldn't get any work out of him."

"Would *get* smitten?" Ira teased. "Looks to me like he already is. They've really been giving each other the eye."

"What?" Parker said. "No, that isn't true. I mean, we were just . . . uh . . . that is . . ."

"Parker, you don't have to explain anything to us," Ira said. "We like the pretty ladies as much as you seem to."

"She's too young," Parker said. "I was just being nice to her, that's all."

Clay and Ira laughed at Parker's obvious discomfort. At that moment a loud, piercing whistle caught their attention and when they looked toward the sound, they saw Sue Reynolds's father, Josh, in the middle of the street. He was mounted on a fine chestnut horse, standing in the stirrups and looking up and down the line of wagons.

"Drivers, to your wagons!" he called.

There was a sudden flurry of commotion as those who were gathered around the wagons shouted their final good-byes, then backed out of the way. Within seconds the street was completely cleared of everyone and everything but the Reynolds wagons.

There was a moment of anticipation, and during that moment Sue, who was sitting on the seat of the lead wagon, turned one more time to look back at Parker. With a dimpled smile, she waved, and Parker self-consciously waved back. At that moment he wished he were going with them.

"Head 'em out!" Captain Reynolds called.

Reynolds's command was followed by whistles, shouts, and the pistol pops of snapped whips as the train started forward. As it rolled slowly toward the west end of town, the sound was like a symphony on the march, a cacophony of clopping hooves, clanking pots and pans, squeaking wheels, creaking axles, and canvas snapping in the wind.

"Will we see them again?" Parker asked as the wagon trail grew smaller in the distance.

"I hope not," Clay said. "If we do, it means they had trouble. They're going to be on the trail a good week before we even get started."

"Oh."

In a brotherly way, Clay playfully ran his hand through Parker's hair. "You know what they say, don't you?"

"What?"

"Sue Reynolds is a pretty little girl, but she isn't the only flower in the desert. You'll find others."

"I wasn't even thinking that," Parker said, though his burning cheeks belied his denial.

"I'm sure you weren't," Clay said.

One week after the Reynolds party left, Clay was in the Brown Dirt Cowboy having a beer with Larry Beeker, the merchant from whom he had bought much of his trade goods. Beeker had been watching settlers leaving Independence since the days of the behemoth wagon parties, and he was considered a source of expert knowledge for anyone who would make the trek West. Beeker took a drink of his beer, wiped the foam from his lips with the back of his hand, then looked at Clay.

"I been thinkin' on this for the last week," he said. "All the signs are that we're goin' to have an early winter this year. That bein' the case, you'd be best advised to wait till next spring before startin' out."

"What?" Clay asked, surprised by the pronouncement. "Are you serious?"

"Yep. Fact is, I'm not sure the Reynolds party will even make it, and they done got a week to ten days head start on you." Beeker said. "Late as it is now, and with winter comin' sooner than later this year, there's a good chance you'll get caught on this side of the Wasatch Mountains with the first snowfall."

"Now is a hell of a time to tell me . . . after you've sold me all the goods."

"I'd be happy to take 'em back," Beeker offered.

"You might take back what you sold me, but what about the other stuff I bought?"

Beeker shook his head. "Can't do nothin' 'bout them things."

"No, nor would I expect you to," Clay said. He stroked his chin. "Well, there's nothing I can do about it now. I thank you for your concern, Mr. Beeker, but I don't figure I've got any choice. I'm going to have to go on."

"I'm just givin' you a friendly word of advice, is all," Beeker said.

"Yes, well, I'm well experienced on the wagon trail, and so is one of my drivers, Marcus Pearson. Even the boy has spent some time on the trail. I think we will make it through, all right. My partner and I have too much money invested in it to wait. We have to go now, or we may wind up losing everything."

"Well, do what you got to do. Ain't no real concern o' mine," Beeker said, taking another swallow.

Unaware that Clay and Beeker were, at that very moment, discussing the possibility of disaster for their freighting venture, Parker stepped into the saloon. His forays into such establishments were relatively rare, thus he was unaccustomed to the noise and the smells that hit him as he walked through the bat-wings, not only of beer and whiskey, but of expectorated tobacco quids, pipe smoke, and body odor. He spotted Clay standing near the bar.

"Hello, Parker," Clay called out, cheerily. "Why don't you come and join me? Barkeep, a sarsaparilla for my friend."

"Thanks," Parker said.

"Mr. Beeker here has been telling me we are too late," Clay said.

"Too late for what?"

"To go to Salt Lake City this year. He claims we're going to get caught on this side of the Wasatch Range before the first snow falls."

""Will we?" Parker said.

"I don't know," Clay answered candidly. "I have to confess that I have never started this late, and I've never gone that far."

"What about the Reynolds company?" Parker asked. "It hasn't been all that long since they left. If we can catch up with them we'd be no farther behind than they are."

"It may be that the Reynolds party started too late as well," Beeker said. "Though, as they are going no farther than Denver, they may not have any trouble."

"I hope they don't have any trouble," Parker said, thinking of the young Reynolds girl.

"I'm sure they won't," Clay said, reading his young friend's mind.

"If you are bound and determined to leave anyway, I can tell you a way to go," Beeker said.

"What way is that?"

"Most folks go north from Pueblo up to Denver, then through the Rockies by Bridger Pass."

"That's the way I'm planning to go."

"There is another, shorter way."

"What way is that?"

"When you get to Pueblo, instead of turning north to Denver, go straight west."

"You can't go straight west from Pueblo. You can get through the Sangre de Cristo Mountains all right, but after that you have the La Garitas, and they are impassable."

"I can see you've been looking at the map," Beeker said.

"Looking at it? I've got it memorized."

"Uh huh. Did you see a place called Demon's Pass?"

"Don't be talkin' foolish, Beeker," the bartender said. He had been listening to the conversation while he was busily wiping glasses. "People have been talkin' about Demon's Pass for years, but even the mountain men say it ain't smart to take it."

"Maybe it ain't smart in normal times, but these here fellas are gettin' started way late. Asides which, this ain't some big train we're a'talkin' about. They don't have but three wagons."

"Demon's Pass? What is it? I've been freighting ever since the war," Clay said, "and I've never heard of it."

"I think it was used a couple of times back when the wagon trains leavin' here was real big," Beeker said. "But it ain't been used in a long time. Everyone agrees that it is real hard-goin', but they also say it'll save purt near three hundred miles to anyone as might use it."

"I'm not about to try anything unless I hear it from someone who actually knows something about this Demon's Pass," Clay said. "Do you know of any such person who has actually been through it?"

"Matter of fact, I do know somebody," Beeker said. He pointed toward the back of the room. "That mountain man back there has been through it a couple of times. Not with any wagons, mind you, but he has been through it."

Clay picked up his beer. "Come on, Parker, what do you say you and I go over there and have a little confab with him?"

"All right," Parker agreed, picking up his sarsaparilla to take it with him.

"Good luck talking to him," the bartender said.

"Is there any reason I shouldn't talk to him?" Clay asked.

The bartender snorted, holding in a laugh. "That all depends on how long you can hold your breath."

"Hold my breath?"

"I've run across skunks that smelled sweeter," the bartender said.

Clay, noticing that the mountain man's own drink was nearly gone, ordered another and carried it with him to the table. He set the beer down in front of the grizzled man and, without so much as a word of thanks, the mountain man quaffed half of it down. Then, wiping his greasy, matted beard, he looked up at Clay and Parker.

"Sit you down, pilgrims," he invited. "Never let it be said that Lou Daws don't share his table with strangers."

The bartender was right. The man's odor was tremendous.

"Thanks," Clay said as he and Parker steeled themselves against the stench long enough to accept his invitation.

Daws studied them for a moment, looking at them with eyes that were more yellow than brown. Parker had no idea what the natural color of his hair might be, because it was so matted and dirty. There were lines in his face . . . maybe more than just a few, though some of them may have been covered by dirt.

"You the pilgrims plannin' on takin' a train out to Utah?" the mountain man asked.

"Yes. You know about us?"

"Heard someone was doin' it. Then I seen you talkin' to Beeker. So I figure he must've told you about Demon's Pass, and now you're wantin' to talk to me about it."

"Yes," Clay said. "Is that really to save time going to Utah?"

"No, it ain't."

Clay was surprised by Daws's answer.

"Oh? I must have misunderstood. I was told

Demon's Pass would save three hundred miles. And I was told you had seen it."

"I have seen it. Been through it, too."

Clay looked at him in confusion. "But I just asked you if one exists and you said no."

"That ain't what you ask, pilgrim. What you ask was, could you save some time, an' what I said was no. Demon's Pass does cut through the Rockies just west of Pueblo, but you can't save no time by usin' it."

"So then, it doesn't cut off three hundred miles?"

"Yes, it does."

"Then, what is the problem? Indians?"

"Nope."

"I don't understand. Why can't we use it?"

"It would be too hard for you to get your wagons through."

"Surely that isn't an insurmountable problem. We only have three freight wagons to get through, and I have the utmost confidence in my men."

"Pilgrim, that there mountain pass would stop a skinny goat. And you're talkin' about crossin' it in wagons loaded down with pots and pans and all sorts of goods. Plus if you do get through it, you'll run into desert that a lizard packin' water couldn't get through."

Clay waved his hand. "Disregard the difficulty for a moment. Is it physically possible for someone to get through?"

"It can be done, I reckon, if you're talkin' 'bout no more than two or three men travelin' with mules," Daws agreed. "The thing is, they's some damn fool folks believe wagons can use it."

"Well, someone must've taken some wagons through, or else people wouldn't be talking about it."

"That's 'cause more'n thirty years ago, some fool wrote a book saying it could be done."

"Did he take wagons through the cutoff?"

Daws shook his head. "You ask me, I don't think the dumb son of a bitch ever even *seen* the cutoff, let alone take wagons or anything else through it."

"Surely, if he wrote a book about it, it was adequately researched. I mean, he wouldn't make such a claim in writing unless he knew for certain that it's true, would he?"

Daws glared at Clay. "Pilgrim, I don't know nothin' 'bout no book," he said. "I ain't never learned to read. But I do know that cutoff, 'cause I'm one of the few folks that's ever took it and lived to tell about it. If it was worth usin', don't you think folks would be usin' it all the time now? I'm tellin' you that, book or no, that there cutoff is a killer. If you try an' take it, you're goin' to leave some bones bleachin' in the sun."

"I see," Clay said, standing up. "Well, I thank you for your advice."

"Advice ain't worth a pitcher of warm piss, pilgrim, if'n you don't use it," Daws said.

"We'll keep that in mind. Thanks for your time. Parker, we'd best be goin'."

"What do you think?" Parker asked after he and Clay left the saloon.

"He was pretty adamant about not using it, wasn't he? Doesn't sound to me like the cutoff is anything we can rely on," Clay replied.

"Yeah, I guess not."

"Still, he has seen it," Clay suggested.

"That's true," Parker said, sensing that Clay was still considering it.

"He's not only seen it, he's actually come through it," Clay said. "And the way I look at it, if he can make it through, we can too. I figure you and I are as good a man as he is."

Chapter 5

Clay had not yet selected the mules, but he had bought the wagons, and they were lined up on the street in front of the wagon yard. Although they were used, the purchase contract guaranteed that the wagons were in top condition, ready to make the long trip out to Salt Lake City.

Because he was getting excited about the prospect in front of him, Parker was down by the wagons, looking them over carefully. That was when he saw one of the wagon yard employees packing the wheel hubs with grease. Or at least, the man was supposed to be packing the hubs with grease. In actual fact, he was doing no more than slapping a gob of grease on and leaving it there, doing nothing to work it into the hub itself. At a casual glance the wheels looked well packed, but the wheel was turning on a dry axle and it would take no more than a couple of days travel for the axle to be so worn that it would break.

"Mister, you aren't doing that right," Parker said to the wagon yard employee.

The employee was a big man, at least three inches taller and, Parker believed, perhaps fifty pounds heavier than Clay, who was himself larger than average size. That the big man was also strong had been proven a few moments earlier when Parker saw him lift the corner of one of the wagons to remove the wheel from some mud. The big man looked over his shoulder at Parker. The expression on his face showed some irritation at Parker's words.

"What did you say, kid?"

"I said, you aren't doing that right. You've got to get that grease well down into the hub, or it does no good."

"Uh, huh. You know all about this, do you?"

"Yes. I packed the wheels on my pa's wagon."

The big man snorted. "Your pa's wagon, huh? Well, kid, this ain't your pa's wagon."

"I know it isn't," Parker said. He waited a beat, then added steadily, "It's my wagon."

The worker stopped, then turned toward him. "What?"

"This wagon," Parker replied. "It belongs to me. And the purchase contract says that it will be fit for travel. The way you are packing the wheel hubs, it ain't fit."

"Get out of here, kid. Go bother someone else." The worker turned back to the wheel.

"No, sir, I'm not going anywhere. I'm going to stay right here and watch you, to make sure you do that right," Parker insisted.

The worker had just scooped out a paddleful

of grease. This time though, instead of putting it around the wheel hub, he turned quickly and wiped it across Parker's shirt.

"Hey!" Parker shouted in surprise and anger.

The big man laughed. "Now, get out of here, kid, and let a man do his work. *Your* wagon," he said, laughing again. "That's a good one."

Parker walked over to a drum of coal oil, wet a cloth, and used it to clean the grease from the front of his shirt. That accomplished, he picked up a bullwhip and returned to the wagon. The worker, who didn't see Parker, was about ready to daub another paddle of grease onto the wheel when, all of a sudden, the end of the whip snapped out rattlesnake-quick, and snatched the paddle from his hand.

"What the hell?" the worker shouted. Turning around, he saw Parker standing there, holding the whip in his hand. "Boy, you better put that rawhide down, or I'm goin' to make you eat it!"

By now the commotion had brought a few others to the scene and they were shocked by what they saw. On one end of the wagon there stood a young, not-quite-sixteen-year-old boy, poised, in control, and showing not one ounce of fear. At the other end of the wagon was a large, angry man the town knew as Arnold Fenton. What Parker had no way of knowing, but what the townspeople knew only too well, was that Fenton was a bully who enjoyed forcing fights. Just last week he had beaten a man so severely that he had required a doctor's care for over a month.

"If you aren't going to do the job right," Parker said, "then quit wasting the grease and get someone out here who knows what he is doing."

"I told you, stay out of this. This is a man's business, and it's none of yours."

"And I told you that these wagons are mine," Parker said. "Or at least, half mine. That makes it my business."

"Boy, you can go to hell for lying, you know. Or I kin send you there myself." Fenton snarled. A few of Fenton's coworkers who had been drawn to the scene by the commotion laughed nervously. In truth, there wasn't one of them who wouldn't enjoy seeing Fenton get his comeuppance, but they couldn't afford to let him know that.

"My partner isn't lying," Clay said, suddenly appearing on the scene. "He is half owner of these wagons. Now, what's going on here?"

"Take a close look at one of the wheels he's packed, Clay," Parker said. "The way he's doing it, we won't make more'n forty miles before we break down."

Clay walked back to one of the other wagons, the wheels of which had already been packed. He leaned down and examined the wheel closely, then stood up and looked back toward Fenton.

"I do believe my partner is right," Clay said. "You're going to have to do these all over."

Fenton growled, then picked up the spanner wrench that would be needed to open the wheel hub. At first, he turned toward the hub as if he were going to comply, but then, instead of opening the hub, he let out a yell of defiance and lunged toward Clay. He lifted the heavy wrench high over his head, preparing to smash it down on Clay.

"Look out!" someone in the crowd shouted.

Clay froze to the spot, completely defenseless. The only way he could shield himself against the blow was to throw his arms up. That would protect his head, but it would also probably result in at least two broken arms.

Before Fenton could bring the wrench down, however, the bullwhip snapped out again, and with a pop as loud as that heard before, the spanner wrench was jerked cleanly from Fenton's hand.

"Why you!!!" Fenton shouted. He turned and started toward Parker. "I'm going to kill you, you little son of a bitch!"

Parker used the whip once again, this time wrapping it around Fenton's feet. Jerking the whip back, he caused Fenton to go down. Screaming in rage, Fenton regained his feet, but by now, Clay was upon him. He spun Fenton around and drove him back against the side of the wagon with a solid blow to the big man's jaw.

With a loud bellow, Fenton sprang back, swinging wildly. Clay was barely able to avoid his punch.

"Fight! Fight!" someone in the crowd shouted and instantly, the crowd doubled in size as nearly everyone in town ran down to the front of the wagon yard. They watched as the two combatants circled about, their fists doubled.

Parker noticed that Clay was holding his fists up in front of him, whereas Fenton was letting his hands dangle much lower, raising them only when the two got close. Fenton swung again, as wildly as before, and Clay countered with a swift left jab that caught Fenton flush in the face. Despite the power of the blow, Fenton just shook it off.

Surprisingly, Parker was able to observe the fight with an almost detached interest, curious as to how Clay would handle his foe. The youth knew it was a contest of quickness and agility against brute strength, and he hoped to learn by watching.

After easily evading another of Fenton's club-like swings, Clay counterpunched with a second quick jab. Again, it caught his opponent square on the jaw, and again Fenton shrugged it off. As the fight went on, it was apparent that Clay could hit Fenton almost at will, but since he was bobbing and weaving, he couldn't set himself for a telling blow, so his punch didn't faze Fenton at all.

Clay hit Fenton in the stomach several times, obviously hoping to find a soft spot, but to no avail. Giving that up, he started throwing punches toward Fenton's head, but they were just as ineffectual until a quick opening allowed him to slam a left hook squarely into Fenton's face. Parker saw Fenton's already flat nose go even flatter under Clay's fist. From that, Parker knew the man's nose had been broken. Fenton started bleeding profusely, and the blood ran across the big man's teeth. It was a gruesome sight, but Fenton continued to grin wickedly, seemingly unperturbed by his injury.

Clay kept trying to hit his nose again, but Fenton started protecting it. Fenton nonetheless continued to throw great arcing blows toward Clay, who managed to evade any real impact, catching them on his forearms and shoulders. Parker feared that if just one of them connected with his friend's head, Clay would be finished.

A moment later, Clay managed to get another sharp, bruising jab through to Fenton's nose, and for the first time, Fenton let out a bellow of pain. But it was clear that the triumph would be momentary, for the thunderous punches that had repeatedly assailed Clay's shoulders and forearms were beginning to wear him down. Then Fenton managed to land a straight, short right, and Clay fell to his hands and knees.

The crowd groaned, for, in numbers, they had found the courage to root for the one they really wanted to win. With a yell of victory, Fenton rushed over and tried to kick Clay, but at the last second Clay rolled to one side. He hopped up again before Fenton could recover for a second kick and, while the big man was still off balance, sent a brutal punch straight into Fenton's groin.

When Fenton instinctively dropped both hands to his groin, Clay slugged him in the

Adam's apple. Fenton clutched his neck with both hands and sagged, gagging, to his knees. Clay hit him one final time right on the point of the chin, and Fenton fell facedown, unconscious.

The crowd was stunned by the sudden change of fortune and for a moment they were silent. Then they gave up a tremendous cheer.

"Did you kill the son of a bitch?" someone shouted.

"No," Clay answered, shaking his head and catching his breath.

"Well, you'd better kill him, 'cause if you don't, he's goin' to try an' kill you when he comes to."

"Yeah, why don't you step on the son of a bitch's neck and break it?" one of the others asked. "It'd save us all a lot of grief if he was dead. Don't nobody like the bastard, and you'd be doin' everyone a favor."

"No," Clay responded. "I have no intention of killing him."

"Well, you might not kill him, but I sure aim to fire him," a voice said from the crowd. Parker saw Charles Garland working his way through the crowd. Garland owned the wagon yard and had been the one who had sold the wagons to them. Garland looked over at Parker. "I'm told you caught Fenton short-packing the wheel hubs."

"Yes, sir."

"Well, I'm glad you caught him, son, 'cause that's not the way we do business. You don't have to worry none about your hubs. I'll get every one of them greased proper for you and, to apologize for what Fenton did, I'm going to throw in two extra buckets of grease for you to carry with each of the three wagons."

"That's very generous of you, Mr. Garland," Clay said.

Fenton, groaning, was just now getting to his feet. He looked around with eyes that seemed to have some difficulty in focusing.

"Fenton, you're fired. Get whatever gear you might have stored back up there in the shed, and get out," Garland said.

"You firin' me over somethin' this fool kid said?" Fenton protested. "Hell, he don't know what he's talkin' about."

"Is that so? Well, he certainly knows how to tell when someone's not doing their job properly."

"Yeah, and the kid can handle a bullwhip pretty damn well too!" someone shouted, and everyone laughed.

By now, the sheriff was on the scene and he was admonishing the crowd to break it up and move on. As the townspeople started to disperse, Clay and Parker looked at each other for a long moment, then both laughed.

"You all right?" Parker finally asked.

"I'm fine, as long as I don't have to actually use my arms," Clay teased. "How about you?"

"I'm fine," Parker said. He laughed again. "And I had a real good seat for the show."

Clay nodded. "Yeah, well, I'd as soon not had

the starring role but, once it started, it was too late to get out of it." Then, Clay abruptly changed the subject. "Oh, I almost forgot why I'm here. Come over to the stable and have a look at our mules. I just bought eighteen of them, and they are the best-looking creatures you ever saw."

Chapter 6

At the Cheyenne Village

"In twelve days you will be married to Two Ponies," Moon Cow Woman said. "There is much to do before then."

"What must be done?" Elizabeth asked.

"You must learn the ways of our people. And you must learn how to be a good wife. That way, you will not be beaten."

Elizabeth gasped. "Beaten? You mean Cheyenne wives are beaten?"

"Only when they are unwomanly, and do not behave as wives should behave," Moon Cow Woman said. "Then it is a husband's duty to beat his wife."

Elizabeth thought of the gentleness she had seen in Two Ponies' face, and she wondered if she had misread him.

"Does Two Ponies beat his wives?"

"I myself have never been beaten," Moon Cow Woman said. "But Willow Branch and Morning Flower have often been beaten. They are Arapaho, and they are sisters. They are Two

Ponies' other wives. They are unhappy that you will be a new wife, for it threatens their rank with Two Ponies."

"I'm sorry they are unhappy," Elizabeth said. "Perhaps I can make friends with them."

"No," Moon Cow Woman said easily. "They have taken a vow to be your enemy. You cannot become their friend."

"Oh," Elizabeth said. "Surely if I try very hard, I can win them over."

"Arapaho are known to lie with dogs when they wish pleasure and no man is present. Willow Branch and Morning Flower are not worthy to be your friends. Do not waste your time with them. They are my enemies as well."

As Elizabeth and Moon Cow Woman walked through the village, Elizabeth looked around, curious to see what was to be her home. Since the council had broken up, things had returned to normal. Women were at work again, and the men had returned to their horses, or had retired to groups where they sat in circles, telling stories and talking. Children ran free, tolerated by their elders as they darted in and out of hogans and teepees without regard to who lived where, laughing and shouting as children do everywhere.

"I am curious. If you do not get along with Two Ponies' other two wives, how do you all live together?"

"We do not live together," Moon Cow Woman replied. "Each wife has her own teepee, as you must."

"What?" Elizabeth asked. "You mean I have to build a teepee? Why, I wouldn't have the slightest idea of where to start."

"I will help you," Moon Cow Woman said. The other two wives of Two Ponies appeared then. They were considerably younger-looking than Moon Cow Woman, but both were just as plump. It became very obvious to Elizabeth at that moment that being the wife of a chief meant that at least you didn't go hungry.

Moon Cow Woman and the other wives began speaking, but Elizabeth couldn't understand what they were saying.

"Look, Willow Branch," Morning Flower said. "Moon Cow Woman has become the slave of Sun's Light."

"Yes, see how she helps Sun's Light," Willow Branch replied, putting the same contemptuous sneer in her voice as had been in Morning Flower's insult. "Perhaps she will also hold on to Two Ponies' penis, to help him mount her."

"As you hold on to the penis of a dog to help him mount your sister?" Moon Cow Woman replied.

"You speak with the tongue of the first wife now, old woman. But soon Two Ponies will tire of you and he will stop coming to your lodge. Then you will beg for scraps, and if I feel kindly toward you, I may feed you along with the dogs of the camp," Willow Branch said.

"I have no fear that I will be discarded," Moon Cow Woman said. "You have the fear, or you would not make a vow to be the enemy of Sun's Light."

"You will see," Willow Branch replied. "It is not only we who shall be the enemy of Sun's Light. Soon, many others will be her enemy as well, for they will learn that the word of a white woman is not to be trusted."

Elizabeth had no idea what Willow Branch and Morning Flower were saying . . . but from the tone of their voices and the looks on their faces, she figured she was just as well off not knowing.

Independence

Clay and Parker were discussing Demon's Pass.

"It's a difficult decision to make because once we start through it, we have no choice but to go on," Clay said. "If we turn back, that means giving up any chance of reaching Salt Lake City this year. We could wind up bankrupt."

"Whatever you decide is fine with me," Parker said.

"No, that's not right," Clay replied. "You are a full partner in this operation, Parker. You have as much to lose as I do. It's a decision we are going to have to make together."

"I appreciate that you call me a full partner," Parker said. "But we both know that this whole thing is your idea, so whatever you decide is what we will do. But, if you must have my opinion, I think we should try the cutoff. How bad can it be, if it saves three hundred miles?"

"I appreciate your support, Parker," Clay said, putting his hand on the boy's shoulder. "All right, let me think about it. I'll come up with something before the final decision has to be made."

The decision was still not made on the morning they were to leave, but that didn't slow their departure. Mounted on the first horse he had ever owned, Parker leaned forward and patted the animal on the neck. With a new rifle stuck down in the saddle holster, and the unaccustomed weight of a Colt on his hip, Parker surveyed the train of wagons that was about to depart.

Although there were only three wagons, each was pulled by a team of six mules, stretching the company out for more than a block. Each wagon had a driver, along with two outriders, in addition to Clay and Parker.

As head driver, Marcus Pearson would be handling the first wagon. Marcus had an unerring sense of direction and could navigate the open spaces by stars and reckoning, as accurately as a ship at sea could be navigated by compass, watch, and sextant. Clay also knew that he could count on Marcus's loyalty. And in an operation such as the one he was undertaking, loyalty counted for a lot.

Jason Mills, the young man who had been working in the livery stable, was driving the second wagon. After meeting him, Parker and Jason became friends. When Jason learned of the excursion to Salt Lake City, and of Parker's unique position within the company, he begged Parker to hire him. Clay cautioned Parker about it, suggesting that Jason might have trouble taking orders from someone who was younger than he was. But Jason insisted that it wouldn't bother him, and he pledged his loyalty.

Despite his young age, Jason was exceptionally good with a gun. Shortly after he was hired, he had given the others an amazing shooting demonstration. He held a washer on the back of his hand, then turned his hand to let the washer fall toward a pie pan on the ground. At the same time the washer started to fall, Jason began his draw, and he pulled his gun, fired, and hit his target before the washer plunked into the pie pan. By his own admission though, Jason had never shot at a man, nor had he ever been shot at.

The driver of the third wagon was Frank Pecorino. Pecorino was a dark, brooding sort of man. He volunteered the information that he was from "back East" without ever saying what city that meant. Some questioned Clay's wisdom at hiring an easterner to drive a freight wagon, but Pecorino proved to be an exceptionally good driver. He explained that his experience came from driving a beer wagon, heavily loaded with oversized beer barrels. It required a delicate touch to maneuver those wagons without spilling your load, and Pecorino had mastered that touch.

The two outriders were Paul Tobin and Greg

Gibson. Paul rode a horse as if he had been born in the saddle, and Clay hired him after seeing him win a horse race, coming in at least ten lengths ahead of his nearest competitor. Greg Gibson had recently taken a discharge from the army. Hearing that an outfit was being formed to take cargo to the Mormons at Salt Lake City, he actively sought the job.

Though Independence had long been the jumping-off point for western adventures, the people of the town were still unjaded to the momentous event of a wagon train hitting the trail. As a result, several of the townspeople had gathered on Independence Avenue to watch the outfit's departure.

True to his word, Charles Garland provided each wagon with two extra buckets of grease, which now hung from beneath the wagons. Garland was in the front of the crowd, waiting to bid good-bye when the company pulled out. Most of the employees of the wagon yard were there as well, though conspicuous by his absence was Arnold Fenton.

By now the final good-byes had been said, the wagon drivers had climbed onto the high-board, and the outriders were mounted. For a moment, all other traffic and activity came to a halt as everyone stood poised for the journey to begin. Clay, who had ridden along the length of the wagons for one last check, now came back to the front, his horse at a clod-throwing gallop. He pulled his horse to a stop alongside Parker, then smiled at his young friend.

"Mr. Stanley, would you like to give the order?" he asked.

A huge smile spread across Parker's face, and he stood in his stirrups to stare back down along the train of wagons. The three drivers and two outriders, all of whom were aware of, and accepted without question, Parker's position as coleader of the outfit, looked at him expectantly.

"Wagon's ho!" Parker shouted.

With whistles, shouts, and cracking whips, the wagons started forward. Within a few steps the mules had reached the speed of two and one-half miles per hour. That half mile per hour advantage over oxen would give them five extra miles per day, thus justifying the extra expense of using mules.

As they pulled out of town, Parker contemplated the trip before them. It would be long, arduous, and perhaps filled with adventure. There was no doubt that it would also be filled with danger.

Traveling by wagon was certainly not new to Parker. After all, he and his family had been on the trail for the better part of two months before they were attacked. Now he found many of the sights, sounds, and smells were so familiar that every time he looked around, he half expected to see his mother, father, and sister.

He wondered about Elizabeth. Was she alive? If so, how was she being treated? The fact that he was now a full partner in a freighting operation, and, quite frankly, having the time of his life, while his sister could be undergoing the harshest kind of conditions, made him feel more than a little guilty. He made a conscious decision not to think about Elizabeth. There was nothing he could do about her condition, and dwelling on it only made it worse.

By the end of the second day, they were sixty miles west of Independence, camped on a grassy glen near a stream of clear water. They ate well that night, then sat around the fire and watched as sparks popped out of the burning wood to rise on a column of heat, joining with the thousands of stars that dusted the night sky.

"Say, have any of you ever met any of these Mormons?" Pecorino asked.

"Sure," Gibson said. "Ain't you?"

"You kiddin'?" Pecorino replied. "I never met anyone who wasn't Catholic till I was a full-grown man."

"Well, I've met lots of 'em," Gibson said.

"What are they like?" Pecorino asked.

"They ain't like nothin'," Gibson answered. "They's just like ever'one else."

"Is it true their men can have more'n one wife?" Tobin asked.

"That's true."

"That would be somethin', wouldn't it?"

Marcus snorted. "Hell, I ain't never wanted one wife, let alone more than one. Whores is better'n wives any time."

"So what you're sayin' is, you ain't goin' out there to get yourself married?" Gibson teased.

"Nope. I'm goin' out there to take me a swim in the Great Salt Lake."

Tobin laughed. "Marcus, you've been saying how you can't sink in the Great Salt Lake, but chances are you'll be so covered with trail dirt by the time we get there, you'll sink like a rock."

"Well, Salt Lake or no Salt Lake, this is the life," Jason Mills said as he poured himself a second cup of coffee. "No more mucking out stables for me."

"Yeah, it beats workin' in a store all to hell, too," Tobin said. Tobin, who was in his midthirties, spoke with the accent of the Mississippi hill country.

"Listen, I don't want you boys to be gettin' the wrong idea 'bout all this," Marcus said.

"What do you mean by the wrong idea?" Jason asked. "You tryin' to tell me this ain't better'n working in a stable?"

"Or driving a beer wagon?" Pecorino added.

"I mean it ain't always goin' to be nice and peaceful and comfortable like this," Marcus answered. "If I've learned anything in this business, it's that things that can get worse, generally do."

"Which brings up something I've been wanting to talk about," Clay said.

"What's that? You mean about things gettin' worse?" Gibson asked. " 'Cause you don't have to tell me about that. Don't forget, I just come out of the army. I know about things gettin' worse. They got officers in the army makin' sure things gets worse as a full-time job."

The others laughed.

"Actually, I've been struggling some with a decision I have to make," Clay said. "We've got two big ranges of mountains to go through. First, there's the Rockies in Colorado, then the Wasatch in Utah. Now, we're going to get to the Rockies before the snow falls, so we should get through them all right. The problem is going to be the Wasatch. It'll be much later by the time we get there, and if we don't get through Demon's Pass before the first winter storm hits, we could wind up trapped on this side."

"Snow. Lord, you're talking about snow when it was so hot today that I nearly melted," Pecorino said.

"He's talkin' about snow because we've got a long way to go," Marcus explained. "And by the time we reach Utah, it'll be a lot colder." Marcus looked at Clay. "Still, we should be able to beat the snow, don't you think, Clay?"

"I don't know," Clay admitted. "Beeker says we're goin' to have an early winter this year. I've known him awhile, and he's generally right about such things."

"So, what do you think we should do about it? Hole up in Denver for the winter?"

"No, we can't do that. Parker and I have every cent we own in the world tied up in this operation. If we don't get through to Salt Lake City in a timely way, we'll lose everything."

"Then, we'll just have to get through, that's all," Marcus said.

"I don't see how we can go any faster," Pecorino said. "Seems to me like the mules are goin' about as fast as they can go . . . and they're fresh and this is flat ground."

"Frank has a point," Tobin said. "We can't go no faster than we're already a'goin'. Fact is, we're probably goin' to have lots of days where we go a lot slower."

"No probably to it. We *are* going to have days when we go slower," Clay said. "That's why I've been giving this a lot of thought." Clay walked over to the fire and held a stick into the flames until it caught, then used the flaming brand to light his pipe. He took several puffs before he spoke again. "The other day, Parker and I heard about something called Demon's Pass. I've been thinking about it ever since then, and I think we should take it. It's supposed to be a shortcut through the Rockies, and it may be our only chance to beat the snows to Reata Pass."

"Clay, you ever seen this-here Demon's Pass?" Marcus asked.

"No," Clay admitted. "But I talked to someone who has."

"Someone who has seen it for sure? Or someone who is just talkin' about it?"

"He's not only seen it, he's come through it."

"And he says we should try it?"

Parker looked over toward Clay to see how he would answer the question.

Clay cleared his throat. "Uh, no," he finally said. "In fact, he advised us against taking it."

"What is Demon's Pass, anyway?" Jason asked.

"It's a southern pass through the Rockies. If we use it, we don't have to go all the way up to Denver before crossing. It will also cut off three hundred miles from the total distance to Salt Lake City," Marcus answered.

The others whistled. "Three hundred miles?" Pecorino said. "You mean this shortcut saves three hundred miles, and here we are just sittin' around here talking about it? Of *course* we should take it."

"It's supposed to be a very arduous route," Clay said.

"How hard can it be?" Tobin asked. "I mean, so maybe it's a little steeper, or narrower or something. Three hundred miles is three hundred miles."

"I want to be honest with you," Clay said. "I'll tell you how hard it can be. Nobody ever takes it, even though folks have known about it for years."

"I'm sure there have been some who have used it," Marcus said.

"'And died trying," Clay replied.

"Wait a minute, now are you for it, or agin it?" Marcus asked.

"I confess that I do want to take it," Clay said. "But I also want you to know the truth about it."

"If you decide you want to take this cutoff, I'll be right there with you," Marcus said. "And you won't hear another word out of me."

"If you're willing to take it, you must think we can get through it. Is the trail really that hard?" Tobin asked.

"Well, there is no doubt that it is hard for the larger wagon trains," Clay answered. "But if you think about it, they were trying to take dozens of wagons through. And, they had men, women, and children, as well as old people with them. Now, look at us. We have only three wagons, we're using mules rather than oxen, and we have no women, children, or old people with us."

"Except Marcus. He's pretty old," Jason joked, to the laughter of the others.

"Don't worry none 'bout me. I say take it," Marcus said.

"Me too. Hell, I'm for anything that will save three hundred miles," Tobin joined in.

"Count me in as well, Gibson added.

"I appreciate that," Clay said. "But, Marcus, I never figured you for anything different. And, Tobin, you and Gibson are on horseback." Clay turned toward Jason and Pecorino. "But you two boys are driving wagons. It's going to be a lot harder for you. So whether or not we try the cutoff depends on what you say."

"I say let's do it," Jason said, quickly. "Sounds like great fun to me."

"Fun?" Pecorino asked. "You think it will be fun?"

"Like I said, it beats mucking out stables," Jason said.

The others guffawed.

"It's up to you, Frank," Clay said. "What's your vote?"

"What about Parker here?" Pecorino asked. "I'd like to know what you think about this?"

"I'm for trying it," Parker said. "And I've been for it from the beginning. But, like Clay said, I'm on horseback. It's you wagon drivers who will have it the hardest."

"And that leaves you, Frank," Jason said. "Are you for it, or against it?"

"I'm not at all for it," Pecorino said. "On the other hand, I don't intend to be the one to stop it. So, I'll go along with the rest of you. You want to take the cutoff, I'll be there with you."

"Thanks, men," Clay said. "I appreciate all of you sticking together on this."

The next day warmed quickly, and with the heat came the clouds. Parker watched them build up into towering mountains of cream, growing higher and higher and turning darker and darker, until the sky in the west was nearly black as night. The air stopped stirring, and it became very hushed, with only the sound of rhythmically clopping hooves, rolling wheels, and the occasional bang of a hanging pan or kettle interrupting the quiet.

There was a strange, heavy feeling in the air, and the men kept a nervous eye on the sky before them. Even the animals seemed to sense that something was about to happen, and were acting skittish.

Parker was riding alongside Marcus. "Marcus,

look at the mules. Why are they shaking their heads like that?" he asked.

"They can smell the sulphur, boy."

"Smell the sulphur? What does that mean?"

"That means that the very gates of hell are about to open."

They could see the lightning first, rose-colored flashes buried deep in the clouds, followed several seconds later by distant thunder, low and rumbling. Then the lightning broke out of the clouds. No longer luminous flashes, the lightning now came as great, jagged streaks on the distant horizon, stretching from the clouds to the ground. The electric streaks were soon followed by booming thunder that made the hairs stand up on the men's arms.

Then the winds came. At first it was no more than a gentle freshening, still hot and dry, laden with the dust of the prairie. But the wind's speed soon increased, and Parker could feel a dampness on its breath.

The intensity of the lightning also increased. Instead of one or two flashes, there were ten or fifteen, and from each major spear there came half a dozen more forking off from it. The thunder which followed was hard and sharp, and it came right on the heels of the lightning. After each flash, the thunder rolled over their heads with a long, deep-throated roar.

"Here it comes!" someone shouted.

The deluge came then, sweeping down on them from the west, moving toward them like a giant gray wall. The raindrops slammed into the wagons, hitting hard and heavy, as if the wagons were being pelted by great clods.

The rain was falling so hard that Parker, who was now riding at the rear, could not even see the front wagon only yards ahead. All about him lightning streaked and thunder crashed, and water cascaded down on him with as much ferocity as if he had been standing under a waterfall. He was wearing a hat and an oiled canvas poncho, but that did very little to protect him. He was drenched clear through to the bone.

Suddenly one of the canvas cargo covers on Jason's wagon caught in the wind and tore loose from its fastenings and came flying back toward Pecorino's wagon. Pecorino's team, already frightened by the thunder and lightning, saw something big and white flapping toward them, and they whirled around and jerked the wagon into a tight turn. Pecorino wasn't expecting it and was tossed from his seat. The mules broke into a gallop.

"Whoa!" Pecorino shouted, chasing after them on foot. "Come back here!"

Parker knew that Pecorino's shouts would have no effect on the runaway team, so, slapping his legs against the side of his horse, he bolted after them.

At first, Parker thought it might be best just to let the mules run until they could run no more. Then he could just ride up to them and lead them back to the group. But as he looked ahead he saw that the mules were making a mad dash for the edge of a fairly deep ravine. The gulley was little more than a rift in the prairie, perhaps cut by some ancient torrential rain like the one they were now experiencing. Nevertheless, it was several feet deep, certainly deep enough to inflict serious, probably fatal injury to any animal that might run into it at full speed.

Parker leaned over the withers of his horse, urging it to greater and greater speed. He drew even with the galloping team, then slowly began to move to the front. The space between the lead animals and the edge of the ravine was rapidly narrowing.

Finally Parker was far enough ahead of the runaway team to put his horse between them and the gulley. He did so and, taking off his poncho, waved it at the team. He was assisted in this effort by a crashing thunderbolt which stuck so close that Parker could feel the electricity crackle in the air around him.

The mules, originally frightened by the specter of a flying canvas, were completely terrified anew. They wheeled away from the ravine edge and started galloping out across the open prairie. Parker chased after them again.

The mules ran for at least three miles before exhaustion overtook them. They slowed, then finally, they stopped. Parker, who had kept pace with them, slowed his horse to a walk, then came up quietly beside them. By now the downpour had eased somewhat, and the thunderheads had passed through, flashing and rumbling now far to the east. Parker rode to the head of the team, talking to them in a quiet and soothing voice, and soon they stood quietly. He tied off his horse on the back of the wagon, then climbed into the wagon to drive them back.

By the time Parker brought the runaway wagon back to the others, the rain had come to a stop. Both men and cargo were soaking wet. After some discussion it was decided that, with the sun now beginning to peek through the gloom, they would stop long enough to allow things to be dried out.

Chapter 7

In the Cheyenne Camp

Elizabeth was glad that Moon Cow Woman had placed herself in the position of being her friend and defender. Because Moon Cow Woman was the first wife of Two Ponies, she was respected within the village, and most of the women, out of deference to Moon Cow Woman, had accepted Elizabeth.

Not so Willow Branch and Morning Flower. As Moon Cow Woman started out to help Elizabeth build her teepee, the other two wives of Two Ponies mocked her. Of course, not understanding their language, Elizabeth had no idea what they were saying, though she could tell from the tone and texture of the conversation that their words were far from friendly.

Moon Cow Woman had gathered several poles together and she indicated to Elizabeth that she should pick up a rather large bundle. As Elizabeth leaned over to pick up the bundle, Willow Branch spit on her.

Elizabeth's reaction was instantaneous. She

lashed out at Willow Branch, bringing her hand up and around in a backhanded slap, mustering all the strength of which she was capable. The result was a blow which not only startled Willow Branch by its suddenness, but also by its strength, and the Indian woman was knocked flat on her backside. She lay on the ground with her ears ringing and her head spinning, surprised that a woman who appeared to be so small and weak could hit with such stunning force.

"Return her blow, my sister!" Morning Flower urged.

"Aiee," Willow Branch said, sitting up and rubbing her eye gingerly. "The white woman has the strength of a horse."

Elizabeth picked up the bundle, determined not to let anyone see how heavy it was. Laughing, Moon Cow Woman began shouting to others nearby.

"I have told them how you bested Willow Branch," Moon Cow Woman explained.

Moon Cow Woman walked for quite a ways through the village and Elizabeth followed, tiring, but determined to bear the load without complaint. Finally, Moon Cow Woman stopped and looked around.

"Have you found no place you like?" she asked.

"I beg your pardon?"

"It is to be your teepee," Moon Cow Woman explained. "It is for you to choose the place."

"How about right here?" Elizabeth asked,

dropping the heavy load at her feet. If she had known that, she would have pitched the teepee right where she had picked up the bundle in the first place.

"Yes, this is a good spot," Moon Cow Woman agreed. "You are near the water, yet far from where the horses are kept. The ground is flat where the teepee will be, but it is higher than the water so you will not get wet during the big rains. You have chosen a good spot."

Elizabeth realized then that by stopping where she had, Moon Cow Woman had actually chosen this spot. But she had done so in such a way as to make it look as if Elizabeth had chosen it herself.

Moon Cow woman began undoing the bundles Elizabeth had carried, and Elizabeth watched carefully, trying to figure out how the thing went together. In addition to the poles, the bundles also held a teepee cover made of buffalo hides, stitched with the same type of sinew that held Elizabeth's dress together.

Quickly and deftly, Moon Cow Woman tied the poles together, using the same cord that had bound the bundle. She tied them at one end, and raised the poles with the tied end up, then she spread the bottoms out so that they formed a tripod. The remaining poles, which were as tall but not as big around, were leaned against the tripod until they formed a cone. Next, Moon Cow Woman put the teepee cover in place by tying it to a stout lifting pole and hoisting it into position. After that, the cover was unfolded around the poles, pegged to the ground along the bottom, then closed at the seam with wooden pins. Finally, two poles were attached to the smoke flaps at the top, and Moon Cow Woman showed Elizabeth how to adjust the poles to vary the size and angle of the opening. The entire operation had taken only a few minutes, and Elizabeth was amazed at how sturdy the finished product was.

"Take it down," Moon Cow Woman instructed.

"What? Why? I think it is good," Elizabeth replied.

"It is good," Moon Cow Woman said. "But you must do it yourself. Take it down, then put it up."

Elizabeth sighed, but she appreciated what Moon Cow Woman was doing for her, so she disassembled the teepee, then started to put it back up.

"No," Moon Cow Woman said. "First you must prepare to move. Then you put it back up."

Elizabeth tried to remember how the bundle had been originally wrapped and how the pegs and poles were arranged, and finally she was able to get it into condition so that it could be moved. Moon Cow Woman inspected everything with a critical eye. Finally, with a grunt, she gave her approval.

"Now, put the teepee up," Moon Cow Woman said.

Elizabeth unpacked the bundle, and, remembering what she had seen, began erecting the teepee. She put up the tripod, then the poles, and finally put the teepee cover in place. When it was all pegged down around the sides and held closed with the lodge pins, she looked at Moon Cow Woman, who smiled proudly.

"I did it!" she said.

"It is wrong," Moon Cow Woman said.

"Wrong? What's wrong with it?" Elizabeth asked.

"Where does sun come up?"

"In the east, of course. What does that have to do with it?"

"The sun comes up there, over that mountain," Moon Cow Woman said, pointing to the east. "The teepee must always open to the direction of the morning sun."

Elizabeth glanced over toward the other teepees and hogans in the village, and only then did she notice that Moon Cow Woman was correct. Every door in the village was facing east.

"Very well," Elizabeth said. "I shall change it."

Patiently, Elizabeth pulled up all the ground pegs, then she took the lifting poles and hoisted the cover around until the door opening was facing east. After that she repositioned the smoke flaps. Finally she looked toward Moon Cow Woman with a hopeful glance.

"It is good," Moon Cow Woman said. "You will live here until you are married." Moon Cow Woman turned and started to walk back to her own hogan.

"Thank you for helping me," Elizabeth said. As she turned back toward the teepee which was now hers, she caught the smell of roasting meat, and suddenly realized that she was hungry.

"Moon Cow Woman, wait!" she called.

The old native woman stopped and looked back toward her.

"Moon Cow Woman . . . I have nothing to eat."

"Until you are married, it is for Elk Heart to feed you," Moon Cow Woman said.

"Elk Heart?"

"It was Elk Heart who killed those who were feeding you," Moon Cow Woman explained. "It is now for him to feed you."

"Oh, great," Elizabeth said sarcastically. "If I have to depend on him, I'll probably starve to death."

Moon Cow Woman turned without another word and started back toward her hogan. Elizabeth watched her for a few moments, then she looked down toward the stream. She squared her shoulders. Surely there were fish there.

Elizabeth walked down to the stream and stood on the bank, looking into the water. After a few moments she saw flashes of silver—trout darting around the rocks, and swimming swiftly through the icy water. Yes, she thought. The trout would make a fine meal. All she had to do now was catch one.

As Elizabeth stood on the bank of the stream looking down at the trout, trying to figure out how to catch a fish, Elk Heart approached the stream from the other side. He was mounted on his horse and he was riding backward. He swung down from his horse and, walking backward, splashed across the stream. He was carrying two rabbits.

"Elk Heart," Elizabeth said. "I wasn't sure you would come back. You were so angry. I thought I would never say it, but you are a welcome sight, especially with the rabbits."

"These are not for you," Elk Heart said, handing the rabbits to her.

"What?"

"These are not for you!" he said again, more impatiently. Again, he handed the rabbits to her.

"Then why are you handing them to me?"

"Do not take them."

"All right, I won't," Elizabeth said, putting her hands behind her back.

"Do not take them!" Elk Heart said again, louder than before.

"Take them, Sun's Light," a voice said, and Elizabeth saw a young boy of about fourteen.

"I don't understand," Elizabeth said. "He says don't take them, but he keeps handing them to me."

"He is a contraire," the young boy explained. "He does everything backward."

"Oh," Elizabeth said, reaching for the rabbits. "Oh, yes, I remember now." As soon as Elizabeth took the rabbits, Elk Heart smiled, and backed across the stream to his horse.

"Will you eat some of the rabbit?" Elizabeth called to him.

"Yes," Elk Heart said.

"Yes? But that means no, doesn't it?"

"No," Elk Heart said. He climbed onto his horse, slapped his legs against the animal's side and the horse started away with Elk Heart hanging on, still riding backward.

"Heavens will he be like that for the rest of his life?"

"No. First, he will go crazy in the head, then he will do something bad," the boy said, matter-of-factly. Smiling, he pointed to the rabbit. "I would eat some of the rabbit if you will have me."

Elizabeth smiled at the young Indian. "Of course I will have you," she said. "What is your name?"

"Running Rabbit," the young Indian said.

"Well, Running Rabbit, let us hope that neither of these rabbits is your relative," she teased.

"All animals are the relatives of all Cheyenne," Running Rabbit said seriously. He looked around. "You do not have a fire?"

"No," Elizabeth said. "And I'm not sure I can even get one started."

"You gather wood," Running Rabbit said. "I will bring fire."

Elizabeth decided to take help when and where she could find it, so she gathered the wood and made a pile in front of the teepee. Running Rabbit returned a few moments later with a burning brand, and he used it to start a fire.

A short time later the rabbits were spitted, and turning slowly over the fire. The aroma of their cooking soon mingled with those of the other fires in the camp.

That night Elizabeth spent the first night in her own teepee. The night was chilly and she shivered with the cold until Running Rabbit came into the teepee and, without waking her, covered her with a blanket.

In her dreams, it wasn't Running Rabbit who covered her. It was her mother, and it wasn't a blanket, it was a beautiful patchwork quilt.

"Why not make the quilt all of one color?" Elizabeth asked her mother.

"Because a quilt like this does more than keep a body warm. It enriches the soul. In years to come, you will be able to look at this quilt and remember." Elizabeth's mother pointed to a piece of green. "This came from the dress your great grandmother wore when she came across the sea. And this is from the trousers your grandfather wore during the War for Independence." Elizabeth's mother pointed to several other patches in the multicolored quilt, telling a story about each one.

When Elizabeth awoke the next morning, she pulled the quilt lovingly around her, before realizing that it was just a simple woven blanket. She allowed herself a few moments of sorrow as she thought about her mother, and the tragedy that befell the family.

Then, she put such thoughts out of her mind. She could not change the past. Her only hope for survival was to adapt to the present, which she intended to do. She looked at the blanket in wonderment, thinking that someone must have brought it to her during the night.

As she was contemplating the blanket, she heard someone calling from outside the teepee.

"Ho, Sun's Light! Come outside."

Elizabeth stepped outside. The village was silent with sleep. It was still very early in the morning, so early that the sun was burning deep red, and the mist upon the valley had not yet burned away. There was dew sparkling on the grass in all the colors of the rainbow. There, standing before her teepee, holding the reins of a horse, stood Brave Eagle.

"I bring you this gift from Two Ponies," Brave Eagle said. He handed the reins to Elizabeth.

"A horse?" Elizabeth said. "You mean I am to have my own horse?"

"It is your wedding gift."

Elizabeth walked up to the animal and patted it affectionately. "Oh, it's beautiful," she said. "'I've never had a horse."

"It is the swiftest of all Two Ponies' mounts," Brave Eagle said. "He honors you with such a gift."

"Tell Two Ponies I am greatly pleased by his wonderful gift," Elizabeth said.

Brave Eagle said nothing. He just mounted his

own horse and started riding back through the early morning quiet of the village.

Elizabeth stood, petting the animal for several moments, talking to him softly, looking down beyond the stream to the rolling prairie which stretched out, endlessly, before her.

Somewhere out there was Oregon, the destination of her parents.

Somewhere out there, too, was the world she had known before entering this world.

Somewhere out there was freedom.

Then, with absolutely no thought or prior planning, Elizabeth decided to leave. She climbed onto the back of the horse, and moving quietly, rode him across the stream away from the village.

As soon as she was far enough away from the village not to be heard, she slapped her legs against the side of her horse to start him running.

"Go, horse, go!" she urged.

The horse burst forward like a cannonball, reaching incredible speed almost immediately. Elizabeth bent low over the pony's neck, holding on tightly, laughing into the rush of wind with the pure thrill of the run and exaltation of the escape. For a moment, she felt as if she and the horse between her legs were one, sharing the same flexing muscles and pounding bloodstream. The horse's hooves kicked up little spurts of dust behind him as he galloped across the plains. Brave Eagle had said this was the swiftest of all Two Ponies' horses, and as she slapped her legs against its side, she believed him. She pushed the horse on, faster and faster, until she had the dizzying sensation that she was going to fly!

Suddenly, and seemingly from out of nowhere, Brave Eagle appeared in front of her. He rode out from behind a rise of ground, and Elizabeth's horse, startled by him, stopped and reared up. Elizabeth slid off the horse's back, falling painfully to the ground.

"What the devil!" she called. "What are you doing here?" She got up and began dusting herself off, thankful that she wasn't hurt. The horse she had been riding turned and ran back into the village without her.

"Where do you go?" Brave Eagle asked.

"Where do I go? I go away from here, that's where!" Elizabeth answered angrily.

"No. You must return to the village."

"Oh, please, let me go, won't you? I won't cause anyone any harm. I just want to go back to my own people. Let me do that, and you'll never see me or hear of me again."

"I cannot do that," Brave Eagle said. "Today you must become the wife of Two Ponies."

"I do not want to become the wife of Two Ponies. Can you understand that?"

"No," Brave Eagle answered. "I cannot understand. You went before the council to ask to be the wife of Two Ponies. Why is it that you no longer want to marry him?"

"I never wanted to marry him," Elizabeth insisted. "I only did that to get away from Elk

Heart, Kicking Horse . . . and to get away from you," she concluded. "I assure you, I have no desire to marry Two Ponies, nor anyone else. Now please, can't you see it would be better for everyone if you just let me go?"

Brave Eagle reached down and grasped Elizabeth by the upper arm, then lifted her onto his horse in front of him. He had incredible strength, and he picked her up as easily as if she had been a child.

"Come," he said, as if tired of the discussion. "We will go back to the village and find your horse. Do not try to leave again. I will not speak of your foolishness to anyone—this time."

"I hate you," Elizabeth said. "I hate all of you, and I want to go back to my own people." She began to cry, and all her pent-up emotions since her capture—fear, heartbreak, grief over the death of her mother, father, and brother, anger, humiliation, and frustration—all burst forth in bitter sobs of anguish.

"We will stay here until all your tears are gone," Brave Eagle said easily.

Elizabeth could not help but wonder if she would ever leave this place . . . or ever see her own people again.

On The Kansas Plains

Arnold Fenton relieved himself.

"Damn, ain't you got no more manners than to piss where we live?" one of the others asked.

"We ain't livin' here, we're just campin'

here," Fenton replied as he aimed toward a grasshopper. He laughed as the grasshopper, caught in the sudden stream, darted away.

"Well, it's where we are livin' now, so don't be pissin' here anymore. Next time you have to shake the lily, go some'ers else to do it."

The man lodging the complaint was lean as rawhide. He had a thin face, a hawklike nose, and gray eyes. His name was Shardeen, but nobody knew if that was his first name or his last.

"I reckon I'll piss about anywhere I want to," Fenton said with a growl. He looked around at Shardeen, and the three other men who were with him. "And there ain't no little dried up toad of a man like you goin' to stop me," he added.

"I've already stopped you," Shardeen answered. "Don't do it again."

Fenton laughed at the audacity of this small man with the big mouth. He started toward him. "How the hell do you plan to stop me, little man?"

In a blink, Shardeen pulled his pistol. "If you do it again, I'll shoot your pecker off," he said easily.

Fenton stopped in his tracks. Most men, especially someone the size of Shardeen, would quake in their boots around Fenton, but clearly Shardeen wasn't intimidated by him. In fact, Shardeen was, and had been, contemptuous of Fenton almost from the moment they had met. There was no mystery to it. Shardeen had the reputation of being someone who was particularly skilled with a pistol. That skill freed him from any fear of Fenton's size or strength. In Shardeen's hands the Colt revolver really was what men called it: an equalizer.

"We ain't goin' to get nowhere fightin' amongst ourselves," one of the other men named Murdock said. Murdock was the oldest of the group. The remaining two men were Boyer and Eakins.

"Hey, Fenton, how long you think it'll be before they show up?" Boyer asked.

Fenton, glad to have the moment diffused, looked back east toward Independence, Missouri.

"They'll make about thirty miles a day," he said. "So I figure they'll show up by midday tomorrow. Three wagons, all loaded with goods."

"How many men?"

"There's two leadin' 'em, man named Clay Springer, and a snot-nosed boy named Parker Stanley. Then there's three drivers, and two outriders."

"Wait a minute. That makes seven of 'em," Eakins said. "Seven of them and only five of us. I thought you said this would be easy."

"Two of 'em is nothin' but boys. Parker Stanley is one, and Jason Mills is the other. And you don't be worryin' none about Springer and the Stanley boy. I aim to take personal care of both of them my ownself."

"What kind of goods are they carryin'?" Boyer asked.

"Some guns, flour, bolts of cloth, cookin' stoves, shovels, nails, and the like."

"Any whiskey?" Shardeen asked, hopefully.

Fenton shook his head. "You can't sell whiskey where they're goin'. They're goin' to trade with the Mormons."

"If they're plannin' on doin' that, they're crazy," Murdock said. "Ever since folks attacked the Mormons in Illinois and Missouri, the Mormons have been just plumb hostile. They don't like visitors."

"Yeah, but Mormons got to have supplies just like ever'one else," Fenton said. "And they'll pay top dollar for the goods. I heard 'em talkin' about it. Springer plans to get twenty-five thousand dollars for deliverin' them supplies to Salt Lake City."

"Twenty-five thousand dollars?" Shardeen asked. "That's a lot of money, just for flour and such."

"I told you, the Mormons are out there all by themselves. They got a need for things like that."

"How's he plan to keep from gettin' hisself killed?" Murdock asked.

"He has a letter to Brigham Young from one of Young's friends, askin' him to treat them real good," Fenton said. "After we get rid of Springer and the others, we've got to find that letter."

"What the hell do we want with that letter?" Boyer asked.

"We're goin' to use it same way as Springer, so's we can trade with the Mormons."

"If it's got Springer's name on it, what good will it do us?" Eakins asked.

"That won't matter none," Fenton replied. "It ain't like Brigham Young has ever met Springer, so that means if any of us says we're Springer, the Mormons won't know the difference. We'll sell 'em the goods, collect the money, then be on our way."

"Why don't we just take the stuff back to Kansas City and sell it there?" Boyer asked. "Be a lot safer, and less trouble."

" 'Cause we wouldn't get no more'n a couple thousand dollars for it in Kansas City," Fenton said.

"Yeah, well, if we're goin' to take this stuff all the way out to Utah, you better be talkin' true when you say we can get twenty-five thousand dollars from the Mormons," Murdock said.

"That's how much Springer was a'tellin' Mr. Garland he was goin' to get when he bought the wagons," Fenton said.

"Whew," Eakins whistled. "Twenty-five thousand dollars? For each of us, that would be . . ." He paused, then began counting on his fingers.

"Five thousand dollars each," Shardeen said.

"Lordy Lord, what I could do with five thousand dollars," Boyer said.

"We ain't got it yet," Murdock said. "And even if we get the wagons, it's a long way to Utah."

"We'll get the money," Fenton insisted. "When we run in to the wagons tomorrow, we'll kill ever'one of 'em. Goin' to be as easy as takin' candy from a baby."

One day east of the outlaws' camp, the Springer-Stanley party was just breaking camp for the morning. Marcus Pearson and Frank Pecorino were nearly finished hitching their teams. But Jason Mills was just beginning to hitch up his wagon. However, with Parker's help, he quickly caught up with the others. In return for Parker's assistance, Jason offered to teach him how to use a gun.

"What's the most important thing? Drawing your gun fast, or shooting straight?" Parker asked, eager to learn all he could.

Jason laughed. "Well, you need both," he answered. "It doesn't do you any good to get your gun out fast if you can't shoot straight. On the other hand, it doesn't do any good to be able to shoot straight unless you can get your gun out in time."

"I've used a rifle for hunting and such," Parker said. "And I know how to use the front and rear sight. But when you shoot a pistol you don't use your sight, do you? Looks to me like you just draw your gun and shoot. Pass that belly brace through."

Jason passed the leather strap underneath the mule. "I do aim," he said. "But it's not the kind of aiming where you actually look through the sights. It's kind of *thinking* about where you want to shoot . . . and willing your gun in that direction."

"I don't understand."

"You can look at something without actually aiming at it, can't you?"

"Sure, I guess so."

"All right, think about having an eyeball on the end of your pistol barrel."

Parker laughed.

"No, I'm serious," Jason said. "Just pretend that the hole in the end of a pistol barrel is an eyeball. Then, use that eyeball to look at your target." Jason nodded toward a nearby tree. "There," he said. "Use your gun-eye to look at the trunk of that scrub tree there."

Parker pulled his pistol and pointed it toward the tree. He started to raise the pistol to look through the sites.

"Huh-uh," Jason said, wagging his finger. "Don't do it that way. Remember. Your eyeball is at the end of the gun. Use it to find your target."

Doing as Jason said, Parker pointed his pistol toward the tree and pulled the trigger. The gun bucked in his hand as if fired, and he saw a puff of dirt kick up from the ground beyond the tree.

The shot didn't alarm any of the others, who continued with their routine of breaking camp after seeing that the boys were just practicing their gunplay.

"That wasn't bad," Jason said. He turned back to the team to buckle the last strap.

"I didn't hit the tree."

"No, but you came close. And you did what

I asked you to do. You let the gun look at the tree."

"You do it," Parker said.

Jason still had his back to the tree when Parker issued his challenge. Instantly, he whirled, and the gun seemed to appear almost as if by magic in his hand. By the time Jason was turned around, he was firing. Parker saw chips of bark flying from the tree trunk.

"You did it!"

"Believe me, it isn't all that hard once you get the hang of it," Jason said.

The other drivers and the two outriders had walked over and joined Clay at the still-burning campfire to pour themselves one last cup of coffee before they left.

"That Mills kid is about as good with a gun as anyone I've ever seen," Marcus Pearson said, as he kicked dirt onto the fire and began stamping out the embers.

"Yes, he is," Clay answered. "I think Parker was right in hiring him. It's good knowing you have someone like that on your side, if you ever need him."

"The way Parker is going at it, he'll be as good as the kid by the time we reach Salt Lake," Marcus suggested.

"That's all we need—two wet-behind-the-ears kids with fast guns," Tobin said, almost bitterly.

"Yeah, especially with Parker making so much of being second in command," Gibson added in a joking tone, that still held an edge.

Clay took a drink of his coffee and looked at

his two outriders over the rim of his cup. "You men knew when you signed on that Parker was second in command," he said. "If you've got a problem with that, turn around right now and ride back to Missouri. It isn't too late."

"I got no problem with it," Tobin insisted.

"Me neither," Gibson said, sighing. "I was just commentin' on it, is all."

"Keep those kinds of comments to yourself from now on," Clay warned. He tossed out the grounds from the bottom of his cup. "All right, men, let's head 'em up and move 'em out!" he shouted.

Chapter 8

In the Cheyenne Camp

True to his word, Brave Eagle said nothing about Elizabeth's attempt to escape, and by noon the rest of the village had already begun the celebration of the marriage which would take place at sundown. Gifts of flowers were piled high around Elizabeth's teepee. In addition to the flowers, there were other gifts, such as eating utensils, robes, blankets, and baskets of corn and turnips.

Moon Cow Woman was in Elizabeth's teepee, having come by to help her prepare for the wedding. As they worked on Elizabeth's ceremonial dress, Moon Cow Woman continued teaching her some of the Cheyenne language, as well as instructing her on the customs of her people.

"Are you a believer in the Jesus-Spirit?" Moon Cow Woman asked.

"Do you mean am I a Christian? Well, yes. I haven't been to church since we left Illinois, but Pa would say prayers and sometimes read from the Bible. I don't want to offend anyone, but I will not stop being a believer in the Jesus-Spirit."

"That is good. You should not stop believing in your Jesus-Spirit," Moon Cow Woman said. "For if you did, then you would have no center, and your medicine would be weak. It is important that everyone have a Great Spirit to pray to. In the life of the Cheyenne, the one thing that is more important than all other things is what the white man calls the soul. When the Cheyenne awakens in the early morning and sees the rising sun, it is a good time to pray. When the Cheyenne sees food which the Great Spirit has put on earth, it is a good time to pray. When the Cheyenne sees lightning, or hears thunder, it is a good time to pray. When the Great Spirit takes the sun from the sky and makes night so that one can sleep, it is a good time to pray."

"Christians pray at all these times as well," Elizabeth protested.

"Ah, then this is good," Moon Cow Woman said. "For if the Jesus-Spirit who came to the white man is the true Great Spirit, then he hears all prayers . . . the prayers of the white man and the prayers of the Cheyenne."

"Moon Cow Woman, you are a good and wise woman, but I am puzzled. Why does it not bother you that I am to marry Two Ponies, who is already your husband?"

"If it pleases Two Ponies to take you as his wife, it pleases me," Moon Cow Woman said.

"And it also pleases me that you will soon be my sister."

When Elizabeth and Moon Cow Woman went to the ceremony that night, there was a ring of campfires burning brightly around the outer edge of the center of the camp. A circle, Elizabeth knew by now, was very important to the Cheyenne. The power of the world worked in a circle, or so the Cheyenne believed. They reasoned that the sky is round, the moon is round, and the earth is round, and that was not without purpose. The seasons also formed a circle, always coming back again. The nests of birds are round, teepees are round, and hogans are round. The teepees and the hogans are always set in a circle, and all meetings and ceremonies took place in the center of that circle.

Elizabeth looked toward the other side of the ring and saw Two Ponies standing there, dressed in his ceremonial finest. He wore a feathered headdress which was so long that the end of it trailed all the way to the ground. He carried a sacred feathered scepter, and his jacket and trousers were decorated with brightly colored beads. His eyes glowed in the reflected light of the many campfires as he looked over the assemblage. The drums and chanting grew quiet.

Two Ponies started toward the middle of the circle, and held his hand out toward Elizabeth. Elizabeth just stood there for a moment, awed by the absolute silence which had fallen over the camp. Over the last several weeks she had grown used to the constant noise of the village; the drums, the chants of the hunting parties, the babble of the women, and the laughter of the children. Now there was no sound except the snapping and popping of the wood in the dozen or so campfires.

Several hundred faces looked toward Elizabeth, all of them bathed in orange by the flickering light of the fires. For Elizabeth, there was a surrealism to the moment which made it all seem like a dream. She was once a farm girl from near Hillsboro, Illinois. And now she was here, in this remote Indian village, about to become the bride of the chief of the Cheyenne.

At Moon Cow Woman's urging, Elizabeth walked into the center of the circle, then sat on the ground before Two Ponies. Two Ponies held his hand out over her, then declared in a loud voice, "I take this woman for my wife." After that, he sat on the ground beside Elizabeth and food was brought to them. Not until they took their first bite did the others in the village start eating.

Midway through the feast, Two Ponies stood and beckoned for Elizabeth to follow him. He led her through the circle and into the darkness beyond the campfires, until they reached her teepee. Just outside the teepee, he motioned for her to go inside.

"It is not for me to enter the teepee before my husband," she said, remembering Moon Cow Woman's instructions.

"I will not be going into the teepee," Two Ponies said.

"What?" Elizabeth asked, surprised by the strange statement. "What do you mean? Why not?"

"Hear me," Two Ponies said. "I am a man of many winter-counts. I am old and set in my ways, and I find peace in the quiet times. You are a young woman, and I fear your blood will be too hot and your desire too strong. I cannot share the hot blood and the strong desire with one as young as you. And I do not wish to try."

"I don't understand," Elizabeth said. "Why did you marry me?"

"Did you wish to marry Elk Heart?"

"No," Elizabeth said. "Absolutely not!"

"Then it was good for you to marry me, for now Elk Heart has no claim on you. You are safe."

Elizabeth realized then what Two Ponies had done for her, and never had she felt a greater sense of gratitude toward anyone.

"Two Ponies, I thank you," she said. "From the bottom of my heart, I thank you for what you have done for me."

Two Ponies nodded once, then, without speaking, turned and walked away. Elizabeth saw him head toward Moon Cow Woman's hogan, and she was glad.

With the Springer–Stanley freight party

As the iron-rimmed wheels rolled across the sun-baked earth, they picked up dirt, causing a rooster tail of dust to stream out behind them. Because the trail was wide enough, the wagons were moving three abreast. That was preferable to traveling in line because it kept anyone from having to eat the dust of the wagon in front of them.

Clay and Parker were riding in front, with Greg and Paul on each flank. As he rode along, Parker made several practice draws of his pistol, though he wasn't actually shooting.

"You're getting pretty good with that gun," Clay remarked.

"I'd like to get as good as Jason."

"I'll admit that he is fast," Clay said. "I just hope he has the maturity to go with it."

"What do you mean?"

"It gives a man a lot of power to be able to draw and shoot as well as Jason can. And a lot of people can't handle that power. They see other people getting scared of them, and it turns something over in them. Sometimes it turns them into very unpleasant people."

"You mean like bullies?"

"Yes."

"You don't have to worry about Jason," Parker insisted. "He's as nice a guy as you might even want to meet."

"He seems that way," Clay agreed. "But, I wasn't only talking about him."

"Who else were you . . ." Parker started, then he stopped. "Clay, you aren't talking about me, are you?"

Clay shook his head. "I'm not talking about

you, the way you are now," he said. "But what if you get as fast as Jason. Or faster."

"Faster?" Parker laughed. "I don't see how anyone could be any faster."

"Well, that's a question, isn't it? The time might come when someone might want that issue settled. And there would be only one way to find out."

"How?" Parker asked. Then, realizing what Clay was suggesting, he gasped. "No, never! You are saying that someday Jason and I might have a gunfight, aren't you?"

"It is not something I would expect," Clay said. "As I said, I'm sure you and Jason can both handle it. But I want you to know all the dangers before they happen. That way it's easier to look out for them."

"You don't have to worry about Jason and me. We'd never do anything like that."

Clay stopped, then held up his hand, signaling for everyone else to stop. Parker heard the squeak of brakes being set, and the commands of "Whoa" from the drivers as they reined in their teams.

"What is it, Clay?"

Clay reached back into his saddlebag and drew out a telescope. Opening it, he looked at something far ahead.

"Do you see something?" Clay asked.

"I saw a couple of men on horseback."

"What's wrong with that? This is one of the main trails, isn't it?"

"Yes," Clay replied. "And ordinarily, seeing

someone wouldn't arouse any suspicions. But for some reason, these men didn't want to be seen. They were bent low over their horses, and they rode quickly across the open gap. Now they're behind that ridge." He pointed out the location.

"So, what do you think?" Parker asked.

"I think we should have a little meeting."

Clay and Parker turned and rode back toward the wagons. By now the two outriders, Tobin and Gibson, had noticed that Clay and Parker were coming back to the wagons and they rode in to see what was going on.

"See something?" Marcus asked.

"Couple of riders who didn't want to be seen," Clay said.

Tobin snorted. "Only two riders? There's seven of us. What's the problem?"

"You ever seen just two cockroaches?" Marcus asked. "You heard him tell they didn't want to be seen. You can count on there bein' more of 'em."

"What do you think they want?" Pecorino asked.

"Probably what we've got," Clay said.

"What are your plans?" Marcus asked. "You want to go in line?"

"No," Clay answered. "We'll stay abreast but we'll alter it a little. Jason, you pull your wagon somewhat ahead. Marcus, you and Frank drop back a little on each side, so you form a V. When they hit, we'll get inside the V. That should give us a little protection. Get your guns ready."

Marcus jacked a shell into his Winchester, then lay it on the seat alongside him. Pecorino broke down his double-barrel greener shotgun, checked the loads, then snapped it shut. The others spun their revolvers, making sure the chambers were full.

With a prickly sensation sneaking up his skin, Parker rode alongside Clay as they continued to move forward cautiously.

"Do you see that opening in the ridge, about a hundred yards ahead?" Clay asked.

"I see it."

"That's where they'll hit us."

Parker tried to answer, but somehow his tongue seemed to have swollen in his mouth and he couldn't speak. Instead, he nodded.

"Are you scared?" Clay asked.

"No," Parker answered. Clay looked at him, then sheepishly, Parker recanted. "Yes."

"Good."

"It's good that I'm scared?"

"I should say so. Only a crazy man wouldn't be afraid. And when I get into a gun battle, I only want levelheaded men around me," Clay said.

They rode on in silence for another few seconds, then, suddenly, five mounted men burst out through the opening in the ridge. With screams of challenge in their throats, they rode at a hard gallop toward the wagon party.

"Back to the wagons!" Clay shouted, jerking his horse around as he yelled. Parker followed, reaching the wagons at about the same time Tobin and Gibson came in from the flanks.

Stopping the wagons, the three drivers jumped down into the barricade within the protective V. All had their weapons ready.

The outlaws, with their pistols extended in front of them, began firing. The flat reports floated across the open ground to them, reaching their ears at about the same time the bullets began whistling by.

"Take aim, but hold your fire!" Clay shouted. Parker aimed at one of the men and, with his hands trembling slightly, held it as the riders swept closer. The outlaws continued pouring in a steady barrage of fire, and as they got closer, their bullets began hitting the wagons, sending out splinters with a solid, thocking sound.

Parker's eyes widened as the riders came closer, seeing that the big man leading them was Arnold Fenton. Steeling his nerves, he aimed directly at Fenton.

"Now!" Clay shouted.

Parker pulled the trigger. Fenton tumbled from his saddle, as did two others.

The two remaining outlaws, suddenly realizing the precariousness of their position, jerked their horses to a halt. Then, turning them around, they started off at a full gallop.

Tobin and Gibson mounted their own horses and started after them.

"No!" Clay shouted. "No, let them go!"

The two outriders paid no attention to Clay's

order. Smelling blood, they intended to make the final kill.

Then one of the retreating outlaws, seeing that only two men were chasing them, turned his horse around and started riding back toward them.

"What's he doing?" Marcus asked. "Has he gone crazy?"

The outlaw fired twice. Gibson was knocked from his horse and Tobin dropped his gun and grabbed his shoulder. The outlaw rode right up to Tobin and Parker thought he was going to shoot him. Instead, the outlaw did something that was totally unexpected. He motioned with his gun that Tobin should return to the wagons and he came riding in behind him, all the while holding his gun on Tobin.

Marcus jacked another shell into his rifle and took aim at the outlaw who was bringing Tobin back in.

"No, don't shoot him," Clay said, reaching his hand out and pushing the barrel of the gun down.

The outlaw came to within about ten yards of the wagons, then stopped. His gun was still trained on Tobin.

Behind the outlaw, on a slight rise nearly a hundred yards away, the other outlaw was sitting on his horse, silhouetted against the sky. He seemed to just be waiting there, looking back toward the wagons as if curious to see what was going on.

"One of you fellas named Springer?" the outlaw with Tobin asked.

"I'm Springer," Clay answered, stepping out from behind the wagons. "Who are you?"

"The name is Shardeen." Shardeen nodded toward the three outlaws who were lying on the ground about thirty yards away. "Are they all dead?"

"I don't know," Clay said. "We haven't gone over to look. What about Gibson?"

"That the fella I shot?"

"Yes."

"He's dead," Shardeen said. He nodded toward Tobin. "He would be dead too, if I wanted him to be."

"What do you want, Shardeen?"

"I'd like you to send one of those boys out to look at my pards," Shardeen said. "I need to know if they're dead or alive before I ride off."

"What makes you think I'm going to let you just ride off?"

" 'Cause you got nothin' to lose now. There's nobody left but Murdock and me. And we damn sure ain't goin' to make another try at you. Also, if you try and stop me now there's goin' to be more killin'. I'll get at least two more of you before you get me."

"Parker, ride over and take a look at them," Clay ordered. "And be careful when you approach them. Could be one or two of 'em's playin' possum."

Climbing onto his horse, Parker rode over to have a closer look at the three men lying on the ground. Two of the outlaws' horses had run away, but one was standing nearby, casually cropping grass.

With his gun held ready, Parker slid down from his horse and walked over to the three prone men. Two were lying facedown, and one face-up. The one who was face up was Arnold Fenton.

Fenton was the one Parker had been aiming at and he had seen him fall just as he shot. Parker had never killed anyone—hell, he had never even shot at anyone before. The thought that he was the one who killed Fenton was a little disquieting. As he examined him more closely though, he saw that the outlaw had been hit by at least four bullets. There was no way of knowing if one of the bullets was his. And even if one of them did come from his gun, he had certainly not been the only cause of Fenton's death. It made him feel a little better.

Leaving Fenton's corpse, Parker checked the other two outlaws. They, too, were dead. He cupped his hands around his mouth and called back toward the wagons.

"All dead!"

"Come on back!" Clay called back to him.

Parker took one more look at Fenton before he mounted and rode back to join the others.

"So, what's it going to be, Springer?" Shardeen asked. "Do Murdock and I ride out of here? Or is there goin' to be some more killin'?"

"You can go," Clay said.

Shardeen started to turn, then he stopped and

smiled. "Wait a minute. What's to keep you from shootin' me as I ride off?"

"Nothing," Clay said.

"Maybe I need to take this fella back with me for a bit," Shardeen said, indicating Tobin. "I'll let him go when we reach the ridge line."

"How do we know you won't take him up there and shoot him?" Clay said.

"I don't reckon there's any way you can know that," Shardeen said.

"Then what we've got here is a Mexican standoff," Clay suggested.

"I'll go with him," Jason volunteered.

"All right," Clay said.

Shardeen scoffed. "You're sending a boy to do a man's job?"

"Were you in the war, Shardeen?"

"Yeah," Shardeen answered. "I was Sescesh. I rode with Bill Anderson. What about you?"

"I wore the blue. But at places like Shiloh and Antietam and Gettysburg, I saw a lot of boys no older than this one, doing a man's job. Don't make the mistake of underestimating him."

"All right, boy, let's me an' you ride out," Shardeen said.

"Put your gun away," Jason said.

Shardeen thought for a moment, then he shook his head. "Naw, I don't think I want to do that. But I tell you what I will do. I'll ease the hammer back down."

"Good," Jason said. "That'll make us even."

Shardeen laughed. "Even? How do you figure that?"

Like a striking snake, Jason's hand went to his holster. As fast as a fleeting thought, the pistol appeared in his hand, and before Shardeen realized what was going on, Jason was pointing his gun toward him.

"I figure it like this," Jason said with a broad smile.

The expression on Shardeen's face went from self-assurance, to shock, to outright fear.

"Like I said, we're even. I don't have the hammer pulled back either," Jason added.

"Still think I'm sending a boy to do a man's job?" Clay asked, chuckling.

Shardeen looked hard at Jason for a moment, then an easy smile broke out on his face. He put his pistol back in the holster. "I reckon he's a pretty good man at that," he said. "Let's go, boy."

Chapter 9

In the Cheyenne Camp

As the late fall rains began to strip the brown leaves from the trees, Elk Heart took a new name. His new name was Bloody Axe. It was the name of a warrior, and it came to him in a vision while he was in the sweat lodge. The vision also told him to abandon the life of the contraire, return to his people, and select a few who would be warriors alongside him.

Because Bloody Axe's new name had come to him in a vision, all who heard him make the proclamation accepted it. A vision was a message from the Great Spirit and it couldn't be questioned.

"Why do they accept him now?" Elizabeth asked. "He struts around the camp as if he were a great chief, when only last month he was riding backward on his horse."

"He has had a vision," Brave Eagle explained to her. "Do you not understand that a vision is a sacred thing? He is no longer bound by his vow to be a contraire."

"How do we know he's really had a vision? He could just be saying that so he wouldn't have to be a contraire any longer," Elizabeth suggested.

"No," Brave Eagle replied. "Maybe when you have lived long enough in your red life, you will forget some of the ways of your white life. You do not understand that a vision is a holy thing that no man would lie about. A vision is as sacred as the medicine bag he carries."

"Brave Eagle, because you are a good, honest man, you see goodness and honesty in everyone. But I tell you that there are some things I learned in my white life which would serve Indians well. And that is that some people may appear to have honor when they have none."

Brave Eagle laughed.

"Why do you laugh?" Elizabeth asked, irritated by his behavior.

"Because you, a woman, think you can tell me, a warrior, about life."

Brave Eagle was still laughing when Elizabeth stomped away from him. She saw several warriors standing in the center circle, listening to a speech given by the one who now called himself Bloody Axe. Moon Cow Woman was standing just on the outside edge of the circle of warriors, and Elizabeth walked over to join her. Elizabeth had been working hard for several weeks now, and had developed a conversational level of the language. With that understanding, and Moon Cow Woman's occasional translation of the words and phrases she didn't understand, she was able to follow most of Bloody Axe's speech.

"Listen," Bloody Axe began. "I have seen a vision of my many victories. I have seen the white men killed by Cheyenne warriors, and in this vision, I, Bloody Axe, have led this brave band of warriors."

"Why should we let you lead us?" one of the warriors asked.

"Yes. You declared yourself to be a contraire, but now you come back and ask us to follow you."

"I tell you this. The vision I had spoke of much glory for Bloody Axe," Bloody Axe said. "Come, if you wish to share in this glory. Come and ride with me, and we will have a great victory over the white men who pass through our country!"

Bloody Axe shouted his last declaration and the Indians cheered, apparently won over by his fierce rhetoric. Then someone broke into song and as he sang, he danced, and the others danced behind him.

Listen, we are warriors.
The God Dogs, our horses,
Run swiftly
Between our legs.
The arrow and the lance
Fly true in their path.
The blood of our enemy
Stains the ground
Beneath the hooves of the

God Dogs.
We will have glory.
We will count many coups.
Listen, we are warriors.

Those who would be warriors joined the dancing men, and Elizabeth saw that the one who danced with the lightest step and sang with the loudest voice was Running Rabbit.

When the singing and dancing was finished, the warriors ran toward their horses. Elizabeth called out to Running Rabbit.

"Running Rabbit, no, don't go! Please, don't go!" she yelled.

Running Rabbit stopped and turned toward her. "I must go," he said.

"No."

By now, Bloody Axe was mounted, and he saw Running Rabbit hesitate. "Running Rabbit, do you stay as Sun's Light pup . . . or do you ride with me as a warrior?" he taunted.

Running Rabbit hesitated no longer. With one final look at Elizabeth, he ran to his horse. Elizabeth glared at Bloody Axe, who was smiling triumphantly at her.

"He doesn't really want the boy," Elizabeth said to Moon Cow Woman. "He is just taking him because he knows I don't want him to go."

"There is truth to your words," Moon Cow Woman agreed. "But you cannot say that to Running Rabbit, for to do so would bring him shame."

When all the warriors were mounted, Bloody Axe held his rifle over his had.

"Yip, yip, yip, aiyee!" he shouted at the top of his voice.

The others yelled as well as they rode out of the village with a thunder of hooves. Brave Eagle watched them disappear, with a firm, pensive look on his face, and ice in his eyes.

When Bloody Axe saw the six wagons moving slowly across the prairie, he hurried back to tell the others of the potential target.

"Why should we attack wagons?" Kicking Horse asked. "They carry farmers, women, and children to far-away places. There will be nothing in the wagons but tools for farming, and the clothes and blankets of white men. These are not things for warriors."

"Not these wagons," Bloody Axe insisted. "Three of the wagons carry farmers, but three are the wagons that white men call freight wagons. Freight wagons carry many things, such as guns, knives, whiskey, axes, and sugar."

"Guns? Knives?" Kicking Horse asked.

"Whiskey?" another eagerly wanted to know.

"Sugar?" Running Rabbit added.

The warriors laughed at Running Rabbit for he was known for his prodigious appetite for anything sweet.

Bloody Axe pointed to a river crossing. "We will wait here for the wagons. When they begin to cross the river, we will attack."

Bloody Axe positioned the warriors so that

they couldn't be seen by the approaching wagons. Then, with everyone in position, he moved back to the ridge from where he had first spotted the wagons, and waited.

A soft breeze moaned through the low scrub trees and shallow canyons. Bloody Axe looked back to see if he could see any of the warriors. At first he saw no one, evidence of their skill at hiding. Then, but only because he knew they were there, they gradually came into view.

One of the hidden warriors was Running Rabbit. He heard the wagons approaching, and though it was cold and he was lying in wet mud, he felt hot in the flush of excitement which had come upon him. He would count coup this day, and when he returned to the village all would see the feathered lance he would carry, each feather dipped in red to denote the counting of coup.

Suddenly Running Rabbit got an idea. He would count coup against one of the white men while they were still alive. If he could ride up to him and touch him with his coup stick while the enemy was still alive, then he would be able to claim the highest honor any warrior can claim. Counting coup against a dead enemy was honor enough, but, once dead, the enemy represented no danger. To count coup against an enemy while he lived would be the cause for stories and songs to be celebrated around many campfires, and surely, it would be entered in the sash of the winter count.

The winter count was the history book of the

tribe. Symbols were painted on a long, winding cloth each winter, in order to designate certain significant events of that year. Though the white man called this year 1868, the Indian had no such numerical system. This year was simply, "this year," and it would not have a name until the winter count was complete. Last year was "the year of the white buffalo calf," because one of the hunters had seen a white buffalo calf during a hunt, a potent and holy symbol to the tribe. Running Rabbit had been born in "the Year of the Spreading Fever," for many in the village were sick that year, and in fact, both of Running Rabbit's parents had died of smallpox. Now, Running Rabbit thought, as he lay in the mud and heard the increasing sound of the approaching wagons, he thought of a name for this year. This year would be known as "the Year of Running Rabbit's touch coup," and he would be remembered forever among his people.

Ira Joyce didn't like it. There was nothing he could put his finger on, but something was bothering him, and the end of his nose began to tingle. Every time his nose began to tingle, it was a sign that something was afoot. He hauled back on the reins and put his foot on the brake.

"Whoa, mules, whoa!" he called.

When he stopped, everyone else in the wagon train behind him was forced to stop as well. Ira could hear the squeaking of wheel brakes and the drivers calling to their teams.

"Whoa!"

"Whoa, there!"

"Hold!"

"Why are we stopping?" Captain Reynolds shouted. Reynolds, who had been riding alongside his family's wagon, slapped his legs against the side of his horse and raced to the front of the small train. When he got there, Ira was cutting off a piece of chewing tobacco.

"What is it?" Reynolds asked. "Why did you stop?"

Ira stuck the plug in his mouth and positioned it against his cheek.

"Somethin' ain't right," Ira said.

"What?"

"They's somethin' wrong."

"What are you talking about? What could possibly be wrong?"

"I ain't sure what it is. I just know that somethin' ain't quite like it should be."

Reynolds breathed out a long sigh of disgust. "You stop us because 'somethin' ain't right,' but you don't have any idea of what it is?"

"No idea a'tall," Ira said. He pointed to the river crossing about fifty yards ahead. "But I don't feel good about goin' through there."

"Do you have a better place in mind?"

Ira spat before he answered. "Nope," he said, wiping his mouth with the back of his hand. "This here's the only ford for ten miles or so."

"Then we're going to have to cross here, aren't we?"

"I reckon we are," Ira agreed reluctantly.

Reynolds took off his hat, stared into it for a

moment as if gathering his thoughts, then put it back on. "Mr. Joyce, this is the third time you've brought this party to a halt because something didn't feel right to you. No doubt, you recall the 'outlaws' who were trailing us a few days ago. Turns out they were nothing more than buffalo hunters. Then you didn't want to take the shortcut to the south because you said we wouldn't be able to find water in that direction. But we did find water. Now you halt us because you say something doesn't feel right, only this time, you don't even know what that is."

"It's a feeling I have in my gut," Ira said.

"Don't give me gut feelings, Ira Joyce. Give me facts," Reynolds demanded. "If there is some danger up there, I want to know what it is."

"That, I can't tell you," Ira said. "All I can say is I have survived a lot of years out here, mostly because I listened to my gut when it had something to say."

"Your gut isn't in charge of this wagon train, Mr. Joyce. *I* am," Reynolds said. "Now, either lead, follow, or get the hell out of the way."

Ira glared at Reynolds for a second, then he snapped the reins over the back of his team.

"Heah, mule! Giddyup!" he shouted.

Reynolds held his place as, once again, the wagon train began rolling. He had positioned a freight wagon in between each Conestoga wagon so that, today, his wagon was second in line. His wife had been ill for several days now, so Sue, his daughter, was driving.

"Hey, Pa," Sue called out to her father as she guided the team by. "What's wrong?"

"Nothin' darlin'," Reynolds replied. "Just keep the team movin'. How's your ma'?"

"Not very good," Sue replied, her voice betraying her worry. "She's runnin' a real high fever. I think she needs to see a doctor."

"Well, honey, 'case you haven't noticed, there's not just a whole lot of doctors out here. You stay with her. If she ain't none better by the time we get to Denver, I'll get us one."

Sue looked back into the wagon to check on her mother as the wagon started down the long, modest embankment, leading to the water. When she turned back around, she saw a single Indian riding toward them. He was carrying a long stick which he held stretched out before him, and he was screaming at the top of his voice.

Because of his uneasy feeling, Ira was ready. His revolver was lying on the seat beside him, and he picked it up and aimed at the charging Indian. Surprisingly, the Indian didn't appear to be armed, except for the stick he was carrying. The Indian swept right up to the side of the wagon and stretched the stick out, trying to touch Ira.

Ira waited until the last possible moment, then he pulled back on the trigger. The gun boomed and bucked in his hand, and the Indian's face turned into a pulp of red as the heavy bullet hit him right between the eyes. The Indian was launched backward from his horse.

"What the hell? Where did he come from?" Reynolds yelled, riding to the front of the column at a gallop.

"They're here!" Ira shouted. "Get ready for 'em."

"What are you talking about? It's only one Indian."

"Get ready!" Ira repeated. "Get the wagons in a circle!"

But it was too late for that. By now, nearly twenty Indians came into view.

"My God, where did they all come from?" Reynolds asked, a quick, nauseating fear building in his throat. Swarming down on the wagons from both sides, the Indians were emitting blood-curdling screams as they fired their pistols and rifles.

Bloody Axe leaped over the rocks and gullies, shouting with joy as he pursued the fight. The men defending the wagon train shot at him, but it was as if he were impervious to their bullets. He surveyed a burning wagon and looked at the battlefield, chortling in glee as the last white man was put to the lance. Now everyone—men, women, and children—were dead.

He and the others looted the freight wagons, taking whatever they wanted. Some of them started drinking the whiskey right away, chopping holes in the end of the barrel and holding their mouths under the issuing stream. Kicking Horse found a hat with red feathers, and he put it on, clowning for the others, who laughed at his antics.

Bloody Axe saw a young girl lying on the ground with a bullet hole in her temple. She didn't look to be much older than Running Rabbit. Neither he, nor any of his warriors, had killed her. She had been killed by one of her own people. The man on the chestnut horse had ridden up to her, put his gun to the side of her head, and pulled the trigger.

She had made no effort to avoid it, but had sat there, unprotesting, as if she welcomed it. He had seen such things before, white women killing themselves or being killed by their men, in order to avoid being captured by the Indians. What cowards white people were.

Chapter 10

When Bloody Axe and his warriors returned to the camp, they were laden with booty from the looted wagon train. He had sent an advanced messenger back with word of his great victory, so the camp was already celebrating by the time the main body of warriors arrived. Elizabeth saw no call for celebration. She remembered her own experience as a helpless victim of a brutal Indian attack, and she was sure that this one had been just as bloody. She stayed in her teepee, refusing even to go outside.

The flap to her teepee opened and brave Eagle came in.

"Here," he said, offering her a pot of black smudge paint. "Put some of this on your face."

"Why?" Elizabeth asked. "Isn't that for mourning? Will it not make it more obvious to everyone if I mourn the death of so many of my people?"

"This is to mourn one Cheyenne that has been killed," Brave Eagle said.

"To mourn for a warrior who does not belong to me would bring disgrace to others who live,"

Elizabeth said, showing that she had managed to grasp some of the customs of her new people.

"You can mourn for one who has no family," Brave Eagle suggested.

"Who would that . . . Brave Eagle, no! Not Running Rabbit?"

"It is so," Brave Eagle affirmed.

Elizabeth thought of the young Indian boy who had helped make her transition into her new life bearable. Tears sprang quickly to her eyes.

"I tried to stop him from going with them. He was just a boy."

"He called himself a warrior," Brave Eagle said. "And he died a warrior. The coward who now calls himself Bloody Axe attacked a wagon train. He made war against women and children.

"You can wear mourning paint for Running Rabbit," Brave Eagle continued. He put his hand to his chest. "And, in your heart, mourn for your own people as well."

"You are a good man, Brave Eagle," Elizabeth said. She walked over to him and put her arms around him. She felt him stiffen in her grasp, then pull away from her.

"We cannot," he said. "You are the wife of Two Ponies."

"Brave Eagle, I didn't mean . . ." Elizabeth started, then she stopped. She was going to tell him that she didn't mean her embrace to be anything more than a gesture of friendship. But she realized at that moment that if the council had voted differently, if she had been made to choose Brave Eagle, that the thought of sharing Brave Eagle's bed wasn't all that unpleasant.

With a look in his eyes that told her Brave Eagle was thinking the same thing, he turned and left her teepee.

Outside, the celebration continued. Bloody Axe had drunk much of the liquor they had brought back from the wagons, and he felt whiskey's fire burning inside him. He was intoxicated, not by the whiskey, but by the exuberance of his own greatness. He listened to the songs which were being sung in his honor, and he heard the praises to his name, and he knew his deeds would help solidify him one day as chief.

When he saw Brave Eagle leaving the teepee of Sun's Light, his blood ran hot with anger. Everyone knew that Sun's Light was the wife of Two Ponies in name only. Everyone knew that she had not shared his bed, even on the night they were married. The marriage was nothing but a means of denying Bloody Axe his rightful claim to the woman who had been his prisoner.

Bloody Axe didn't like the arrangement, but he had accepted it for what it was. Until now. When he saw Brave Eagle leave her teepee, he was convinced that Brave Eagle was enjoying what rightfully should have been his. Bloody Axe was being played for a fool!

The anger he felt at seeing Brave Eagle leave the teepee passed quickly, however, when he realized that here was his opportunity. He looked toward Sun's Light's teepee. She was still inside.

Bloody Axe felt a quick-building need for her, and he rubbed himself through his loincloth and thought of what it would be like to be with her. Looking around, he saw that Brave Eagle was nowhere in sight. He started toward the teepee of Sun's Light.

Bloody Axe slipped through the open flap of Sun's Light's teepee and stood there glaring defiantly for a moment.

"Brave Eagle, I'm glad you've come back," Elizabeth said, turning toward him with a smile on her face. When she saw who it was, though, her smile was replaced by a combination of terror and revulsion. "Elk Heart!" she gasped. "What are you doing here?"

"Elk Heart is no more. You will call me by my new name," Bloody Axe demanded. His painted face was underlit by the dull glow of the teepee fire, and the fire and shadow gave him the look of a demon. He stared down at her menacingly.

Elizabeth realized that it had been a foolish and dangerous thing to taunt him by calling him by his old name. "I apologize. I meant to call you Bloody Axe," she said. She was frightened, but she tried not to show it. She looked behind him, hoping that Brave Eagle was with him.

Bloody Axe smiled, but rather than making his face more pleasing, the grin seemed to pull his fire-lit features into an even more hideous countenance.

"Why have you not come to celebrate my victory?" Bloody Axe asked.

"I . . . I am in mourning," Elizabeth explained.

"You mourn for the white dogs who were killed?"

"I mourn for Running Rabbit," Elizabeth said.

"Running Rabbit was a fool," Bloody Axe said. "He tried to make a coup, to take the glory that was mine. And as that glory was mine, so shall you be." Bloody Axe gloated.

"What?" Elizabeth gasped. "What are you talking about?"

"You belong to me," Bloody Axe said and he touched his chest. "It was Bloody Axe who captured you. You should be in my teepee, cooking my meals and warming my blankets."

"It was not Bloody Axe who captured me," Elizabeth said. "It was Elk Heart, and Elk Heart is no more."

Suddenly, and without warning, Bloody Axe swung the back of his hand across Elizabeth's face, sending her sprawling. She was so surprised by his action that she didn't even cry out.

"Now I will show you what it is like to be taken by a warrior." Bloody Axe grunted. The light gave his eyes a demonic glow of lust. Elizabeth opened her mouth to scream, but a wicked blow from Bloody Axe's fist cut her scream short. She tasted blood, and realized that her lip was cut. She tried to scream but couldn't, because Bloody Axe was holding his hand across her mouth.

Elizabeth let her body go limp. Bloody Axe,

thinking she was giving in to him, grinned and relaxed his grip. It was the opening Elizabeth was seeking, and she rolled over and struggled to get up.

Bloody Axe perceived then what she was doing, and he gave her a wicked kick in the stomach, knocking her back down. She became dazed, barely aware of Bloody Axe spreading her legs apart.

Suddenly, through the numbing haze of near unconsciousness, Elizabeth saw the shadow of another man in the teepee. It was Brave Eagle!

Brave Eagle bellowed in rage, and he grabbed Bloody Axe by the hair, jerked him up, and threw him outside the teepee. He followed outside, and as a stunned Bloody Axe scrambled to get up, Brave Eagle savagely punched him in the face, knocking him down again.

"You are but a cur that eats its own vomit," Brave Eagle cursed. "You are a worm, crawling in human dung!"

Every time Bloody Axe tried to get up, Brave Eagle would knock him down again, uttering a curse each time he did so.

The celebration which had continued unabated even as Bloody Axe was in Elizabeth's teepee, had now stopped abruptly, and people began to gather to watch the confrontation.

"Give me a weapon so that we may fight!" Bloody Axe finally called to the assembled group.

Brave Eagle grabbed the lance of a warrior who had came from the dancing circle, and threw it at Bloody Axe's feet, where it stuck in the ground. Bloody Axe pulled it out, then turned it toward Brave Eagle.

As Brave Eagle turned to arm himself with another lance nearby, Bloody Axe made a thrust at him, cutting him off.

"Unfair!" Kicking Horse called. "Let him pick up a weapon!"

But Bloody Axe paid no attention, and continued to thrust the lance toward Brave Eagle, who could do nothing but dance out of the way of each deadly thrust.

"Tonight you will see me lie with Sun's Light," Bloody Axe boasted. "Your severed head will be hanging from the lodgepole, and I will prop your eyes open so that you will see everything!" He made another jab with the lance, and Brave Eagle avoided it deftly as he had the others.

Elizabeth, alarmed by the urgent cries outside her teepee, came out to see Bloody Axe facing Brave Eagle with murder in his eyes. Bloody Axe lunged viciously at Brave Eagle, who managed to avoid his thrust yet again, and as Bloody Axe was trying to recover, Brave Eagle cuffed him on the back of the head, sending him sprawling, facedown, in the dirt. Bloody Axe dropped the lance and Brave Eagle swooped in to pick it up. Then, as Bloody Axe turned over onto his back, Brave Eagle put the point of the lance against Bloody Axe's throat.

"Kill him!" someone shouted. "You have bested him fairly!'

Bloody Axe looked up at Brave Eagle with hate and defiance in his eyes, preparing to die. "Kill me," he said. "I will wait for you in the other world."

But Brave Eagle pulled the point away. "You are the grandson of my grandfather. I have no wish to kill you," he said.

Brave Eagle dropped the lance, then turned away from him. He started toward Elizabeth, and she knew that, if he wanted her, she would share his bed this night.

Then, with horrifying suddenness, the point of the spear burst out of Brave Eagle's chest. Blood pumped out from around the shaft and Brave Eagle, more surprised than in pain, put both hands up to feel the lance before falling forward.

"Brave Eagle!" Elizabeth cried out in shock and horror. She looked up and saw Bloody Axe on his feet. Bloody Axe had picked up the spear Brave Eagle had dropped beside him, and hurled it at Brave Eagle's back. So great was Bloody Axe's anger-induced strength, that the lance had penetrated all the way through Brave Eagle's body.

"Seize him!" Two Ponies shouted, for he, too, had been drawn from his lodge by the fight. Two Ponies pointed toward Bloody Axe, and two nearby braves darted toward him to obey Two Ponies' command.

"No!" Bloody Axe said, knocking the two Indians away. He took a couple of hesitant steps backward, looking into the faces of those who, only a short time before, were paying him honor. Now they were ready to put him to death.

Bloody Axe turned and ran toward the remuda. He leaped onto the back of the first horse, grabbed the line of another, and rode quickly, into the night. The other horses, spooked and alarmed, ran through the remuda's open gate.

"Get the horses!" Two Ponies commanded. "Get the horses, then ride him down and bring him to me."

The Indians, many of whom were drunk from the stolen liquor, ran stumbling and bumbling into the night, trying to catch the skittish horses as Bloody Axe made his escape.

With the Springer–Stanley freight party

Clay held up his hand and the wagons behind him stopped.

"What is it?" Parker asked.

Clay pointed. "Buzzards."

It wasn't uncommon to see one or two of the scavengers making long, slow circles in the sky. But here was a whole flock of them, gathered as thick as blackbirds.

"A dead coyote, maybe?" Parker suggested.

Clay shook his head. "Too many for a coyote. Too many for a person even, unless there's more than one."

"Well then, what do you think it is?"

"It's hard to say."

"Want me to ride over there and see what it is?"

Clay shook his head. "No," he said. "We'll all check it out together."

With another hand signal, the wagons started forward. Ten minutes later they crested a small rise and saw, for the first time, what was drawing the buzzards. Scattered piles of blackened ash, half a wheel here, a tongue there, fire-rusted iron, and bits of charred canvas were all that remained of the Conestoga and freight wagons that once made up the Reynolds party.

But it wasn't the wagons that had drawn the buzzards. They were feasting with relish on the mules, dead in their harness, and what was left of the men, women, and children, their bodies black and bloating in the sun.

"My God," Marcus said. "It's Reynolds and his bunch!"

"That there is the little Reynolds girl," Tobin said, pointing to a lump on the ground.

Just as Tobin pointed out Sue's body, a buzzard spread his wings to halt his descent over the dead young girl.

"No! Get away from her!" Parker shouted. Before he realized what he was doing, he drew his pistol and fired at the buzzard. The buzzard fell to the ground, frantically flapping its wings a few times before it died. It all happened so quickly that Parker didn't even realize he had drawn and fired his pistol just as Jason had taught him.

Clay put his hand out toward Parker. "Put

the gun away, son," he said sympathetically. "You can't kill them all. Besides, they're just doin' what God intended them to do."

Marcus set the brake on his wagon, then climbed down and started walking toward the bodies, carrying a shovel. A moment later Jason started toward the bodies with his own shovel, then Pecorino, and finally Tobin, the wound in his shoulder nearly healed by now.

"You goin' to help bury them, or are you just goin' to sit there?" Clay asked.

It was all Parker could do to get the words out. "I'll help," he said.

The Cheyenne Camp

Elizabeth stood with the others as Brave Eagle's body was raised onto the burial platform, right alongside the platform holding the body of Running Rabbit. She had thought the words spoken over the bodies by Brave Eagle's friends, and by the elders of the village, were particularly moving. And though there was no representative of her own religion, Elizabeth quietly prayed for Jesus to accept the souls of the two Indians who had been so meaningful in her life since her capture.

"Hear the names of Brave Eagle, and Running Rabbit," Two Ponies called out to the others. "These are the honored names of those who now reside in the spirit world. I call now upon the spirit world to give Brave Eagle and Running Rabbit lodging. Give them horses to ride, and guns so that they may hunt. Give them food to eat and water to drink. Give them warm fires in the winter and cool breezes in the summer.

"And I call upon Brave Eagle and Running Rabbit to remember that you are Cheyenne. Do nothing in the spirit world that will bring dishonor to the people you have left behind. And now, we will say these names no more."

As the villagers returned to the village, Moon Cow Woman told Elizabeth that the council had expelled Bloody Axe so that he would never again be able to return to the village of the people. Elizabeth knew that "the people" meant the entire nation of Cheyenne, and not just the village.

Brave Eagle's belongings were disposed of later that same day, and though the virtues of "he who once owned this buffalo robe" were extolled, never once was Brave Eagle's name mentioned.

Elizabeth heard a sound. She wasn't sure how long she had been asleep. In fact, it was a moment before she even realized she had been asleep, and now, she floated back to consciousness only with effort.

She lay in the quiet darkness of her teepee, listening for a long time, to see if the sound returned. It was the stirring of the camp dogs she had heard, she decided. That, and nothing more.

The blankets were warm, and her senses were still groggy from sleep. Soon, Elizabeth drifted off again.

Elizabeth was awake less than a minute later, startled wide awake, her eyes open and her heart pounding in fear as rough hands grabbed her. But as soon as she perceived the danger and could cry out, she was gagged, and saw Bloody Axe kneeling over her, smiling evilly down at her.

"You are my woman!" Bloody Axe said. "You are coming with me!"

Elizabeth tried to call out against the gag, but she managed only a small, whimpering noise. Soon, even that was muffled as she felt herself being bound up in a buffalo rug, wrapped from head to toe so that she was unable to see or to cry out. Bloody Axe tied rawhide thongs tightly around the buffalo rug, so that she was unable to move an inch, completely helpless.

Elizabeth was scooped up and carried out of the teepee. She felt herself thrown across the back of a horse, then Bloody Axe climbed onto the horse with her. He gigged the animal's sides and Elizabeth, belly down over the horse, was spirited away into the night.

Chapter 11

Elizabeth had been Bloody Axe's captive for ten days. During that time, they had not seen another human being. Bloody Axe went high into the mountains, keeping away from main trails and waterways to make certain they went undetected. They may as well have been on the moon, so alone were they.

Bloody Axe knew that his life would be worthless, whether he was captured by the Indians or the white man, so he moved from campsite to campsite and never stayed in any one site longer than a single night. They traveled without a teepee, and Elizabeth had only the robe in which she had been wrapped to warm her against the chilly nights of late fall and higher elevations.

During her ordeal, Bloody Axe took Elizabeth forcibly, many times. The loss of her virginity, which had once meant so much to her, was not even a consideration in Elizabeth's determination to survive. It was just one more thing she had to endure, and she didn't even try to fight him off—not because she had succumbed, but because she realized that fighting was futile, and it was much easier to bear up under it until it was over. She had developed the art of making herself go numb, completely closing her mind and body to the degradation she was suffering.

Sometimes when they traveled, Bloody Axe allowed her to ride on the horse with him, but more often than not, she was forced to trail behind on foot, at the end of a long tether, with her hands tightly bound.

Elizabeth had grown much stronger during her time with the Indians. She had hauled wood, erected teepees, and skinned game. All that had a tremendously beneficial effect on her endurance. It was only because of that strength that she was able to survive the ordeal, and even then, she was tried to her utmost capacity.

Elizabeth was allowed to eat, but only after Bloody Axe had eaten. She was always very careful to break the bones and suck the marrow, in order to utilize as much as she could from the scraps she did get. On the night of the tenth day, as she was sitting quietly, waiting for him to finish a game bird, agonizing because it was so small that she knew there would be little left, Bloody Axe told her to get some water.

"Aren't you afraid I will run away?" she asked.

Bloody Axe pulled the meat off a bone, then smiled at her. "You will not run," he said.

"How do you know?"

"I have the horse," Bloody Axe answered. "I

can find you. You are hungry, and cannot run for long. If you run, I will catch you."

"And if you catch me, what will you do? Will you kill me?" Elizabeth asked in a voice that was totally devoid of expression.

"Yes."

"Good. Kill me now," Elizabeth said.

Bloody Axe looked at Elizabeth for a moment, surprised by her response. Then, he realized that she was not bluffing.

"No, I will not kill you. That is what you want. But if you run, I will beat you. Get the water," he demanded again.

Elizabeth picked up the buffalo stomach flask and started down toward the stream. The stream had not yet begun to ice over, but the water was running so cold that if she jumped in, her breath would be taken away, and she would quickly drown.

The thought of suicide, once no more than a point of philosophical interest to her, began to look attractive to Elizabeth. For the first time since her capture, she considered suicide as a serious alternative. Elizabeth put the flask down and took a few more steps toward the water.

The sudden, unexpected blow to the side of her head made her see stars and set her ears to ringing. She was knocked to the ground, and when she looked up, she saw Bloody Axe standing over her.

"No! You will not kill yourself," he said, menacingly, seeing her intention.

"Then you had better kill me," Elizabeth said

flatly. "Because, if you don't, I will kill you the first chance I get."

"You, a woman, would kill me, a warrior?" Bloody Axe laughed harshly.

Pueblo, Colorado

Although railroads were springing up all over the West to connect with the great transcontinental railroad that was being built, Pueblo's main connection to the rest of the world continued to be by stagecoach and wagon. Thus, when the three wagons rolled into Pueblo, their arrival garnered a good deal of interest from the citizens of the town. Pedestrians stopped and gawked, shoppers in the stores came to the windows and stared, and several young boys darted out into the street to great them. They ran alongside the wagons, keeping pace with the train as it moved down the street.

"Hey, where'd you come from?" one of the boys shouted up to Parker.

"We came from Independence, Missouri," Parker replied.

"Did it take you a long time?"

"It's taken long enough," Parker said.

"How come you ridin' up front? Ain't that where the wagon boss rides?"

"I *am* the wagon boss," Parker said.

"You're lyin'. You ain't old enough," the young boy said.

Clay, who had ridden ahead of the wagons earlier in order to make a few necessary arrangements, now rode back to meet them. As he approached, Parker held up his hand and signaled for the wagons to stop, and the street soon echoed with the drivers' shouts to their teams and the squeak of breaks.

"For law's sake, lookit that!" one of the boys said in surprise. "Did you see how he stopped them wagons? He *is* the wagon boss!"

"I've made a deal with the livery," Clay said to Parker. "They'll keep the mules in the corral and feed and water them for three days, and there's a place out back for the wagons."

"All right, I'll get the wagons in position before we disconnect the teams," Parker said. With a motion of his hand, the three wagons started moving again, leaving the pack of young boys behind.

Because the livery stable was at the extreme western end of town, wagons filled the streets with the hollow clopping sound of the mules, grinding wheels, clanging pots and pans, cargo-banging, and canvas-flapping.

The wagons were soon moved into position against the back wall of the livery, then the mules were disconnected and turned loose into the corral. The animals shook their heads, brayed, then trotted out into the open area, enjoying their freedom from the yokes.

The men, too, felt a sense of release as they stretched and walked around, restoring circulation to limbs too long cramped by saddle or wagon seat. Pecorino relieved himself against the back wall of the livery while Marcus checked the canvas covers on all the wagons.

"So, what do you want us to do now, boss?" Tobin asked.

"I want at least two of us to be with the wagons at all times," Clay said. "But if you don't happen to be one of the ones watching the wagons, you can do pretty much anything you want."

"That sounds good to me," Tobin said with a broad grin, his shoulder wound healing nicely.

"Who's going to get first watch?" Pecorino asked, coming back to join the others.

"I'll take first watch," Marcus offered.

"Good," Clay said. "I will too. Marcus and I will stay here tonight, so you boys are free to go on into town and do whatever you want to do. But don't get into any fights. In these trail towns, the sheriff always sides with the locals."

"You don't have to worry none about that," Pecorino said. "Fightin' ain't what I've got on my mind."

"Also, don't be talking too much 'bout our business," Marcus warned.

"Good point," Clay agreed. "I don't particularly want anyone to know what we are carrying. Especially the rifles."

"What about this Demon's Pass?" Tobin asked. "This might be a good time to see what we can find out about it, seein' as this is the closest town to it."

Clay shook his head. "No, I'd rather you not say anything about it. I've already talked to someone who's been through the pass, and I know pretty much what to expect. If we talk about it here, there's no telling who might be listening. And there's sure to be some place where a few enterprising outlaws could ambush us, if they were of a mind to."

"If you recall, we've already been through one outlaw attack and it cost us a good man," Marcus said.

"Yeah," Tobin said. "I bet ole Gibson would have had himself a time here."

"Boss, is that all you want to say to us?" Pecorino asked.

Clay laughed. "You sound like you're anxious to get started. Go ahead, we'll see you boys tomorrow."

"Clay, you want me to stay with you and Marcus?" Parker asked.

"No, go on into town with the others. Have yourself a good time. It'll do you good."

"Come on, Parker, let's go," Jason said eagerly.

"So, what are we going to do?" Jason asked the others a few moments later as the four walked back toward town.

"I tell you what *I'm* going to do," Pecorino said. "First thing I'm going to do is get me a good, sit-down meal. Then, after I've had myself a good meal, and maybe a little whiskey, I figure on gettin' me a woman."

"How are you going to do that?" Parker asked.

"Well, hell, I'm just going to go into a restaurant and order it," Pecorino replied.

"No, I don't mean the meal. How are you going to get a woman? We're only going to be here for a couple of days. How are you going to meet one that fast?"

Pecorino, Tobin, and Jason stopped walking and looked at Parker for a moment as if not sure he wasn't putting them on. Then they burst out laughing.

"What is it? What's so funny?"

"I didn't say nothin' 'bout *meetin'* a woman," Pecorino said. "I said I was goin' to *get* me a woman. There's a difference."

When, by his expression, Parker showed that he still didn't understand what Pecorino was saying, Jason interpreted for him.

"He's talkin' about a whore," Jason explained.

"Oh," Parker replied. And, with his understanding, came embarrassment over his earlier naïveté. He blushed.

"You know what we ought to do," Tobin said as they resumed walking. "We ought to break ole Parker in."

"Break me in how?"

"You ever had a woman, Parker?"

"Well . . . uh . . . no, I haven't," Parker admitted.

"I didn't think so," Tobin said. He looked at Jason. "What about you, boy? You ever had your ashes hauled?"

"Sure, lots of times," Jason replied.

"Then that just leaves you, Parker. How about it? You going to get yourself a woman tonight?"

"I don't know," Parker said.

"What's there not to know? Clay did tell you to go into town and have a good time, didn't he? I believe he even said it would be good for you. Haven't you ever even thought about it?"

Parker couldn't say that he had never thought about it, because he had thought about it, many times. And, he noticed, such thoughts seemed to creep into his mind with more frequency of late. But he had never actually considered contracting the services of a prostitute.

On the other hand, he certainly knew that it was something men did. And, it was a surefire way to accomplish that objective. He recalled the two women who had accosted him back in Independence. What is it they asked him about wanting to "see the varmint?"

Parker smiled.

"All right," he said. "I'll go see the varmint."

"Now you're talkin'!" Jason said enthusiastically.

"What kind of woman do you like, Parker?" Tobin asked.

"I don't know, I never stopped to think about it. I mean, a woman is a woman, isn't she?"

"No, a woman ain't just a woman," Tobin said. "There's all different kinds. I don't know, maybe you ought to let me pick out this first one for you. I mean, seein' as you ain't never done it before, you're liable to make a mistake your first time in the saddle. And somethin' like that could mess you up good from now on. They say that's what makes some men not do too good with women. So, how about it? You want me to pick one out for you?"

"No, thank you. I'll pick out my own. If I'm going to make a mistake, it'll be my own."

"All right, all right, have it your own way," Tobin said, holding up his hand in surrender. "I was just tryin' to be of some help, is all."

"Hey, let's ask that fella over there where we can find a whorehouse," Jason suggested, pointing to a man standing on the corner. The man was wearing a three-piece suit, and a gold watch chain stretched across his vest. When all four approached him, he looked at them with some apprehension.

"Is there something I can do for you gentlemen?" he asked a little nervously.

"Yes," Jason asked. "Where at's the whorehouse in this town?"

"I beg your pardon?" the man responded, a shocked look on his face.

"The whorehouse. Where's it at?"

"I assure you, gentlemen, if there is such an establishment, I am not a habitué," the man replied. Drawing his jacket together indignantly, he walked away quickly to put some distance between himself and the four men.

"Well, hell, mister, you don't have to get into a piss soup about it," Jason called after him.

The others laughed loudly.

"Jason, I have to hand it to you," Pecorino said. "You've got a real way with strangers."

"What the hell is a habitué?" Jason asked.

"Damned if I know," Pecorino said.

"Yeah, well, if that fella ain't one, whatever it is, it's probably somethin' I'd like to be," Jason said.

"Why don't we find us a saloon?" Tobin suggested. "We could maybe get us a drink or two, then find out where's the best place to eat. And I'm sure the folks at the saloon will know where the whorehouse is at."

"Good idea," Pecorino agreed.

When they came across a tavern a short while later, they paused out front to give it a quiet assessment. Then they pushed through the batwing doors and strode up to the bar, catching the bartender's eye.

"Parker, I don't want to embarrass you or anything in here, so, what'll it be? Beer or sarsaparilla?" Tobin asked.

Parker thought for a moment. He had tried beer before, and he didn't particularly like the taste, whereas he did like the taste of sarsaparilla. On the other hand, if he actually was going to go through this thing tonight, then beer seemed to be a more apt choice.

"I'll have a beer," he said.

"Good man," Tobin said.

After ordering beers for each of them, Tobin asked the bartender where they might find a whorehouse.

"Ain't nothin' exactly like that in Pueblo," the bartender replied. He pointed toward the stairs. "But we got a top floor here with private rooms and beds, and half a dozen whores that look as good as any you're goin' to find in one of them fancy places. I'm sure you will find them most satisfactory."

"All right, we'll give 'em a try. After we've had a good supper. Know any good places to eat?" Tobin asked.

"Sure—the City Café, just down the street," the bartender answered. As he spoke, he saw Parker take a sip of his beer, then make a face. He looked at Parker and then at Jason as if just noticing them for the first time.

"Have we suddenly turned green?" Jason asked the bartender. "What are you looking at?"

The bartender didn't answer Jason, but spoke instead to Tobin. "These here boys is just pups," he said, indicating Jason and Parker. "They're kinda young to be runnin' with you two, ain't they?"

Jason's eyes narrowed. "Mister, you got somethin' to say about me or my friend, you say it to us directly."

"All right, I'm tellin' you, I think you boys are still a little too wet behind the ears to be in here."

Jason took another swallow of his beer before he answered. "You know, I heard there was lots of young fellas no older'n my friend and me, killin' and dyin' in the late war. If it was to come down to that again, do you think we would be old enough to die? Or, let me put it this way." He leaned across the bar and said, in a cold, menacing voice, "Do you think we're old enough to kill?"

"Yes, I suppose you are," the bartender replied, unexpectedly intimidated by Jason's demeanor.

"Then, how old do we have to be to get a drink and a woman?" Jason asked.

"You're old enough, I reckon," the bartender mumbled.

"I'm glad you see it our way," Jason said, easing back onto his stool.

"Listen," Tobin said. "Me an' my friends is goin' out to get somethin' to eat now. Then we're goin' to come back for some serious drinking, and to make a run on them whores. Don't you let them get away."

"Oh, don't worry none about that. They're goin' to be here all night."

"So are we, mister. So are we," Tobin said.

The four left the saloon and strode a few doors down to the City Café. Their orders came quickly, but while Pecorino, Tobin, and Jason wolfed down their meals, Parker merely picked at his food.

"You plannin' on eatin' the rest of them taters?" Tobin asked Parker. When Parker shook his head no, Tobin took Parker's plate and shoveled the uneaten potatoes onto his own. Tobin had spent the whole meal instructing Parker on the proper techniques of "whoring," as he called it. He was now telling him, "You're probably figuring you should have yourself a real young whore, maybe someone about your own age.

But if you was to do that, you'd be makin' a big mistake."

"Why would that be a mistake?" Parker asked.

"Because if she's that young, she wouldn't be knowin' a whole lot more about it than you," Tobin explained. "What you need is to find yourself the oldest one in the place. See, that way, there ain' no kind of way she ain' never been rode, an' no kind of man she ain't never throwed. Besides which, the older the whores get, the younger they like their men. An old whore would be a real good one for breakin' you in."

Pecorino laughed. "Tobin, you're as full of shit as a Christmas goose, you know that? Don't go listening to him, Parker. He's just tryin' to make sure he gets the youngest and prettiest one for himself. By the way, you goin' to eat the rest of your steak?"

Without answering, Parker forked the rest of his steak off his plate and onto Pecorino's.

"You're wrong, Frank. I for sure don't want the prettiest one," Tobin said. "You see, that's another thing about whores. The prettiest ones, now, they think their good looks is all they need. What you want to do is get you one that's just a little bit ugly. Most of them that's ugly know they're ugly, so they'll kind of go out of their way to treat you right." Tobin cut off a piece of his steak and chewed it thoughtfully for a moment before he continued with his lecture. "Of course, every now and again you're likely to get you one who's ugly, but she don't *know* she's ugly. Now, them's the worst kind, 'cause they figure they're pretty enough for looks to get them by, and they don't try none at all. An ugly woman that thinks she's pretty and don't try . . . well, you sure don't want that kind of whore if you can help it."

"Tobin, it's too bad you can't write," Pecorino teased. "Hell, I'll bet there ain't nobody in the country knows as much about chasin' whores as you do. You could do a fine book on the subject."

"Well, now, I could write a book on it, an' that's a fact," Tobin said. "If I could write," he added.

Parker laughed, then put the uneaten portion of his apple pie on Jason's plate.

"Damn, boy, what's wrong with you?" Tobin asked. "You give me all your taters, Frank your steak, and Jason your pie. You feelin' all right?"

"Sure, I feel fine. I guess I'm just not hungry, is all," Parker said.

Though he wouldn't tell the others, he had butterflies in his stomach, nervous just from thinking about being with a woman for the first time.

When they returned to the saloon after their meal, all the whores were working the tables for drinks, as the bartender told them that none of the women could go upstairs before eight.

"Well, then, we'll just sit over at that table

there and have us a few drinks while we're waitin'," Pecorino said.

The bartender chuckled. "Yes," he said. "That's the whole idea."

As they waited, Parker watched the women work the customers and made up his mind which one of them he wanted. In fact, he made up his mind that if he didn't get her, he wasn't going to go upstairs at all.

Though none of them looked under thirty, the one he picked out seemed to have a softer smile and a gentler disposition than the others. Somehow she seemed less threatening to him. He had heard one of the men call her Penny.

"I want Penny," he said to the others. It was the first comment he had made in several minutes.

"Penny?" Tobin replied. He twisted around in his chair and looked at the women. "Which one's Penny?"

At that moment, Penny was sitting in the lap of a big, bearded man, twisting the hair of his beard around her fingers. When Parker pointed her out, Tobin nodded. "She looks like she might be a good one for you. Which one do you want, Jason?"

"The one in the green dress," Jason answered.

Tobin looked at the girl Jason pointed out, then back at him. "You sure? Damn, look how skinny she is. Doin' her would be like pokin' it through a knothole in a board."

"Maybe so, but that's the one I want," Jason insisted.

"You got one picked out, Frank?"

"That's the one I want." Pecorino pointed to an exotic-looking, dark-haired, Mexican girl.

"Yeah, she's a pretty one, all right. But I want the one in blue. You know, if a fella was to fall down the front of her dress he'd like as not smother before he could get hisself excavated."

At eight o'clock, the woman in blue came over to the table where the four men had been sitting patiently for just over an hour. Putting a hand on her hip and thrusting it out provocatively, she leaned over the table. "Roy says you fellas want some company tonight."

"You said it, honey," Tobin replied.

The woman straightened up. "First, we must get the unpleasant business of money out of the way. Our company will cost you gentlemen a dollar and a half, each, or three dollars apiece for the whole night."

"I reckon we'll each one of us take about three dollars' worth," Tobin said.

"Oh, my. Big spenders, are you? Well, I'm sure we'll have a wonderful time." The woman smiled. "My name's Amy."

"Amy, I done laid a claim on you," Tobin said. "My pards has chose up the ones they want, too. Frank here wants the little Mex gal. Jason wants the skinny one in the red dress, and Parker here, wants Penny."

"Have you ever been with a woman before, honey?" Amy asked Parker, eyeing him up and down.

Parker felt his cheeks burning in embarrassment. "No, ma'am," he answered, barely mumbling the words.

"Then you've made a wise choice," Amy said. "Penny's real good with young boys who're doing it for the first time. It's almost as if she has a calling for it."

Amy signaled the other three, and they came over to the table to stand beside her. She made the introductions, ending with Penny.

"Penny, this little sweetheart is one of your specials, if you get my meaning," Amy said.

"She means he ain't never done it before," Tobin added, and Parker felt his cheeks flush again.

Penny reached out to take Parker's hand in hers. She smiled, and Parker saw a few lines around her eyes that he hadn't noticed before. Perhaps she was older than he thought, maybe even older than the other girls. He liked her eyes, though. They were bright blue, and were clear and deep and somehow not quite as hard as the other girls' eyes.

"There's no need to embarrass the young gentleman," Penny admonished Tobin. "We're going to do just fine."

"Well, shall we all go upstairs?" Amy invited.

"I reckon so, unless you're wantin' to do it right down here on the table," Pecorino said. "And I'm that ready."

"Well, we certainly don't want to see him bust, do we?" Amy said, laughing. "Come on, ladies, I do believe these gentlemen are badly in need of our services."

As they all climbed the stairs, Parker was acutely aware that everyone else in the saloon knew exactly what was going on. He thought he could feel their eyes burning into the back of his neck. But as they reached the first landing, he happened to glance into the mirror hanging behind the bar, and it didn't appear that anyone in the saloon was paying the slightest bit of attention to him and his friends. He was surprised by that, but it did make him feel a bit less embarrassed.

Once in her room, Penny shut the door behind them, then lit a single candle. She turned and smiled at Parker as she began stripping out of her clothes. Parker watched, spellbound, as the smooth skin of Penny's shoulders was exposed. Then she turned so that he saw only her back as she removed the rest of her clothes. Calling on all the tricks of her professional experience, she used a shadow here, a soft light there, a movement to hold her body just so. As if by magic, she seemed to lose so many years in age and gain so much in mystery that she became as sensual a creature as anyone who had ever appeared in Parker's fantasies. Finally, raising the corner of the sheet, she managed to slip into bed using the shadows in such a way that he wasn't sure whether he had seen anything or not.

"Are you going to keep your clothes on?" Penny asked.

"No," Parker said as he began to undress.

She folded the corner of the sheet back, inviting him into bed with her, and showing herself from one breast all the way down to one side of her hip. He got the tiniest glimpse of a black, triangular patch of hair before she readjusted the sheet. He inhaled quickly.

"Oh, my, look at that," Penny said when Parker was completely nude.

"I'm sorry," he apologized.

"Don't apologize, honey. The time to apologize to a woman is when it *doesn't* do that. That's the way it's supposed to be."

Parker slid in under the sheets. She reached over to touch him, and her hand felt as if fire and ice were contained in her fingertips.

"Should I . . ." Parker started, but Penny shushed him, much as one would a small child.

"You just let me take care of everything, honey," she said. "It'll be all right. Trust me."

Chapter 12

A fly landed on Parker's face, and though he brushed it away, it returned. It came back a second and then a third time, until finally the irritation of it penetrated Parker's sleep and he was forced to open his eyes.

For a moment he didn't know where he was. Then he remembered what had happened the night before, and he turned his head to see a woman in bed with him. She was on her back, her head was turned away from him, and the bedcovers had slipped down from her left shoulder, allowing Parker to closely examine her exposed breast, which was lighted by a beam of sunlight stabbing between the bottom of the dark green shade and the edge of the windowsill.

Penny's position had pulled her breast nearly flat so that the globe of flesh Parker had made a thorough exploration of last night, was now just a gentle curve. Quietly, gently enough so that Penny wasn't aware of what he was doing, Parker lifted off the cover, then rolled it all the way down to the bottom of the bed. With her body fully revealed, Parker was able to see in person, for the first time in his life, a totally nude woman. He lay with his elbow bent and his head resting on his hand, studying her.

"Enjoying the show?" she finally asked, without opening her eyes.

Parker, who had thought she was asleep, was startled by her unexpected remark, and he jumped. "I'm sorry," he said quickly.

Penny laughed, then pulled the cover back over her. "I'm glad you enjoyed it," she said. "But I'm chilled, so, if you don't mind."

"No, ma'am," Parker said quickly. "No, ma'am, I don't mind at all."

"You're just passing through town, aren't you, Parker?"

"Yes, ma'am."

"It's a good thing."

"It's a good thing?" Parker replied, surprised by her comment. "Why?"

"Because you are the kind of young man I could corrupt very easily. And that's something I would not like to see happen. Promise me you won't be corrupted."

"Yes, ma'am, I promise."

"Good. Now, run along. Go eat breakfast, join your friends, or go back to your wagons. If you stay here any longer, I might start trying to get you to go back on that promise right now."

Parker got out of bed and dressed, acutely aware of her eyes on him the whole time. Then, when he was fully dressed, he started for the door.

"Parker?" she called to him.

"Yes, ma'am?" He looked back toward the bed.

"I hope you have a good rest-of-your-life," she said.

"Thank you, ma'am. You too," Parker said as he stepped out of the room and closed the door behind him.

With their water kegs full, the stock well rested, and the wagons in good repair, Clay and Parker led the train out of Pueblo. After going north for a few miles, as if heading for Denver, they turned west to pick up the trail to Demon's Pass.

Clay had examined the map several times, and no matter how one looked at it, this route would save them three hundred miles. Under normal conditions, three hundred miles would translate into two weeks, and this late in the fall, two weeks could be the difference between an unfettered passage and being caught in a deadly winter blizzard.

Because of the mountain man's warnings about the difficulty of the route, Clay confessed to Parker and Marcus that he continued to have some reservations about it. However, the fact that there were only three wagons in his train made Clay confident that they would succeed where others, apparently, had failed.

The first day of travel was one of the easiest days they had had since leaving Independence, and when they camped that night, the party was in very high spirits. Travel was much more difficult the next day but no one worried about it. "After all," Clay assured them, "we're goin' to have as many hard days as we have good."

Thanks to bad weather and a thrown wheel on one of the wagons, the third day was more difficult, and some were beginning to get disheartened. Pecorino even suggested that maybe they would have been better off going the other way.

"No, I'm with Clay on this," Marcus said. "We can put up with some hard traveling if it saves us three hundred miles."

On the fourth day they reached a valley that was lush with grass and had an excellent source of water. Their spirits brightened again.

Late in the morning of the fifth day, the wagons followed the creek into a canyon. The walls of the canyon were a foreboding red color, and they loomed three hundred feet or more above the canyon floor. Because the wagons were closed in by walls on either side, the canyon filled with the ricochets of the fall of every hoof, the creak of every wheel, and the whistle of each driver, bouncing back from the walls in an avalanche of sound.

Parker looked high up on either side, feeling dwarfed by the steep, rocky cliffs.

"Sort of awesome, isn't it?" Clay said, riding up beside him.

"I didn't know there was country like this anywhere in the world," Parker said.

By the sixth day, the trail had climbed to an elevation of several thousand feet, and squeezed down to the point that it was barely passable by the men on horseback, and even more difficult for the wagons. In fact they saw the remains of some wagons that didn't make it, including one which had fallen into a deep crevice, killing the oxen. Wolves had already visited the site, and along with the buzzards, had long since picked the bones so clean that they shone brightly in the sun.

They stopped for a moment to look down at the wreckage, taking a drink of water as they rested.

"How long you think that's been down there?" Parker asked.

"You ask me, it's been down there for twenty years or more," Clay replied. "I expect it's left over from the days of the big wagon trains."

"Wonder if any of the people went over with it?" Jason asked.

"Probably not," Marcus answered. "Comin' through here, they was probably leadin' their teams rather than drivin' 'em. Especially if they had big trains."

"Maybe we should be leadin' our teams as well," Pecorino suggested.

"Naw, we got mules, not oxen," Marcus said. "Mules is more surefooted, and the faster we go, the sooner we'll get through here."

"I don't know, maybe I've made a big mistake," Clay said, giving voice to the doubts that had begun to plague him. "I'm beginning to think I should have never insisted that we come this way."

"You weren't the only one wanting to do it, Clay," Parker said.

"But I forced the issue," Clay insisted.

"You're not planning on turning back, are you?"

"No, no, it's too late now. If it were earlier in the season I might, but we can't turn back now. We must go on. We have no choice."

The drivers, who had been standing on the edge of the crevice, looking warily down at the wreck, climbed back onto their wagons and wearily continued on.

Later that day, Clay and Tobin rode ahead to scout the trail. When they reached the top of a long, sharp-spined ridge, they got off their mounts and walked out to the end of a flat rock. Ahead, there appeared to be two possible ways to proceed.

"Which way do we go, boss?" Tobin asked.

"If we continue straight ahead, we would go that way," Clay said, pointing in front of them. He turned a little to the right and pointed toward a long, upward sloping canyon. "But I've got a feeling that's the way we should go."

"Yeah, well, it has to get easier, because it sure can't get any harder," Tobin replied.

The new route proved to be no easier than the old had been. In fact, as they progressed up the canyon, the route became much steeper and choked with slippery trails. They had to pick their way slowly, cutting timber and moving rocks, working until the blisters on their hands broke and bled. By evening, everyone was so exhausted that they fell asleep immediately.

The next day, there were times when the going was so difficult that roads couldn't even be made. They were following nothing but a small Indian trail and the wagons had to be hauled up to the top of the ridge by windlasses and doubled teams, then lowered down the other side.

They moved out of one canyon and into another, where they encountered a small creek. Although it didn't seem possible, this canyon was worse than the previous canyon had been. Its bottoms were crowded with boulders and wild growth, and by now they were making no more than a mile or two per day. Six days later, they left the main canyon and started up a side canyon. So far, each day, and each turn, had made the situation worse.

It was now two weeks since they had taken the cutoff. It was nighttime and the little party made what camp they could. Parker was leaning against the side of the lead wagon, so exhausted he could hardly stand, drinking a cup of coffee, when Clay came up to stand beside him.

"Some coffee over there," Parker said.

"Thanks."

"I can't believe there was ever a time when I

didn't like this," Parker said as Clay poured his own cup and freshened Parker's.

Clay put the pot back on the hot embers, then looked over at Parker. "I'm sorry, kid," he said.

"Sorry for what?"

Clay sighed, then took in the wagons and teams with a wave of his arm. The men were lying or sitting around on the ground, in various poses of fatigue. "For this," he said. "Bringing you, and them, through this hell. We never should have tried this cutoff."

The next day Parker, who was riding in the lead, reached the top of the pass. As he did so, he was overwhelmed by what he saw in front of him. The sun glared brightly from the white surface of a desert that stretched, unbroken, from here to the shadowy suggestion of a mountain range far, far, on the distant, shimmering, horizon. Not only was there no water, there was not one tree, shrub, or blade of grass to be seen. The desert was at least seventy miles wide. It looked impassable, but they had no choice. They could not go back.

As the others reached the top of the pass their reaction was the same as Parker's had been. The wagons stopped, and everyone just stood there for a long moment, looking ahead, shielding their eyes with their hands and trying to imagine if they would survive the crossing.

"It looks like we are going into the bowels of hell itself," Jason suggested.

"We'll never make it across," Pecorino added worriedly.

"We ain't got no choice," Marcus reminded them.

"We're wasting time standing here." Clay growled. "Let's move 'em out."

Mouthing a prayer and gathering what strength they had remaining, the little party started out into the arid desert.

As the mules plodded and the wagons rolled, the wheels lifted a fine, powdery dust from the ground, which hung in the air, clogging the nostrils and burning the skin. With red-rimmed eyes, chapped lips, and grim, determined expressions, they continued their trek out into the yawning wasteland.

They camped the first night on the desert, building fires from the greasewood to help push back the cold. Almost total exhaustion made for a very quiet camp. They ate little and drank even less, then turned in for a few hours of fretful sleep. Before dawn they were up and going again.

As they moved farther out into the desert, the sand became deeper and harder to move through. The hooves of the mules sank into the sand and the wagon wheels cut grooves almost halfway up to the hubs, making the pulling much harder. The merciless sun continued its agonzingly slow transit across the bright blue sky, punishing everyone with its heat and glare. Despite their best efforts to conserve what they had, parched throats and chapped lips demanded water, and the men went to their containers time and time again. Often as not, when the water vessel was empty it would be cast aside so that, soon, the little train could be traced by the empty canteens, jugs, bottles, and barrels which littered their route.

When they stopped for the second night they realized a grim truth. The mountain range on the distant horizon looked as far away now as it did when they had entered the desert yesterday morning.

There was no water left for the animals by midmorning of the third day. There was no grass either. There was only the great desert reaching out before them in a blazing white that glistened in the distance, giving the tantalizing but false impression of water.

The men urged the teams on, sometimes getting behind the wagons and pushing when there was a particularly difficult place for them to negotiate.

That night, their third night on the desert, they sat around the fire, watching the sparks ride a rising column high into the night sky until the tiny red embers mingled with the distant blue stars. Finally, the fire burned down.

"We aren't going to make it out of this damn desert, are we?" Pecorino asked.

"Sure we are," Parker said.

"No, we aren't," Pecorino insisted. "We're going to die out here, all of us." Pecorino's words were not those of a frightened man, but rather those of a man resigned. He said them as if he really didn't care whether they survived or not. "Someday someone will find our bones and if they know who we are, I want them to put on my tombstone; 'Here lies Frank Pecorino. He never should'a left New York.' "

"Why did you leave New York?" Jason asked.

"On account of my sister."

"Your sister made you leave New York?"

"My sister was to be married . . . but the man who proposed to her changed his mind. The only problem is, he didn't tell my sister. He said nothing to no one, and just took off."

Pecorino paused for a moment, as if gathering his thoughts.

"On the day of the wedding my sister put on her beautiful white dress and went to the church. My father was there to give her away. My mother carried flowers, The church was full as we all gathered to watch my sister be married."

Pecorino poked at the fire with a long stick. It was several seconds before he spoke again. "Everyone was there for the wedding: family, friends, the priest, the bride, the bridesmaids. Even the best man was there. Only one person wasn't there—the groom."

There was another beat of silence.

"And that's it?" Parker asked. "You left New York because you were embarrassed that the groom didn't show up at your sister's wedding?"

"Not exactly," Pecorino said. He put the end of the stick he was holding into a flame and held it there until it ignited. Then he raised the stick and examined its end closely. "I left New York because I went after the son of a bitch who left my sister standing at the altar. I found him . . . and I killed him."

"Damn! Remind me never to make you mad, Frank," Clay said.

The others laughed, and the mirth had the effect of breaking the tension. When they went to sleep that night, after more joking and bantering, there was a mutual belief that the desert would not beat them. They would survive

That feeling of transcendency over all obstacles was put to a test the very next afternoon when they crossed over a great saltwater sink, covered by a thin veneer of sand. The hooves of the mules and the wheels of the wagon cut through the crust easily, bringing saltwater to the surface.

The mules, with very little water for the last thirty-six hours, were nearly mad from thirst. The men weren't faring much better than their animals. Marcus told Parker of an old trick he had once learned of sucking on rocks to fight the thirst, and Parker did so, though he didn't know whether it helped or not. He rubbed eyes which were nearly blinded by the sun and irritated by blowing salt.

"Parker," Clay said, finally coming to a decision, "I'd like you to ride ahead to find water. As soon as you do, bring some back to us."

"All right."

"What about the mules, Mr. Springer?" Jason asked. "Parker can't bring back enough water for them too, and if we keep on drivin' 'em like this, we're goin' to kill 'em."

Reed rubbed his chin. "You're right," he said. "All right, if Parker finds water we'll cut the mules loose and take them on ahead. After they've drunk their fill, we can bring them back for the wagons."

Parker began gathering what canteens had not been discarded, and tied them to his saddle pommel.

"Parker," Clay said, just before Parker was ready to ride off.

"Yes?"

"Don't tarry, boy," Clay said. "For if you do, when you get back, you'll find nothing but bleached bones."

"I'll be back as soon as I can," Parker promised.

Leaving the others behind, Parker rode on ahead, fighting the heat and the sun throughout the rest of the day. At about dusk his horse smelled water and, without Parker's urging, broke into a gallop. Parker hung on until, finally, he saw grass and trees and knew that there had to be a spring there.

When he reached the small spring he leaped from the saddle and ran to the water, then lay on his stomach and after dunking his head under, he sucked up cool liquid in such long drafts that he got stomach cramps. He had to get up and walk away from it, and he began throwing up.

When, finally, he got control of his retching, and drank some more water to replace that which he had regurgitated, he began filling the canteens. Once they were full, Parker started back, continuing all through the night until he finally reached the wagons just before dawn. He found Clay and the others waiting patiently by the inert wagons. He gave them all water to drink, then, because he had not slept in over twenty-four hours, he crawled into one of the wagons to sleep. There would be nothing else to do until Clay and Marcus brought the refreshed mules back for the wagons.

When Parker woke up it was midafternoon and he was sweating in the terrible heat.

"Jason?" he said, sitting up.

"Yeah, I'm right here," Jason answered.

"Where is everyone?"

"We're down here," Jason said. "Sitting in the shade of the wagon."

Parker crawled out of the wagon and looked around. They could have been on the surface of the moon, they were so alone. The mountains rose in the distance and a hot, dry wind moaned across the desert.

"Clay and Marcus aren't back yet?"

"Not yet."

"Maybe they ain't comin' back," Tobin suggested.

"They'll be back," Parker said.

"What makes you so sure of that?" Tobin asked.

"Because I know Clay Springer. He's not the kind of man who would abandon us."

"Then how come he's not back yet? He's had plenty of time to get there and back."

"Could be the mules are too tired," Jason said. "You know what ornery cusses them critters can be."

Jason's suggestion turned out to be correct. It was absolutely impossible to get the mules away from the spring and moving again before the next morning. As a result, by the time Marcus and Clay returned to the wagons with the animals, the supply of water for those who had waited behind was nearly exhausted again. Anticipating that, Clay and Marcus had brought back two barrels of water.

Returning to the spring, it was five more days before mules and men were sufficiently rested from their ordeal in the desert to continue. Two more days of hard travel beyond that brought them to a small lake with green grass. It was such an inviting oasis and the mules were so exhausted, that the train wanted to rest again.

Clay, however, was anxious to go on as quickly as he could. He was beginning to grow more and more concerned about the lateness of the season and in order to discuss his concern, he called a meeting.

The men gathered around with gaunt faces,

sore bodies, and diminished spirits. How different this meeting was, Parker thought, from the ones they had had early in the journey. At those earlier gatherings there had been jokes and good-natured ribbing. Now, everyone was silent.

"Men," Clay started, "I don't have to tell you that we're in a bad fix here, and I have to take the blame for it. I thought that by taking the cutoff, we would be gaining time. Instead, we've lost time, and we're beginning to run low on provisions. I know you want to stay here and rest some more, but if we do that, we'll never make it through the mountains before the snows come. We can't stay here and rest. We have to get going, and we have to do it now."

Grumbling over the fact that their rest period was being cut short, the men nonetheless left to begin hitching up their teams.

"I don't know, Clay," Marcus said as he walked over to stand beside Clay and Parker. "The way you're driving these men, you may wind up with a mutiny on your hands."

"Well, if it does come to a mutiny, it'll be three against three," Clay said. "And I reckon we'll just have to handle it."

"It'll be four to two," Parker said.

"Four to two? What are you saying, boy? That you would join with them?" Marcus asked in surprise.

"No," Parker answered. He smiled. "I'm saying that Jason would throw in with us."

Clay looked over at the young man, who was, at that very moment, busily connecting his team.

"I have to admit," Clay said, "Jason has worked out a lot better than I thought he would. You have an eye for good men, Parker. You are going to be a fine leader."

Chapter 13

Because Bloody Axe knew Elizabeth had wanted to leap into the cold stream, the brave now kept her wrists bound together all the time. He didn't untie her when she ate, nor when he forced himself upon her. He even kept her tied when she had to answer the call of nature, laughing at her awkwardness. At first her cheeks flamed in embarrassment as he watched her during these most private moments, but eventually she got used to it and she was able to totally close him out of her mind.

It was midmorning now, and Bloody Axe was on horseback. Elizabeth, with her wrists tied and a long cord keeping her attached to him, walked along behind the horse, often having to break into a shuffling run to keep up.

"Stop," Bloody Axe called to her as he halted his horse, then slid down to the ground. Putting his hands to his groin, he started pulling the breechcloth to one side. At first, Elizabeth steeled herself for another assault, but from the expression on his face, she knew that sex wasn't on his mind.

Ironically, while Elizabeth had learned to adjust to the lack of privacy when she was called by nature, Bloody Axe had not. Walking a few paces off the trail, Bloody Axe turned his back to her, then began urinating on a tree.

A stout hickory limb about two inches in diameter and about three feet long gave Elizabeth the opportunity she had been looking for. She walked toward it quietly, utilizing the skill of silent movement she had acquired since being captured by the Indians. Watching him intently, she bent down to retrieve it.

"I think you do not walk fast enough," Bloody Axe said without looking around. "If you cannot keep up, I will drag you like a travois," he added.

Elizabeth wrapped her hands around the stick, getting as good a grip on it as she could, given that her wrists were tied together. She raised herself up again, then took another step toward him. Now, with the hickory club firmly in her grasp, she drew her arms back, ready to strike.

"We go now," Bloody Axe said, adjusting his breechcloth as he turned away from the tree.

Bloody Axe barely had time to perceive the danger. His eyes grew wide in fear an instant before Elizabeth brought the club smashing down on his skull. There was a loud thunking sound as club hit flesh, and Bloody Axe fell back like the pole-axed pigs Elizabeth used to see during slaughtering time on her father's farm back in Illinois.

By the way Bloody Axe lay on the ground, Elizabeth believed he was dead, but she intended to be certain of it. Though it unsettled her to do so, she brought the club down on his head again and again, until his face was nothing but bloody, disfigured pulp. Not until then did she realize that she had been screaming at him with every blow of the club, cursing in both English and Cheyenne.

Finally, exhausted and emotionally drained, Elizabeth dropped the stick and sat on the ground beside Bloody Axe's body.

It was several moments before her breathing returned to normal. When she recovered, she took his knife from his belt and began sawing at the rawhide thongs. Because of the way she had to hold the knife, it was much more difficult to free herself than she thought it would be but, finally, she was able to cut through them.

Her wrists were abscessed and bloody from the several days of tight binding, and as she pulled the rawhide strips away, she began to gently rub the festering sores. Then, with some degree of circulation restored, she climbed onto Bloody Axe's horse and rode away. Not once did she look back at the body of the man who had been her captor.

With the Springer–Stanley Party

When Tobin came back to report that he had seen a buffalo herd, everyone's spirits lifted.

"If we could kill a buffalo, we'd have enough meat to last us a month," Clay suggested.

"Yeah, well, who are you going to send to kill one?" Tobin asked. " 'Cause I don't want nothin' to do with 'em. They're mean-tempered sons of bitches."

"Me neither. They're as big as a house," Pecorino said.

Marcus laughed. "They're nothin' but oversized squirrels," he said.

"I'd like to go," Parker volunteered.

"Me too," Jason added.

Parker, Jason, and Marcus were selected to make the hunt, and Parker was excited as he rode out with the others. But he was a little frightened too. Suppose they failed? Suppose the buffalo got away from them, and they had to return to the camp empty-handed? It would be awfully embarrassing to disappoint everyone like that. Parker made a vow to himself that he would not fail. He would kill a buffalo, no matter what it took.

They approached the herd from downwind with Marcus in the lead. They could smell the herd before they heard it, and heard the animals bellowing before they came into view. They had a wild, tangy smell, which filled the nostrils and excited the senses of the hunters as they approached.

As they got nearer, they could hear all of the bawling and coughing, grunting and squeaking, rumbling and clacking as the herd moved.

Finally they saw them.

When the three hunters crested the last little hill, they saw thousands of buffalo stretching in an unbroken carpet of brown from horizon to horizon.

Parker felt his heart in his throat, for never in his life had he seen a sight so magnificent.

"All right," Marcus said. "We'll ride toward them. If they start to run, pick one of them out and stay with him. Watch out for yourselves, though—don't get unseated. If you do, their hooves will ground you up like sausage meat."

"I'm ready," Parker said. Despite his assurances, however, the palms of his hands were sweating and he wiped them on the leg of his trousers to dry them before he pulled his pistol.

"Let's go," Marcus ordered and started toward the herd. Parker and Jason followed.

As they approached the herd they began to spread out so that by the time they reached the buffalo they were separated from each other by several yards. At first the buffalo just stood there. Then one of them saw the hunters approaching and started running. That started the others, so that the entire heard was quickly set in motion. From Parker's perspective, it looked like the flowing of a great, thundering brown river.

Parker locked on to a buffalo that he wanted, and holding the reins in his left hand, guided his horse toward the creature. He spurred the horse into a full gallop but the buffalo was much faster than he thought it would be. It was taking some effort to catch up with it.

One of the bulls suddenly thrust his great shaggy-maned head toward Parker, trying to hook Parker's horse with a horn, but Parker managed to pull away at the last minute. His horse seemed to show no particular fear of the creatures, drawing its courage from its rider's steady, guiding hand.

Finally Parker managed to close up on the buffalo, and raising his pistol, he put the barrel right behind the bull's ear, no more than six inches away. When he pulled the trigger he saw the flash of fire, then the impact of the bullet as hair and a little spray of blood flew up from the point of entry.

The buffalo continued to run for a few more steps as if it hadn't even been hit. After a minute, Parker saw it jerk its head, wobble slightly, then fall. The stampeding buffalo behind it veered to the right, opening up a little space around it. Parker stopped his horse, jerked it around sharply, then approached the fallen bull, ready, if need be, to finish him off.

No final coup was required, however. The buffalo lay dead.

Clay and his men were not the only ones who knew about the buffalo. A band of Shoshoni had tracked the herd from the south. When they saw that a group of white men had taken a buffalo, some of them became very angry and they held a brief council to determine what they should do about it. Many wanted to attack the white men and steal whatever they might have in the wagons.

Black Crow was the leader of the wandering band of Shoshoni, assuming that position by virtue of his age and experience. That night, around the council fire, he spoke to the others, urging restraint.

"These white men are not like those who hunt buffalo for the hides. They took only one, not many, and they did not leave the meat rotting on the plains, as do those who hunt for the hide only. The buffalo has been placed here by the Great Spirit to feed all his people, red and white. If we attack the white men for killing one buffalo and eating it, then we will anger the Great Spirit."

Black Crow sat down to be immediately replaced by Yellow Hand. Yellow Hand, who wore his name in the form of a yellow handprint on his face, was young and ambitious. He had not fought in as many battles as Black Crow, and he was hungry for the opportunity to prove himself before the others. He believed this to be a chance to do just that, and he didn't want to let it slip through his fingers.

"I have listened to Black Crow," Yellow Hand said. "I know that he is a man of many fights, and so when he counsels us against war, I know it is not because he is frightened, but because he is tired, like an old man."

There were a few grunts of displeasure, but no one spoke out directly, because to do so could have brought a challenge to fight from

Yellow Hand. Also, though Yellow Hand dismissed Black Crow's precautions as those of a tired, old man, he did so in such a way as to continue to pay respect for Black Crow's past accomplishments.

"The white men are few," Black Crow said. "We are many. What honor would there be in making war against so few?"

Black Crow won several converts to his position with this approach, and Yellow Hand saw his opportunity to lead men in battle beginning to slip away from him. He played his strongest hand.

"Have you seen the wagons of the white men?" he asked the others. "These are not the wagons of the men and women who come to settler on the land and make farms. There are no women with these wagons. These wagons are loaded with many wonderful things that they will use for trading."

"What sort of things?" one of the warriors asked.

Yellow Hand saw that a couple other young men were interested as well, and he knew that he was beginning win some to his side.

"Such wagons carry many things that are of great value," Yellow Hand said. "They will have guns and knives, sugar and warm blankets. They will have hatchets and gunpowder, and lead for making bullets."

"Will they have whiskey?"

Yellow Hand had no way of knowing that the wagons were carrying trade goods for the Mormons, and thus had no whiskey, coffee, or tobacco. He did know, however, that the prospect of whiskey was an appealing one.

"They will have much whiskey," he declared resolutely.

"Then I will come with you to attack them."

"And I!"

"And I!"

Several more warriors declared their intention to join with Yellow Hand in his attack. For a while, it looked as if the entire band would join him, and Yellow Hand smiled broadly, victoriously, as the men got up from the council fire and moved toward him to make their positions known.

When all was finished, nearly fifty had agreed to come with him. Fifty, out of a band of just over two hundred, including women, children, and the elderly. To assemble such a large war party from such a small group was quite an accomplishment, and Yellow Hand looked on with pride as the warriors lined up behind him.

"Yellow Hand," Black Crow said, "if you attack the white men, you will bring trouble upon all of us. You have taken all the young warriors with you. Only those who are old and sick have remained behind. If we are attacked, we cannot mount a proper fight. Stay with us. We will have a good buffalo hunt, then we will find a place to make our winter camp."

"No!" Yellow Hand said. "Those who joined me are brave of heart. They are not like the cowards who will stay in the village and warm themselves in lodges built for them by their women, filling their bellies with food cooked for them. Come, brave hearts, if you would be men. Come with me now!"

Yellow Hand started toward the remuda where the village kept their horses. He made no effort to look back until he climbed on his horse. Only then did he see that every man who had joined him initially was still with him. Black Crow's entreaty to them to stay had failed. Yellow Hand felt a tremendous pride inside, for he knew that when he and the warriors returned, he would be the new chief.

When all were mounted, Yellow Hand held his rifle over his head, let out a loud yell, then slapped his legs against the sides of his horse. His horse leaped forward, reaching full gallop in a couple of strides. Those who chose to ride with him urged their own horses forward as well, and the warriors made a grand show as they left the camp, splashing through the stream that ran by the encampment. A shower of silver was kicked up as the horses flew through the stream, and a fine rain was churned by the horses' hooves. It was a magnificent sight, and several of the very young boys crowded to the edge of the village to watch in awe as the warriors left to make war.

Chapter 14

Elizabeth stood in the swift-running stream, the cold water numbing her legs from the knees down.

Spotting a trout working hard to fight the swift current, Elizabeth raised her hand and held it, palm open, just above the surface. Exercising a patience she wouldn't have had a few months earlier, she waited. Finally the trout came closer toward her outstretched hand.

"Hold still, little fish," Elizabeth said under her breath. "You are going to be my breakfast."

She watched as the fish slowly fought the current toward her, then as quick as a striking snake, her hand flashed down into the water just ahead of the fish, just as it reached her.

She felt the fish's firm, scaly body under her hand and jerked her arm up and out of the water, catapulting the fish onto the bank. It was exactly as Moon Cow Woman had taught her.

The fish lay alongside the stream, flopping about frantically, trying to propel itself back into the water. Elizabeth quickly climbed out of the water then fell on the fish, trapping it under her body. She lay there, holding it down until it quit fighting. After the trout died, she gutted and cleaned it with Bloody Axe's knife. Spitting it on a green willow limb, she started a fire with the flint and steel she had taken from her captor. Moments later the aroma of broiling fish assailed her senses.

As the sun rose over the mountain range, Yellow Hand and his men stood just below the crest of a ridge, looking down on the ranch below. They had happened across the ranch on their way to locate the wagons of the men who had taken the buffalo. Yellow Hand made the decision to attack the ranch first.

They saw three men come out of the house and begin their morning chores, and they smelled the smoke of their breakfast fire, hearing the woman inside the house call to the children. One of the men outside walked toward the outhouse, and it was while he was in there that the two braves Yellow Hand had sent as decoys made their false attack. They fired their rifles and let out bloodcurdling screams as they rode at the house. Yellow Hand smiled, for his warriors made as much noise as three war parties.

"My God! Where the hell did they come from?" one of the other men shouted, and started running for the house. "Edith! Injuns! Injun attack!"

The man's call was shut off by the sharp whistle and thud of an arrow. It was a shot of nearly one hundred yards, and when the bowman saw he had hit his mark, he let out a victory whoop.

The man who had been in the outhouse stumbled out with his pants down around his ankles. He hopped around, trying to pull them up, but he was hit with perhaps a half-dozen arrows. The third man tried to run away, but at a signal from Yellow Hand, two warriors chased him down, then dispatched him with brutal blows from their war club.

With the three men dead, the warriors began moving toward the ranch with less fear now, for only the woman and children remained.

Suddenly a series of shots rang out, and Yellow Hand and his men all dove for cover. They looked toward the house to try and determine from which window the shots had come. They couldn't tell, so one of the warriors stood up in a show of courage and ran from one window to another. He shouted to attract the woman's attention, hoping to draw her fire.

But no more shots were fired.

Another warrior tried the same tactic, but he, too, was unsuccessful. The one inside the house with the rifle simply did not fire.

Finally, moving one at a time, the entire war party advanced to the house; then Yellow Hand kicked in the door and leaped into the house. What he saw there made him stop short, for there, sitting up against the wall were two little girls and a grown woman, all dead. It didn't take that long for Yellow Hand to realize what had happened. The woman had shot the two children, and then had taken her own life. She was sitting there with her eyes still open, but with her head twisted grotesquely on her neck. There was a blackened hole in her temple, and a stream of blood and brain tissue ran down the side of her head, soaking the shoulder of her dress.

"We should not let the breakfast go to waste, should we?" one of the braves asked, reaching for a pan of fresh biscuits. The pan, sitting on top of the stove, was still hot, so the Indian burned his fingers when he reached for a biscuit. He let out a yelp of pain and stuck his fingers in his mouth. The others laughed, then they, too, began poking through the kitchen to find something to eat.

Yellow Hand walked out onto the porch of the ranch house and stood there with his hand on one of the roof support posts. Behind him he could hear his men laughing and talking and reliving the "battle." It was the sign of a good leader to win a victory with very little fighting, for that showed that he was a good tactician, and able to outsmart his enemy. He knew, though, that attacking a ranch house was not like attacking a wagon train, guarded by armed men. Still, it gave them a taste of the warpath and that was his purpose, along with the chance to pick up a few more guns, as most of his men were armed only with bows.

"Yellow Hand," one of the warriors called out, rushing out onto the porch. "Look—three rifles and three pistols. We have done well!"

"Burn the white man's lodges," Yellow Hand said. "Now we will travel to attack the wagons."

Parker, Clay, and the others rested for two days while they cut up and dried strips of buffalo meat, letting their mules rest from the ordeal of the desert. During that same time, they also made repairs to the wagons. Using the extra buckets of grease Charles Garland had given them, Parker repacked every wheel of every wagon.

"Clay, we have got to get along today," Marcus said. "Look at the sky. There's snow in those clouds."

Clay thought about it for a moment, then nodded. "You're right," he said. "It's time we got going again."

"Wait a minute, you promised us five days of rest," Pecorino complained. "Besides, we couldn't go on now, even if we wanted to. Look at the mules. Do you really think they can pull a load? We'd be lucky if they can walk by themselves, let alone haul a wagon."

"We've got to try," Clay insisted.

By now, the others had gathered around to listen to the conversation.

"I think Frank is right," Tobin said. "We've been here a few days now and the mules don't seem one bit stronger."

"Then maybe we should go on before they get any weaker," Jason suggested.

"Hold it, boys," Marcus said quietly. "It

doesn't look like we're going anywhere for a while. At least, not now."

"What do you mean?" Clay asked. "You're the one who said we should go."

Marcus carved off a piece of chewing tobacco and stuck it in his mouth before he answered. "Looks like we got company." He pointed to a distant ridge line. At first, there were only a few shapes outlined against the sky, then more joined them, then more still, until finally they appeared to fill the whole top of the ridge.

"Indians!" Pecorino said. "Son of a bitch, look at 'em! Where'd they all come from?"

"You think they're the same ones who attacked the Reynolds party?" Tobin asked.

"I hope they are." Parker seethed. "I'd like a little revenge."

"Revenge?" Tobin said. "There are six of us. There must be forty or fifty of them. Who's going to get revenge on who?"

"They ain't the same ones anyway," Marcus said. "Them that attacked Reynolds was Cheyenne. We've done passed through their territory. More'n likely these fellas are Shoshoni."

"Any chance they're friendly?" Clay asked.

"I doubt it. Look at that big fella, the one with a yellow handprint on his face," Marcus said. "Friendly Indians don't paint themselves up like that. No, sir, they've come for a fight."

At that moment, the Indian with the handprint raised his rifle and fired at them. They could see the white puff of smoke, followed an instant later by the whine of the bullet as it whizzed by.

Clay began unhitching one of the mule teams.

"Boss, you crazy? You better get back behind the wagon," Tobin said.

"If they kill our mules, we'll be stuck right here," Clay said as he continued to loose the team.

"I'll help," Parker said, and started disconnecting the second team. Marcus began unhitching the third team.

Clay led the mules, keeping them together as a team, and bringing them around behind the wagons. Parker was just behind him.

But Marcus didn't make it. Parker was looking right at him when he went down. Clay heard the sound of the bullet hitting flesh, and when he turned around, he saw Marcus holding his hand in front of him, looking surprised at the blood that filled his palm from the hole on his chest.

"Marcus!" Clay shouted, running back to him.

"Oh shit," Marcus said. He wavered, then fell down on one knee. "It don't look like I'm going to be able to take me that swim in the Salt Lake."

The Indian with the yellow hand on his face was evidently the one who had shot him, for he held his rifle over his head and let out a loud victory yell.

"Get back behind the wagons, you damn fool," Marcus said in a pain-wracked voice. "I'm already kilt . . . ain't nothin' you can do for me."

Disregarding Marcus's warning, Clay started to pick him up. At that moment Yellow Hand fired again, and Clay went down as well.

"Jason! Clay and Marcus are both down! Help me bring them in!" Parker shouted, running toward the two men.

"Start shooting!" Jason yelled at Tobin and Pecorino, both of whom were taking cover behind the wagons. Not until they were galvanized into action by Jason's shouts did the two men begin firing at the Indians. With their rifles providing some cover, Jason hurried out to help Parker.

"Clay," Parker called, kneeling down beside him. "Clay, talk to me."

Clay opened his eyes. "What are you doing out here, boy?" he scolded. "Get back behind the wagons."

"Not until I get you in," Parker said.

One of the Indians, thinking it to be an easy target, pulled away from the others and started riding hard toward Parker and Clay, holding his lance out in front of him.

Jason watched for a second, as if unable to believe the Indian would subject himself to such exposure. Then, when he realized that it wasn't a trick, that the Indian actually intended to come all the way to them with nothing but a lance for a weapon, Jason shot him.

"How bad am I hit?" Clay asked, his voice strained.

"I don't know," Parker answered. "But I don't

think the bullet hit any of your vitals. It looks like it's too high in the shoulder for that."

"What about Marcus?" Clay asked.

"I just checked Marcus," Jason said. "I'm sorry, Clay. He's dead."

"Damn," Clay said. He sighed. "Listen, you boys get back, or you're going to join him."

"We aren't leaving you," Parker said. "Come on, Jason, help me get him behind the wagons."

Just as they reached down for Clay, another Indian broke away from the group and started toward them. This time it was Parker who saw him, and he whirled and fired. The Indian went down.

"You're getting pretty good with that iron," Clay said.

The boys helped Clay up, but his wound was such that he could only use one arm, and they couldn't support him from both sides. Parker held him up as best he could while Jason helped them back toward the wagons, providing covering fire. Another Indian came toward them, close enough to send an arrow whistling between them, and Jason brought him down. Finally, they reached the relative safety of the wagons, and Clay sat down behind one of the wheels.

"Here they come!" Tobin shouted. "This time the whole bunch of 'em is comin' at once!"

The Indians came hard, galloping through the dust, shouting and whooping their war cries. They charged almost all the way up to the wagons, firing from horseback. Those without firearms loosed arrows or hurled lances toward the little huddled group of defenders.

Parker, Jason, Tobin, and Pecorino took very careful aim, making every shot count. Four Indians went down, and their empty horses whirled and retreated, leaving their riders dead or dying on the ground behind them.

Over the next two hours, the Indians attacked several more times, getting a little closer each time before being driven away by their deadly gunfire.

"As many of them as there are, why don't they come all the way in?" Pecorino asked, nervously. "Seems to me like they're just playing with us."

"There are a lot more of them than us, that's true," Clay said. "But not that many of them have guns. We're pretty even with them on that score, and my bet is we've got more ammunition than they do."

"Maybe if we can hold 'em off till dark, they'll go away. I heard Indians don't like to fight at night," Tobin said. "Somethin' about the Great Spirit not bein' able to find 'em in the dark."

"Well, Indians don't like to fight at night, that's true. But they won't leave, either. And we could wake up in the morning to find 'em right on top of us," Clay said. "No, if we are going to get rid of them, we're going to have to do it now, before the sun goes down."

"How we going to do that?" Pecorino asked. "Run 'em down and club 'em?"

"Tell me that . . . and we'll both know," Clay

answered, his voice weak and halting. "You boys may have to hold on without me for a while," he said in an even weaker voice. His head fell forward and his eyes closed.

"Clay?" Parker asked anxiously. "Clay, are you all right?"

Tobin checked him. "He's still alive," he said. "He's just passed out, that's all."

"Damn, what'll we do now?" Pecorino asked.

"We do the same thing we've been doing," Parker said. "We fight them off."

"What do you mean?"

"I mean we can light a shuck out of here," Tobin said.

"You mean run?"

"Yep," Tobin answered. "Think about it. They don't want us. They want what's in these here wagons."

"How we goin' to run?" Pecorino asked. "There's not horses enough for all of us, and we sure can't go on foot."

"Frank is right," Parker said.

"Maybe not," Tobin said. "We got three horses amongst the four of us. Frank can ride Clay's horse. You two boys are light, you can double up. Hell, the Indians will be so interested in what's in the wagons, they won't pay us no never mind."

"What do you mean he can ride Clay's horse?" Parker asked. "Don't you think Clay ought to have something to say about that?"

"He ain't got nothin' to say about it," Tobin

said. "Like it as not, he won't live through the night anyway. We'll leave him here."

"Leave him to the Indians?"

"It's a hard life out here, boy," Tobin said. "Sometimes choices has to be made."

"When you were wounded, we could've left you with Shardeen," Parker said. "We didn't leave you behind then, and we aren't leaving Clay behind now."

"The hell you say," Tobin growled. He looked over at Jason. "What do you say, Jason? If Parker stays, we'll have a horse apiece."

"I'm staying," Jason said.

"Suit yourself," Tobin said. He started to turn away.

"Tobin," Parker called menacingly to him, "I said you aren't leaving, and I meant it. Neither of you are."

"Who's going to stop us?" Tobin asked.

"I am."

Tobin laughed. "I know you been practicing with that gun, learnin' how to draw and all. I hope you don't think you're good enough to stop both of us all by yourself."

"He won't be by himself," Jason said, stepping over to stand beside Parker.

"What the hell?" Pecorino shouted. "Are all of you crazy? The Indians can't kill us fast enough that now we've got to start killing each other?"

For a long moment, Tobin glared at Parker and Jason, then he let out a long, surrendering sigh.

"Ah, what the hell," he said. "Even if we got

away, we'd probably starve to death trying to make it back through the canyon. All right, kid, you win. I'll stay here and let the Indians slaughter us all."

"I'm glad you feel that way," Clay said, speaking for the first time in several minutes.

"Clay, you're all right!" Parker said excitedly. He dropped down beside him for a closer look.

"Depends on what you mean by all right," Clay replied. He turned and looked toward the Indians, who were now gathered in a little cluster about five hundred yards away. "Anyone figured out who their leader is yet?"

"I reckon he's the one with the yellow hand on his face," Jason said. "He's the one that done shot Marcus and you. And he's the one been doing most of the yellin' and pointin'."

"Good," Clay said. Grunting against the pain, he stood up, then leaned against the wagon wheel and looked out toward the Indians. "Parker, hand me the spyglass," he said, holding his hand out.

Parker pulled the telescope out of Clay's saddlebags then handed it to Clay, who opened it and held it up to his eye, studying the Indians. After a moment, he snapped it shut.

"I think you're right," he said. "The fella with the yellow hand is the one we want."

"The one we want for what?" Jason asked.

"The one we want to kill," Clay said easily. "Parker, you think you can snake one of those fifty-caliber Sharpes out of the back of Marcus's wagon?" he asked.

"The Buffalo rifles? Sure, I can get one."

"Do it," Clay said. "Then get me a couple rounds of ammunition and a candle."

"A candle?" Parker asked, not sure he heard right.

"Yeah, a candle."

"What are you going to do?" Pecorino asked.

"I told you, I'm going to kill an Indian," Clay said in a strained, matter-of-fact voice.

"What do you mean you're going to kill an Indian? Hell, that's all we been doin' since this started," Tobin said.

"Yes, but we haven't killed the right one," Clay said. "Sometimes, when the leader gets killed, the rest of the Indians give up the fight."

A few moments later Parker gave Clay the buffalo rifle, ammunition, and a candle he had taken from the wagon. Clay, fighting the pain, which still had a grip on him, sat down again and took two of the fifty-caliber shells out of the ammunition bag. He separated the bullets from the cartridges, then started pouring powder from one of the cartridges into the other.

"What the hell are you doin' now?" Pecorino asked.

"Damn!" Jason said, his eyes shining brightly. "I know what he's doing! He's doubling the powder load."

"You gone crazy?" Tobin asked. "You do that, you're goin' to bust a barrel."

"It's a chance I have to take," Clay said as he continued to work on the bullet.

"So, what are you going to do?" Tobin asked. "Try and get him next time they come down?"

"No. I'm going to get him now."

"Now? He's better'n five hundred yards away," Tobin said with a scoff. "Ain't no way you can get him from here."

"Light that candle, then hand it to me, will you, Parker?" Clay asked.

Parker lit the candle. Clay tapped the bullet back into the cartridge, then used the dripping candle wax to help seal it.

"You really think you can hit him all the way from here?" Pecorino asked.

"I don't know if I can or not," Clay admitted. "But I'm damn sure going to try."

Pulling himself up again, Clay rested the barrel on the side of the wagon. He aimed, then lowered the rifle. "Damn," he said.

"What is it?" Parker asked.

"I just happened to think. This thing kicks like a mule as it is. With a double load it's going to really kick hard. And with this shoulder, it's going to hurt like hell."

"You want me to try the shot?" Jason asked.

"You as good with a rifle as you are with that pistol?" Clay asked.

"I don't know," Jason admitted. "I've never really shot a rifle."

Clay shook his head. "Anyone else think they can make the shot?"

There were no takers to his offer.

Clay sighed. "That's what I was afraid of. All right, all I have to do now is put it out of my mind. Otherwise, I'll flinch for sure and I'll miss by a mile."

Clay adjusted his sights, raised it to his shoulder, aimed again, then lowered it for another adjustment.

No one said a word.

Clay aimed a third time. Then the rifle roared, bucking hard against his shoulder.

"Ow shit!" Clay shouted, grabbing his shoulder.

Parker had been looking through the telescope at the Indian with the yellow hand on his face. He saw the brave suddenly jerk, then look down at the hole that appeared in his chest.

"You got him!" Parker shouted excitedly.

An Indian named Crow Dog was seated on his horse next to Yellow Hand, looking toward the wagons. He heard an angry buzz, then the smack of a bullet hitting flesh, then he heard Yellow Hand grunt. Looking toward him, he saw dark crimson blood pouring from a very large hole in his chest. Yellow Hand tumbled backward from his horse.

"Yellow Hand!" Crow Dog called.

"What happened?" one of the other Indians called.

"Yellow Hand is shot!"Crow Dog announced.

The Indians were disoriented. Surely, no ordinary rifle could kill from this far away.

"What manner of weapon is this that can kill from so far away?" Young Calf asked Crow Dog.

"The medicine of these white men is strong,"

another said. "Surely, if we stay here longer, we will all be killed."

"Crow Dog, what shall we do now?" Young Calf asked.

Crow Dog had not declared himself in charge, nor, while Yellow Hand was leading them, had Crow Dog been considered as second in charge. In fact, the Shoshoni had no concept of second in charge, but because he was asked by the others, the position of leadership was suddenly thrust upon him. All turned toward him to hear what he would say.

"We will leave this place of death," he said. "Come, let us return to Black Crow and our people."

Pecorino and Tobin patted down the mound of dirt that covered Marcus's grave. Clay read the same passages over the grave that he had read over those of Parker's parents.

"You knew Marcus a long time, didn't you?" Parker asked as they made camp that night.

"Since the war."

Parker held out Marcus's hat. "If you don't mind, I'm going to keep this."

"No, of course I don't mind. Don't know what you want with it, though."

"It's just a memento."

"I think Marcus would have liked for you to have it."

The pain of his wound kept Clay from sleeping that night so, as the others snored, he stared up at the stars and remembered the day he first met Marcus Pearson.

Shiloh, April, 6, 1862

Lieutenant Clay Springer was having breakfast when the earth shook with the sound of distant thunder.

"Damn, that's all we need now. Another thunderstorm," one of General Sherman's staff officers said.

Immediately thereafter came the sound of whistling cannonballs. Tree limbs crashed to the ground as the heavy balls ripped through the timber. The balls were interspersed with shells that burst loudly, throwing out singing shards of shrapnel.

One of the pickets came running into camp, shouting at the top of his lungs. "The Rebels are coming! The Rebels are coming!"

A cannonball crashed heavily through the nearby trees and Clay tossed away his coffee, then hurried over to the headquarters of the Seventh Kansas Volunteers to spread the alarm. When he arrived, he found everyone bunched together in a ravine. Colonel Sweeney, the commanding officer of the Seventh Kansas, was lying facedown behind a tree.

"Colonel Sweeney, we are being attacked!" Clay shouted. "What are you doing? You have to form your men for the defense!"

Another barrage of incoming artillery smashed through the trees and exploded in rosy plumes of fire, smoke, and whistling death.

"This is no place for us!" Colonel Sweeney said. "This is no way to fight . . . not against cannons!

Why don't the Rebels come out and fight us like men?"

"Colonel, you must form your men, sir! You must deploy in a skirmish line! Otherwise the rebels will roll right over you!"

Sweeney raised his head and looked around, his eyes glowing with a wild look. "Yes!" he said. "You're right, we do need to deploy, but not here! Fall back, men!" he shouted, standing up and running toward the rear. "Fall back!"

"Sweeney, you cowardly son of a bitch! Come back here!" Clay called after him.

When Sweeney broke and ran, the other officers on his staff, then the rest of the Seventh Kansas, started running as well, many of them throwing down their rifles so they could run faster.

The one exception to the mass retreat was a small, wiry private, who at that moment happened to be driving a wagon toward the front, coming up from the rear. He saw everyone running, but he didn't stop his wagon until he reached Clay, who was still standing there in frustration. Calmly, the wagon driver took out a plug of tobacco. He carved off a piece for himself, then extended the plug to Clay.

"Chaw?" he asked.

"No, thanks," Clay replied.

"The name's Pearson. The army told me my first name is supposed to be Private, but I'd just as soon be called Marcus, if'n you don't mind."

A cannonball exploded not fifty yards away, and shrapnel whistled through the tree leaves. The team Marcus was driving reared up in terror. Marcus showed no reaction at all, but talked soothingly to his team, managing to calm them down.

"You handle a team pretty well," Clay said.

"Learned it from my pa," Marcus said. He looked around. "Have you noticed that we seem to be alone here?"

"Yes, I've noticed."

"Bein' as you're the officer, I was sort of hopin' you'd taken notice of that. What do you plan to do?"

"Do you have any ideas?" Clay asked.

Marcus nodded toward the abandoned weapons. "I figured I might pick up a few of those," he said. "No sense in leavin' 'em for the Rebs. Then, if you don't have any objections, I thought we'd go find some of our own folks to join up with. I'd rather go this way or that to look for them, though," he said, nodding to the left and right flank in the line. "I'd just as soon not go back there." He nodded toward the rear. "I don't want to be confused with that bunch of yellow bellies that skedaddled out of here."

"Believe me, Marcus, no one will ever confuse you with a bunch of yellow bellies."

Marcus smiled. "I appreciate that, Lieutenant."

"It's Clay," Clay said, disregarding the wall of rank that was between them.

On that bloody battlefield was their friendship born.

As Clay lay there in the dark, he felt a lump in his throat, and tears in his eyes as he remembered his old friend. He was glad the others were asleep, and that there was no one to see him grieve.

Chapter 15

It was now six days since Elizabeth had killed Bloody Axe and made good her escape. But the question was, escape to where? During the time she had been with Bloody Axe he had wandered around so much, climbing, descending, twisting back on himself, that Elizabeth lost all sense of direction.

For a while she could tell east from west by the rising and setting of the sun, but for the last two days the sun had been obscured by low-hanging clouds. And even if she could see the sun, even if she could ascertain the cardinal points of the compass, what good would it do her? She didn't know if Two Ponies' village was north, south, east, or west of her present position.

That brought up another question. If she did know where Two Ponies' village was, would she want to go there? Or, would she rather try and find a white settlement?

Elizabeth was also desperately hungry. Since her escape from Bloody Axe, she had only caught two fish. Yesterday, she found some wild onions. But, realistically, if she didn't find some sort of civilization soon, she feared she would starve to death. Or, she thought as she shivered with the cold, she would freeze to death. She had no idea what the date was, but she was well aware of the fact that each day was colder than the last.

As darkness fell, she burrowed into a pile of dead leaves, pulling them around her for what little heat they could provide. Lying there, waiting for sleep to come, she mouthed a prayer. "Oh Lord. Deliver me from my travail soon, or take me now."

When Elizabeth awoke the next morning, she heard voices. Although there were a few words she could understand, most of the conversation was unintelligible to her. She thought it significant, however, that none of the voices seemed excited or angry. Only curious.

When she sat up, she saw that she was surrounded by Indians; men, women, and children. All of them, young and old, male and female, looked at her with uninhibited curiosity. At one time in her life Elizabeth would have been terrified, but her experience with the Cheyenne had changed all that. Intuitively, she knew these people were no danger to her. On the contrary, they now represented her only hope of survival.

"Have you anything to eat?" Elizabeth asked, speaking in English.

One of the men said something, and a woman unfolded a bundle, then removed a piece of dried meat which she gave to Elizabeth. Elizabeth thanked the woman for the meat, then began eating ravenously, aware of their intense stares, but so absorbed by her hunger that she paid no attention.

"Who are you?" the same man who had translated her request for food asked her. Elizabeth didn't know if he was their leader, or if he was their spokesman, merely because he could speak English.

"I am Elizabeth Stanley of Illinois," Elizabeth answered. "How are you called?"

"I am Standing Bear, of the Ute."

"I thank you, Standing Bear of the Ute, for the food." Elizabeth spoke the words in English, but she made the universal hand signs that she knew were understood by all the tribes. Turning to the woman who had provided the meat, she made the sign of gratitude a second time. The woman smiled.

A young girl approximately seven or eight years old moved unabashedly toward Elizabeth and reached out to take a strand of her blond hair in her fingers. Holding the hair in her hand, she looked at it in wonder.

The woman who had given Elizabeth the meat spoke harshly to the girl and pulled the girl away.

"It's all right," Elizabeth said. Then, smiling at the little girl, she used Bloody Axe's knife to cut off a lock of her own hair, which she extended toward the little girl. The little girl looked at the woman for consent. The woman nodded, and the little girl took the hair and began examining it closely.

"You are riding an Indian horse," Standing Bear noted.

"Yes."

"How did you come by such a horse?"

"It was the horse of Bloody Axe, the Cheyenne who captured me," Elizabeth said.

Standing Bear laughed, then spoke to the others, who joined in the laughter.

"Why do you laugh?" Elizabeth asked.

"It is a good trick for you to steal the horse of the Cheyenne who stole you. Now he has no horse to ride to find you."

"He has no need of a horse," Elizabeth said, now speaking in Cheyenne. Her words were understood by nearly all of them, and many of them gasped in surprise.

"You speak the language of the Cheyenne," Standing Bear said, expressing the astonishment of them all.

"Yes."

"Why is this?"

"Because I am Sun's Light, wife of the Cheyenne chief, Two Ponies."

"You are from the village of Two Ponies?"

"Yes."

There was some discussion among the Indians, then Standing Bear spoke again. "We know many in Two Ponies' village, but we do not know Bloody Axe."

"Ah," Elizabeth said. "That is because he has

only recently taken that name. Before he was Bloody Axe, he was known as Elk Heart."

There were several grunts and comments before Standing Bear spoke again. "Yes, we know Elk Heart. He is the grandson of Two Ponies. Why would he steal you from his own grandfather?"

"He wanted me to be his woman," Elizabeth said. "I would not be, so he stole me."

Again, there was a quick consultation among the Indians. Then Standing Bear asked, "Why is it that Elk Heart has no further need for his horse?"

Elizabeth took a deep breath before she answered. She wasn't sure how they would take it, but she decided to be truthful. "He will have no need of it because he is dead," she said. "I killed him," she added.

Standing Bear nodded. "It is good that you killed him."

"Standing Bear, can you take me to the village of Two Ponies?"

"The land of the Cheyenne is on the sun-coming-up side of the mountains," Standing Bear said. "Now is the season of snow. It is not a good time to cross the mountains."

Have I come across the mountains? Elizabeth wondered. She thought of the weeks she had spent as Bloody Axe's prisoner. She was aware of her hunger, the exhaustion, and the increasing cold. And, yes, she could also remember the narrow, twisting trail that climbed higher and higher until her breathing came as labored gasps, and she felt as if she could reach out and touch the clouds. She had come over the mountains, though she didn't realize it until this very moment.

With the Springer–Stanley Party

Three weeks after the Indian fight, with his shoulder wound still sore but healing without putrefying, Clay and his reduced party reached the eastern slope of the Wasatch Mountains, at Devil's Pass. Leaving the three wagons at the bottom of the trail, he and Parker rode halfway up to have a closer look at the high pass they were expected to negotiate.

It was cold, and as the men and horses breathed, vapor clouds formed around them. The top of the pass was shrouded by a low-lying bank of clouds and here and there Parker could see patches of snow, lying brilliantly white in the sunshine and dark azure in the shadows. The horses were breathing heavily in the thin air, and a couple of times Clay and Parker were forced to dismount and walk so as not to overtax their animals.

The exertion made Parker breathe hard as well, and the cold air hurt his lungs. The thought of pulling heavily loaded wagons up a grade this steep seemed overwhelming, and Parker cringed at the difficulty of the task that lay before them.

Clay must have read his mind. "It's not going to be a walk in the park, is it?" Clay asked.

"No, it sure isn't," Parker agreed. Nervously he patted his horse on the neck.

"The horses will be all right," Clay said. "Especially if we get down and walk them through." He pointed to the cloud-covered spine at the mountain's top. "But that hogback up there is goin' to cause the wagon teams a lot of trouble."

"Maybe we can group all the mules together and pull the wagons over one at a time," Parker suggested.

"That's a good idea," Clay agreed. "In fact, that's exactly what I plan to do."

"How much farther is Utah, do you think?" Parker asked.

"You mean after we clear this pass?"

"Yes."

"I'd say it's a little over one hundred miles," Clay said.

"That seems so far."

Clay laughed. "Yes, it is, but compared to what we've traveled, it's just across the street," he said. "The thing we have to worry about now is gettin' our wagons through this pass."

"It looks like we got here before the heavy snow," Parker said.

"Yes, we seem to have caught one good break, at least."

They rode back down to the others to explain to them how they would negotiate the pass. Tobin, who had started the journey as one of the outriders, was now driving what had been Marcus's wagon. He and Jason were standing in front of Pecorino's wagon. Pecorino was on the ground underneath, examining it closely.

"What is it?" Clay asked. "What's wrong?"

"I think I cracked an axle back there," Pecorino said.

"You think? What do you mean? Don't you know?"

"I heard a loud crack," Pecorino said. "I've been looking at it pretty close, but I haven't found anything yet."

"Maybe the wood just flexed and popped back," Clay suggested. "Cured wood will do that sometime."

"Maybe," Pecorino agreed, sliding out from under the wagon. He stood up and wiped his hands together.

"What's it look like up there?" Tobin asked, nodding toward the top of the pass.

"Oh, it's not so bad," Clay lied. Parker knew that Clay said that so as not to discourage the others. "But Parker and I were talking about it, and we think it might be better if we grouped the teams and pulled the wagons over one at a time."

"Well, if we're going to do it, let's do it," Tobin said. "The sooner we get on the other side of the pass, the better I'll like it."

"I agree," Clay replied. "Come on, boys, get your teams hitched up to Tobin's wagon, and let's go on."

All worked together as they began chaining up the three teams of mules to Tobin's wagon. The mules balked at being connected to their burden, but the teamsters persisted until the job was done. Then, when all the mules were connected and the wagon was ready, Clay gave a whistle and they started up the road toward the top of the pass.

"Look at that," Jason said. "We're going right up into the clouds."

Pecorino chuckled. "Well, they say every cloud has a silver lining. You boys see any silver up there?"

Jason studied the clouds carefully. They were gray and dingy.

"Can't say as I do," Jason answered.

"It's just as well," Pecorino said. "I don't think our wagons could stand to carry anything else."

Clay made the decision that rather than get the wagons too far separated, he would haul one of them partway up the pass, leave it, then return for the others. In this leapfrogging way, he had all three wagons halfway up the pass by early afternoon. It was, however, very difficult going and the mules were blowing hard now.

One by one, the wagons passed under the boughs of tall, dark pine trees. As they went higher in elevation, though, the trees stopped, replaced by a scattering of gray rock and patches of snow.

What little sun there had been earlier this morning was gone now, and it became a dark, dreary day, so heavily overcast that the position of the sun couldn't be made out, even by the faintest glow. Individual clouds couldn't be seen either—a thick blanket shrouded the towering mountains so effectively that the peaks disappeared into the slate gray sky itself.

As the trail curved upward, the patches of snow grew more numerous, and deeper. Before too long the patches increased in number and crowded closer together until finally the ground was completely covered.

At first the snow was shallow enough that larger rocks and gray boulders would poke up through it. But the higher they went, the deeper the snow became. It eventually got so deep that the bottoms of the wagons began scraping down into the frosty crust. This had the effect of creating a plow so that snow piled up in front of the wagons, making the passage even more difficult. The mules, already weak, started losing their footing in the loose snow, and the wagon was in danger of slipping back.

"Boss! Boss, hold it!" Tobin shouted.

"What is it?" Clay called back. He had been riding in front of the team, pulling and urging them on.

"These mules aren't in any shape to pull these wagons over this pass, loaded like they are," Tobin said. "Maybe we should disconnect the teams and load what we can onto the backs of the mules and try it that way."

Clay shook his head. "No, if we do that, we may as well go back," he said. "We couldn't get half our load through that way. It would break Parker and me."

"You're going to have to make up your mind

pretty soon," Tobin said. "You can see for yourself we ain't gettin' anywhere with the wagons."

"I think Tobin has a point," Pecorino said.

"Yeah, well, whether he has a point or not, I've got no choice but to try it," Clay replied. "I've got to get over the pass . . . with everything."

"What about packing the stuff over on mules, make as many trips as it takes, then pull the empty wagons across?" Pecorino suggested. "We can load 'em up again on the other side."

Clay was quiet for a moment, then he nodded. "All right," he finally agreed. "We'll try it that way. Come on, boys, let's get these critters cut loose from the wagons. Then we'll see what we can do about packin' 'em."

For the next few hours the party worked hard to unload the wagons and to construct packs which would allow them to put their belongings on the backs of the mules. As they were team mules, not pack mules, they were unused to carrying a load. They fought hard to resist carrying the packs but the men persisted until the mules were forced to accept their fate. Finally the animals settled down and were formed into an orderly line. The line was necessary because by now the road was so narrow that it could only be traveled in single file. Slowly, they plodded up the trail.

The footing was treacherous and both man and mule slipped and fell many times. It was extremely rough going, even though Clay and Parker made it somewhat easier by going out front, using their horses to break a path through the snow. In most cases the snow was nearly up to the horses' bellies, but they didn't balk and they managed to do a pretty good job of clearing the way for those who followed.

The wind was blowing hard and carrying before it crystals of ice which cut into the skin like a million tiny knives. It was cold and painful, and it caused everyone to bend his head, or to look away, unable to face it head-on.

"I thought the desert was hard," Jason said. "I was so hot, I thought I would never be cold again. But this is beatin' it all!"

"Come on, keep going everybody," Clay shouted. "We're nearly to the top! When we get there, it's all downhill."

Despite the path that Clay and Parker had cleared, the men were having a hard time keeping their animals going. Sometimes they would lose their load, and when that happened everyone would have to stop until the load was recovered and repacked. The day grew darker, and though they couldn't see the sun, they knew that it was about to set.

Suddenly there was a loud hurrah from the front of the column.

"We're here, boys, we're here!" Clay shouted down at them from the peak. "We've made it to the top! Come on, it's just a little way now!"

The trail was at its steepest and most difficult near the very top, and it became much, much harder to move forward. It seemed as if they were slipping back at least two steps for every three they went forward. They could see Clay and Parker waiting for them at the top of the pass, yet they didn't seem to be making any real progress toward the summit. Finally, in exhaustion and frustration, Pecorino stopped and sat down.

Clay came back down the trail. "Come on, Frank, what are you doing?"

"Look, you don't want half your load on that side, and half over here on this side, do you?" Pecorino asked.

"No, of course not."

"Well, face it, boss, we ain't gettin' any closer and it's gettin' too dark to see. And I, for one, ain't got no intention of fallin' over the side of a mountain in the middle of the night."

"Frank has a point, boss," Tobin said. "Why don't we just wait here for a while?"

"It's getting darker by the minute. We wait here any longer it'll be too dark to try," Clay said.

"That's what I'm talkin' about," Pecorino said. "You ask me, we should spend the night right here."

"No, no," Clay warned. "We've got to keep going until we get over the pass! We can't stop here!"

"Think about it, boss, we sure ain't gettin' nowhere this way," Tobin said. "Maybe a fresh start in the mornin' when the mules are more rested will do ya'll some good. That way we can go over the pass in the daylight."

"But it's just a few yards farther! Don't you

see? We've got to get over it and down the other side before the snow starts falling. If we get a good storm, we'll never get out of here!"

"Come on, let's give it one more try," Jason suggested.

Reluctantly, the men made another attempt, but despite Clay's exhortations, they were no more successful this time than they had been before. Then, as darkness closed around them, Parker went over to speak to his partner.

"Clay, I hate to admit it, but Pecorino is right. Even if we do get the mules over now, the wagons are still back there, half full of goods."

"All right, we'll camp here for the night," Clay said in disappointment. "I can't help but think we are going to be sorry, though. We are almost there!"

They camped where they stopped that night, no more than two hundred yards down from the top of the pass.

"Where do you think we should bed down?" Parker asked.

"I don't know. Probably up at the head," Clay answered. "If we wind up having to break through the snow again tomorrow morning, the further up trail we are, the easier it will be."

"All right," Parker said. Later, when they threw their tarpaulin and blankets out on top of the snow and were sitting there, Parker saw the look of frustration in Clay's eyes. "Clay, I'm sorry if you think I betrayed you."

Clay looked over in surprise. "Betrayed me? What do you mean?"

"I know you wanted to go on."

Clay was holding a stick and he began scratching in the snow with it. "Listen, I said we are equal partners in this operation and I meant it," he said. "That means you have every right to express your opinion. And the truth is, I think you are right. There's really no way we could have gotten more than half the load across tonight, no matter how hard we tried. And I sure wouldn't want something to happen that would leave half our goods on one side and half on the other."

A flash of golden light suddenly illuminated the area. Along with the light came a wave of heat. Parker looked toward the source of heat and illumination and saw that Tobin and Jason had set fire to some mossy scrub brush that was standing away from the camp.

"Hmm, good idea," Clay said. He and Parker moved their tarp and blankets closer to it, joining with the others who were finding positions around the fire.

They sat there for a long moment, as if mesmerized by the flames.

"Moses and the burning bush," Pecorino said.

The others laughed.

"Moses . . . if you are here, part this snow the way you did the Red Sea," Tobin said.

"Clay, you think we'll get over the pass tomorrow?" Parker asked.

"Yeah, I think so," Clay said. He paused for a long moment before he spoke again. "At least, I hope so," he added, a little less sure of himself.

They all fell silent then, but the night wasn't quiet. The burning shrub popped and hissed and snapped as it was consumed. And, because they were exhausted by their labors, they fell asleep easily, warmed by the fire.

They were oblivious to the cold, oblivious to the precariousness of their position . . . oblivious to the large flakes of snow which, just after midnight, began tumbling down through the blackness.

The snow fell silently, moving in unnoticed by the sleeping crew.

When Parker woke up the next morning, he was immediately aware of the change. Last night he had gone to sleep on top of the snow. This morning, he awoke under it. A pristine blanket of snow covered everything in sight. No longer was the trail ahead that he and Clay had broken visible. No longer was the trail behind them, made by the pack mules, visible. There were no footprints, no signs of encampment. Even the shrub they had burned last night was completely covered in a mantle of white. It was as if man had never been here before. When he looked up toward the pass, Parker saw that it was packed solid and piled high with snow. There was no way anyone could get through. The thing they had feared most had happened.

Chapter 16

In the winter camp of Standing Bear

When Elizabeth first joined Standing Bear's group, she was concerned as to how they might treat her. Would they treat her as a captive, and thus make a slave of her? Or would they force her into another "marriage" similar to the one she had been forced into with Two Ponies of the Cheyenne.

As it turned out, Standing Bear and his band recognized Elizabeth's marriage to Two Ponies, and thus did not require that she marry again. In this case, the fact that she was a woman worked to her advantage, for, whereas the men could have more than one wife, women could not have more than one husband.

Elizabeth had not told them that she was a wife to Two Ponies in name only. Because Elizabeth was married to a chief, Standing Bear offered her membership in his family. Standing Bear's wife—and he had only one—helped Elizabeth erect a teepee right next to theirs. Quiet Stream was much closer to Elizabeth's age than had been Moon Cow Woman.

Quiet Stream became a good friend to Elizabeth, but Standing Bear's young daughter, White Feather, practically became Elizabeth's shadow. Using the lock of blond hair Elizabeth had given her, White Feather wove a bracelet, interlacing the blond strands with tiny beads of turquoise and garnet. It was White Feather's proudest possession and she wore it constantly.

Elizabeth had been in the Ute village for six weeks when she laced her teepee shut for the night and settled into the warm buffalo robes near the small fire she had built herself. As she lay there, staring at the flickering flames, she considered her situation.

She really had no desire to return to Two Ponies' village, and she didn't know if she would ever again live among the white people. A part of her was quite willing to accept her current status as a permanent condition. After all, she had no living relatives, and there was not one white person this side of Illinois whose name she could call upon for help.

Except one.

She thought of the big, red-haired man who had ridden with the Indians who had attacked her parents' wagon. His name was Talbot. Red Talbot. She could never forget that name.

Outside it began to snow, but inside, Elizabeth was warm and snug. An untroubled sleep came quickly.

All through the night, the snow fell heavily in

large white flakes that drifted down from the black sky and settled upon the village of Standing Bear. It fell silently, and its presence deadened all sound, so that the movement of horses, and the stirring of the villagers in their robes and blankets were unheard.

The doors of all teepees were laced tightly shut, and wisps of blue smoke curled up from the smoke flaps, providing a scene of peaceful tranquillity to the village. The smell of a hundred simmering stews told the silent story of a night when no one went hungry, and when everyone was warm and snug against the harsh elements.

Two hundred yards away from the village lay the lower reaches of a great pine forest, and from the darkness of those trees, came the emerging shadows of a long line of riders. The horses moved silently, as if treading on air, and only their movement and the blue vapor of their breath gave any indication of life. A small, clinking sound of metal on metal came from the party, a sound which contrasted sharply with the drift of snow and the soft whisper of trees.

In the village, Standing Bear heard it while in the deepest recesses of his sleep, and his eyes snapped open. As he lay beside Quiet Stream, he wondered what could have caused the sound. But the bed robes were too warm, and the flesh of his woman too sweet, and as he looked at White Feather sleeping undisturbed, he realized that he must have dreamed the unusual sound. He rolled back against the inviting curve of the sleeping body of his wife and went back to sleep.

Outside, the silent horses and the quiet men approached.

Red Talbot sat in the saddle and looked toward the sleeping Indian village which lay before him. A rider, whose name was Pugh, came up beside him and spat a stream of tobacco into the snow. The snow browned for a moment, but was quickly covered by new fall.

"Looks like we caught 'em sleepin'," Pugh said.

"Yeah, well, we'll just make sure their sleepin' is permanent," Talbot replied.

"You got that right, Colonel."

Talbot called himself a colonel now. If his rank lacked the legitimacy of an official appointment, so, too, did the body of men he commanded. The "Righteous Militia," as he called his organization, was the latest in a long line of Talbot's schemes.

Although he claimed to have been a colonel during the late war, in truth, Private Talbot had deserted the Union Army on the first day of fighting at Wilson Creek, fleeing the battle in panic. Working his way back up along the Missouri–Kansas border, he threw his lot in with the Rebel guerrilla, Quantrill. He hadn't changed loyalties—he simply saw an opportunity to use the war for his own gain.

The war had ended for the rest of the country, but not for Talbot. Now addicted to violence as a way of getting what he wanted, he engaged in a series of activities, all of them criminal. At one point, he allied himself with renegade Indians to attack small parties of immigrants moving West. That proved to be a less than successful scheme, however, as the settlers rarely traveled with any significant amounts of cash. In addition, Indians as partners proved too volatile and unpredictable.

Then he hit upon his present scheme. Instead of riding *with* the Indians, he would ride *against* them. He formed the Righteous Militia, a group of mercenaries, and began selling his services as an Indian fighter. His customers were citizens in those dangerous areas that were too remote to be protected by the regular army.

If no Indian trouble presented itself, Talbot was perfectly prepared to create some. In this case, however, that wasn't necessary, for recently the Cooper ranch has been attacked and everyone, including Mrs. Cooper and her two daughters, had been killed. The neighbors were outraged, and terrified by the incident. When "Colonel" Ted Talbot offered the services of his militia to hunt down and kill the offending Indians, the citizens' commission, backed by banks and other businesses, willingly paid the three thousand, five hundred dollars Talbot demanded of them. He and the forty men with him were now gathered outside Standing Bear's village in the early-morning darkness to fulfill that mission.

Two more men approached, bringing with them an Indian captive.

"Look what we got," one of them said.

"Who is that?" Talbot asked.

"She's some squaw woman we found gatherin' wood."

"Did she have time to sound the alarm?"

"No," one of the two men said. "We seen her comin' and we grabbed her 'afore she knowed what hit her."

"Do you speak English?" Talbot asked the captive woman. She didn't answer.

"Look at this, Colonel," one of her guards said. He put his hand on the buffalo robe the woman was wearing and jerked it open. The Indian woman was young, beautiful, and, beneath the robe, naked.

Talbot heard the quick intake of breath from the men who were close enough to see what was going on. He was himself affected by the sight, and for a moment he thought of declaring her "spoils of war," so he could enjoy her later.

"Cover her," he said quickly. "She could be a distraction to the others."

"You got that right," the guard said, putting the woman's robe back in place. "I just thought you might appreciate a little peek, that's all."

"Girl, how many Shoshoni are in the village?" Talbot asked.

"I am not Shoshoni. I am Ute."

Talbot grinned broadly. "Ah, so you do speak English. All right, so you are Ute. Is everyone in the village Ute?"

"One is not. Sun's Light is Cheyenne," the girl replied. Regardless of the fact that Elizabeth was white, the fact that she was married to Two Ponies and had introduced herself in such a way made her a Cheyenne in this young woman's eyes.

"What are we goin' to do now, Colonel?" Pugh asked.

"What do you mean? We are going to do what we came out here to do."

"But you heard the girl. These here Indians is Ute. The ones that attacked the Cooper Ranch was Shoshoni."

"Shoshoni, Ute, Cheyenne—what difference does it make? Indians is Indians," Talbot said. "We're gettin' paid to kill Indians, and that's what we're goin' to do."

Suddenly the girl escaped from the grasp of the two guards. She did it by simply slipping out of the robe, leaving them holding her coat while she started dashing stark naked across the snow, heading back for the village.

"Don't let her get away!" Talbot called. "She'll give the alarm!"

One of the militiamen drew his rifle from the saddle scabbard, aimed, and fired. The bullet hit the fleeing girl in the back of the head and she pitched forward, staining the snow with crimson. Her nude body lay facedown on the snow.

There was a shout from the village.

"Damn!" Talbot staid. "Let's go! Hit 'em now! Hit 'em now!"

An explosion of sound invaded the peaceful

silence. Voices shouted in fear and anger, guns fired, and horses neighed.

Then the savage butchery began. The militia chased down the running Indians and shot them at point-blank range with pistols, or clubbed them with rifle butts. Women were murdered without mercy, and children and babies were run down and trampled. Old men and unarmed warriors were killed, and teepees were set ablaze.

It was a grotesque montage of sound and fury, savagery and color; black smoke, orange flames, red blood, and white snow.

Elizabeth had no idea what was going on, or who was doing all the shooting. She knew only that someone had attacked a peaceful village in the middle of the night. Slipping her feet into a pair of moccasins, she wrapped herself in a blanket and stepped out of the tent. The first thing she saw was a woman running from someone on horseback. The rider was carrying a pistol, and when he drew even with the woman he leaned over, put the barrel of his pistol right up to her head, and pulled the trigger.

"No!" Elizabeth screamed, watching in horror as blood erupted from the wound. The woman went down.

By now, several of the Indian warriors had managed to arm themselves, and they stood in a tight group, firing into their attackers. The mounted riders were so intent upon shooting and slashing the helpless women and children that they weren't aware that a defense was being mounted. A volley of fire from the Indians brought down three of Tobin's men.

"All right, men, we've done enough here! Let's go!" one of the attackers shouted.

"Talbot!" Elizabeth said, recognizing the red-bearded man who had ridden with the Indians in the attack on her parents. Now he was riding with white men, attacking a peaceful Indian village.

Elizabeth looked around for a gun. Seeing a pistol on the ground beside a dead warrior, she ran for it, picked it up, and aimed. Talbot was looking the other way. He would never know what hit him.

Elizabeth pulled the trigger . . . and heard only the dull click of a hammer falling on an empty chamber. With a cry of frustration, she hurled the gun at him. It fell so far short of its mark that Talbot never even saw her.

The attackers galloped away, leaving as quickly as they had come. Within a moment, nothing was left of their visit but the sound of the crackling fire and the angry shouts and wailing curses of the Indians left behind.

Cries of anguish and grief drifted through the camp as the Indians began to find the slaughtered bodies of their loved ones. Some of the Indians began weeping aloud, while others walked around with shock and disbelief etched on their faces.

More than two dozen teepees had been burned, and several were still in flames, the skin burned away and the burning poles forming glowing cones in the predawn darkness.

By first light, the villagers were able to count their dead. Elizabeth stood over one of the bodies, covered now by a brightly colored blanket. A small arm protruded from beneath the blanket, and around the wrist of that arm was a bracelet made of blond hair, interlaced with turquoise and garnet. Eighty-eight had been killed. Eighty-eight out of a village of two hundred, nineteen of them children.

The Ute held funeral ceremonies all that day, and Elizabeth stayed with them, helping to prepare the dead and to clean up the village. Finally, three days later, after the last body was wrapped and placed on the massive burial platform, Elizabeth went to see Standing Bear. Though they could no more speak White Feather's name, the grief over the loss of Standing Bear and Quiet Stream's daughter was still etched in their faces as they received her.

"I thank you for allowing me to live with you," she said. "But I fear I have brought evil to this place. I think I should go now."

"I will have food prepared for your journey," Standing Bear said quietly.

Elizabeth thought it was significant that he made no effort to talk her out of leaving.

Two hours later, mounted on the same horse that she had ridden in on, and carrying a good supply of salted meat and dried fruit, Elizabeth said good-bye to the Indians who had befriended her, and rode away from the village in the direction of the setting sun.

With the Springer–Stanley Party at Demon's Pass

After waiting almost a week for the snow to clear, Clay called the men together to discuss whether or not they would try the pass the next day. Even though the snow had not melted as much as they had hoped, they now had a week's rest, and had recovered some of their strength. They were fairly sure they could make it, though they were no longer that confident in their stock.

"The problem is, our animals haven't been able to recruit," Jason said. "What grass there was has been covered over with the snow. They can't eat."

"They're probably getting more than you think," Tobin suggested. "I've seen animals find browse in deeper snow than this."

"Yeah, well I would've felt a heap better if the sun had come out today," Pecorino said.

"We're not getting anywhere by waiting here," Clay said. "Hook up the teams and let's go."

"Hey, Jason," Pecorino teased as they began hooking up the teams, "you ever eat mule meat?"

"Don't know as I have," Jason replied.

"Well, we might get to pretty soon, if we don't get out of here."

"I've et mule meat," Tobin said. When the

others looked at him, he continued. "Durin' the war, I was with Pemberton's troops outside Vicksburg. Mule meat can be quite tasty if you know how to cook it."

"We won't be eating our mules," Clay insisted. "We'll need them."

Almost immediately after starting their second attempt at the pass, they ran into difficulty. The snow, which was less than knee-deep where they had made their temporary camp, grew deeper as they climbed higher. They struggled against it, flailing at it with their arms and hands as it reached waist-deep. Still they pressed onward.

The snowdrifts varied in depth, making it very slow and very difficult to walk. At first Clay and Parker rode side by side, then they decided it would be better to let just one of them break the trail while the other followed behind. They took turns that way so that neither one of the horses would get too tired from plowing through the snow.

The crystal-clear air made the pass seem agonizingly close, much closer than it actually was. But in actual fact, they weren't even able to get as close to it as they had gotten on that first day with all the pack animals. One of the ironies of this attempt was that they were able to see just how close they had come on that first day.

"We should have gone on!" Pecorino said to the others. "If we could just get that close now, I know we could make it. Me and my big mouth. I shouldn't of said anything that day." Clay said nothing in response.

As night fell, they knew they were going to fail. They turned around and started back, their spirits even lower than they had been before they had tried. It was as if they were now being forced to accept the brutal truth. The nightmare that had plagued them for the entire journey had come true. They were trapped here, and there was every possibility they would be here for the entire winter.

"You know, we could starve to death here," Pecorino suggested the next morning.

Clay shook his head. "We won't starve," he said.

"I've heard of it happenin' before," Pecorino insisted. "There was them people several years ago that got caught in the snow and they wound up eatin' each other."

"What? You're making that up," Jason said, wide-eyed.

"No, he's telling the truth," Clay said. "It was the Donner party."

"And they actually began killing each other?"

"No. They didn't eat anyone until they had already died."

"I ain't too keen on anything like that happening here," Pecorino said.

"It won't," Clay insisted.

"How do you know it won't?"

"Because we're carrying enough foodstuffs in our cargo to keep that from happening. We've got beans, sugar, flour, and coffee. The more we get into it, the less profit we'll make, but, I promise you, I will get into it before I let any of us starve."

"So . . . what are we going to eat between now and then?" Pecorino asked.

"There should be plenty of game around," Clay suggested. "In fact, I saw some ducks yesterday. We ought to be able to shoot a few of them."

Even as Clay was talking, Parker was pulling a couple of rifles from one of the wagons. He tossed one of them to Jason.

"Come on, let's go hunting," Parker invited. "I'm getting hungry just *talking* about getting hungry."

"All right," Jason replied. He smiled at the other three. "You men have the fire started and the pot ready," he said. "We'll bring back the meat."

"You better bring something back," Tobin teased. "The more I look at you, the tastier I think you would be." He laughed out loud.

"That ain't funny," Jason said sternly. "Don't even make jokes about it."

Tobin was still laughing as Parker and Jason walked away from the camp. After their second unsuccessful try at negotiating the pass, the rest of the men had come back down from the mountain to make their camp in the little valley, where they set up alongside a lake. Most of the lake was frozen, though here and there a few patches of water peeked through, and it was that water that attracted the birds.

"You like duck better roasted or stewed?" Jason asked as they walked along the lake's edge.

"I like roasted duck, with maybe some apples and a few carrots cooked with it," Parker said. "My mom makes . . ." He paused. It was the first time he had even thought of his mother in a long time and it seemed odd to him, how naturally it slipped out. "I mean, my mom used to fix it that way."

"I'm sorry about your mom," Jason said softly, seeing the hurt on Parker's face.

"Yes, well, what's happened can't be changed. Anyway, how do you like your duck?"

"I like it with gravy made from the drippin's," Jason said.

"Your mom make it like that?"

"Nah, my mom's a whore, remember? 'Bout the only thing I can ever remember her fixin' me is scrambled eggs. Mrs. Pratt makes it like that, though. She was the store owner's wife. I used to clean up for Mr. Pratt a bit, and sometimes Mrs. Pratt would let me take supper with 'em. She was real good at makin' gravy. What you do is, you take some flour and brown it in the drippin's, then you add milk. Water will do if you've got no milk. Then you whip it together in a skillet till it thickens up. Then you spoon that over mashed potatoes."

"Irish potatoes, or sweet potatoes?" Parker asked, keeping the conversation going.

"Either one. Or you could serve the gravy over biscuits. That's always good too."

"Then you want to top that off with a big piece of hot apple pie," Parker suggested.

"With cheese melted on top," Jason added. "Now, when it comes to apple pie, couldn't no one beat Mrs. Yates. Fact is, she runs a business makin' and sellin' pies. Sometimes I would buy a whole pie from her and eat it all by myself before I got home."

"Don't know if I could eat a whole pie."

"Sure you could. You just never tried, is all. But once you get started, they're so good, you can eat a whole pie easy."

"You know what we ought to do? We ought to just shut up," Parker said. "What we're doing is punishing ourselves. We don't have any potatoes or carrots, and we sure don't have any apple pie."

"Maybe not, but we're damned sure goin' to have us some duck," Jason said in a low, excited voice. "Look over there."

Parker looked in the direction Jason pointed and saw two ducks coming toward them, flying low and fast over the water.

"Give 'em plenty of lead," Jason said, cocking the hammer and raising his rifle. "You take the one on the left, I'll . . ."

"Jason! Forget the ducks!"

"What?"

"Forget the ducks! Look at that. There's a hell of a lot more meat over there," Parker said.

Parker pointed to the edge of a clearing where a big, brown grizzly bear was rooting through the snow.

"Jesus! Look at the size of that son of a bitch!" Jason said. "How come he's not hibernatin'?"

"I don't know, maybe he's not quite ready yet. You know they store up a whole winter's worth of food before they go in. Look at him—there's enough meat there to feed us for a month," Parker said.

"If we can kill him," Jason replied. "From what I hear, those things aren't all that easy to bring down."

"We've got no choice. We have to kill him."

"All right, I'm ready if you are," Jason said. "But if we only wound him, there's goin' to be hell to pay, 'cause he's goin' to come after us."

"Then make sure and shoot straight."

The two boys raised their rifles and took aim. Jason fired first and, out of the corner of his eye, Parker saw a flash of light and a puff of smoke. Then Parker pulled the trigger, and the gun banged and kicked back against his shoulder.

The bear, who had his back to the two boys, was hit. He fell and rolled once, flinging blood onto the snow. Though hit hard, he managed to get up and turn toward the upstart and puny creatures who had dared to attack him. He bolted forward, nostrils flared, teeth bared, and eyes flashing. The bear roared an angry challenge as he came crashing down the mountainside toward them, dislodging snow and loose gravel during his lumbering descent.

"Shoot the son of a bitch, Parker! Shoot him! Use your pistol!" Jason shouted.

The boys stood their ground, peering over the

barrels of their pistols, watching as the bear loomed bigger and bigger. The bear was running in a loping gate, sometimes raising both front legs at the same time. They awaited their opportunity, timing it just right.

"Now!" Jason shouted, firing his gun.

Parker pulled the trigger just as the bear's front legs were raised, presenting its underbelly as a target. The balls from both pistols crashed into the bear's chest.

The grizzly fell a second time and slipped forward on his belly, all four legs stretched out and useless. A swath of pink appeared on the snow behind it as it slid the last few feet down the side of the mountain, piling snow up in front of it. Finally, it came to a halt no more than five feet away from the two boys.

"Damn!" Jason said excitedly. "We got him! We killed the son of a bitch!"

Jason's triumphant shout was a little premature, for the bear raised its head and glared at them through narrowed, yellow eyes. It growled again as blood bubbled from its mouth.

"He's not dead yet," Parker said. He raised his pistol to shoot again.

"No, wait," Jason said, holding out his hand to stop him. "Let's don't waste any more ammunition on the son of a bitch. Pick up a club somewhere. We can finish him off that way."

"Good idea," Parker agreed.

The two boys looked around until each of them found a large branch they could use. Thus armed, they moved cautiously toward the bear.

Parker raised his club and the bear looked at him. For a moment Parker hesitated. He felt a sense of guilt. Like him, the bear was just trying to survive the winter. It was one thing to shoot him when he was charging . . . quite another to club him to death when he was down.

Jason had no such reservations. While the bear was looking at Parker, Jason hit him a blow, spattering more blood onto the snow. The bear jerked his head toward Jason then, and Parker, recovering from his moment of indecision, took his own swing. The bear roared again, a terrible, frightening bellow, but Parker knew that it was its death knell, for there was no challenge left in its cry—only fear and pain.

Finally, exhausted and exhilarated, the two boys stopped clubbing it, realizing at last that it was dead. They stood there looking down at its still form for a long moment, the vapor clouds from their gasping breaths curling around their heads.

"What do you think he'll weigh?" Jason asked.

"Easily five or six hundred pounds," Parker replied.

"Think we got a pot big enough to cook 'im in?" Jason asked.

They laughed until their sides hurt.

Chapter 17

When Elizabeth's horse went lame on her, she had no idea what to do. She looked at its foot and rubbed its leg, but the horse's limp got so bad that she couldn't bring herself to add to the poor beast's misery by riding.

"I think people shoot horses when they are like this," Elizabeth said to the animal. "But I don't have a gun. And, even if I did, I don't know if I could bring myself to shoot you. So, I'll just turn you out on your own."

Elizabeth disconnected the buffalo hide bridle, then swatted the horse on its rump. It tried to run, but the injured leg buckled and it nearly went down. The horse recovered enough to move off, though with such a severe limp that Elizabeth felt bad for having ridden it as long as she had.

It had been two weeks since the raid on the Indian village, and during that two weeks, Elizabeth had seen no one. She had eaten the last of the food Standing Bear had given her on the previous day. Now she had neither food nor water. She did have a buffalo robe which protected her from the cold, and she was very thankful for that, for without it she would have surely frozen to death. She continued to walk west for the rest of the day, having no idea where she was going.

Fred Sargent stopped the team and set the brakes on the wagon. Beside him was his wife Mary and their infant child, Timmy. Behind were three other children: Becky, who was three, Billy, who was five, and Sara, seven.

The baby was crying.

"He's hungry," Mary said, opening her dress to free her breast. Timmy took to the nipple immediately.

"I'm hungry too, Mama," Billy said. "When are we going to eat supper?"

"As soon as we get home."

"Come on, Papa. Make the team go, so we can get home faster."

"We've just come up a long hill," Fred said. "If I don't give the team a few minutes to rest, they'll fall down in their traces and we'll never get home."

"Mama, can I get down and walk around a little?" Sara asked.

"Yes," Mary replied, "but don't wander too far."

"I won't."

Sara climbed down from the wagon, then began singing a little song, skipping in time.

"You need someone to help you with the house, Mary," Fred said. "You know you do."

It was the continuation of a discussion they had been having all during the long drive back from the meeting at Elder Ben Malcolm's house. "You saw how well Elder Malcolm's wives got on, didn't you?"

There had been many people at the meeting, but Elder Malcolm's three wives worked together as a team to make sure things went quite smoothly.

"Fred, our religion says that a man can take on more wives. You certainly don't need my permission to do so, so don't make excuses by saying I need someone to help around the house."

"You know you would always be my first wife," Fred said. "No matter who else I might take into the house, she could never take your place."

"I know that," Mary said. She smiled at her husband. "And, it might be nice to have a sister."

"Eeeeeek!!!"

Sara's scream interrupted whatever reply Fred might have made. Reacting quickly, he grabbed his rifle and jumped down from the wagon. "Sara!" he called.

Sara came running over the top of a small rise. "Papa, there's an Indian back there! An Indian!"

"Just one?"

Sara nodded. "She's the only one I saw."

"*She*? You saw an Indian woman? Where?"

"She was sleeping," Sara said, pointing toward

the rise. "But I saw her get up when she heard me. There she is!"

Fred raised his rifle and pointed it at the woman who was just now coming toward them. "That's far enough!" he called.

"Fred, she's no Indian. She has blond hair," Mary said.

"Who are you?" Fred asked, lowering his rifle.

Before the blond woman in the Indian dress could answer, she passed out.

When Elizabeth came to, she was in bed. It was the first time she had seen a real bed, room, or house in nearly a year.

"Here, try to drink some of this," a woman said, holding a cup toward her.

Elizabeth took it, realized at once that it was a clear broth of some sort, and began to drink it eagerly. She could almost feel the strength returning with each sip of the soothing broth.

"Thank you," she said. As she sipped the broth, she looked around the room. Curtains hung at the windows. On the wall a sampler read, "God Bless This Home."

A man came into the room. "How is she?" he asked.

Elizabeth gasped and jerked back, spilling some of the broth. "You!" she said, glaring at the man. "You were going to shoot me."

"I'm sorry about that," the man said. "We thought you were an Indian."

"Yes," the woman said. "You gave us quite a

scare, first because you were dressed like a wild Indian, and secondly because you passed out. We didn't know if you were going to live or die."

"It's been a while since I've had anything to eat," Elizabeth said. "I guess I was weak with hunger."

"We're the Sargents," the woman said. "My name is Mary, and this is my husband, Fred. What is your name, dear?"

"Sun—" Elizabeth started to say, then caught herself. "Elizabeth Stanley."

"Do you have people around here, Miss Stanley?"

Elizabeth shook her head. "I have no people anywhere," she replied. "My mother, father, and brother were killed by Indians."

"Oh, my," Mary replied, her hand covering her mouth. "Such a tragedy."

"Did it happen near here?" Fred asked.

"I don't know. I don't know where 'here' is."

"This is Utah," Fred said.

"Utah?" Elizabeth said in surprise. "My, I have come a long way."

"Would you like some more broth, Elizabeth?" Mary asked.

"Yes, thank you. And if you have it, perhaps a piece of bread?"

"Of course, my dear."

Several days of sunshine and above-freezing temperature had its effect. Although all the snow didn't melt, enough of it was cleared away to enable the men to make another try at the devilish pass.

Ironically, the enforced waiting had some beneficial effect. At the lower elevation where they had made their camp, the mules were able to forage quite easily. Food, water, and a prolonged period of rest enabled them to regain much of their strength. The bear provided an ample supply of food for the men so that on the day Clay pronounced the snow in the pass low enough to give it a try, men and animals were stronger than they had been on the day they had first arrived.

The wagons, too, had benefited from the delay. Further inspection of Pecorino's wagon showed that the popping noise he heard was, indeed, a cracked axle. They had brought some spare parts with them, so they used this opportunity to replace not only Pecorino's axle, but one of the wheels on Jason's wagon. Also, the last of the grease was used, and all bolts and fittings were tightened.

They began readying the wagons shortly after sunup, and by midmorning all the teams were in harness, the wagons brought into line, loads secured, and drivers seated. Clay and Parker moved to the front of the train, then Clay stood in his stirrups and looked up the trail in front of them. Although most of the trail was still white with snow, there were a number of areas where the ground showed through.

Tobin was in the front wagon, Jason was in the second, and Pecorino was bringing up the rear.

"All right, men, let's go," Clay said.

"Hear, giddup!" Tobin called.

"Yah, now!" Jason yelled, snapping his reins.

"*Avante!*" Pecorino shouted, then he whistled shrilly. The mules started forward, almost as if they were as anxious to leave this place as the men. The wagons rolled easily across the level ground where they were camped, then they started up the long, sloping rise leading to the pass.

Two-thirds of the way up the pass, Clay stopped the train to give the mules a rest. The snow was practically inconsequential, but here the grade steepened sharply.

Clay went on up to the top of the pass. When he did so, he let out a shout. "Hey! Come here, all of you! Look!"

Setting the brakes on the wagons, the others hurried up to the top of the pass. Parker was the first one there. When he looked in the direction Clay was pointing, he felt a sense of elation. There in the distance he saw a large body of water, shimmering in the sunlight.

"What is that?" Jason asked, joining them then. "Is that the ocean?"

"No, it's a lake," Clay said. "But it's like the ocean, because the water is salty."

"That's the Great Salt Lake, isn't it?" Parker asked, grinning wildly. "The one Marcus wanted to swim in."

"Yes, it is," Clay said. "And around on the other side of that lake is Salt Lake City, the Land of the Saints."

"Why do they call it 'Land of the Saints'?"

"Well, because that's what the Mormons call themselves," Clay said. He laughed. "But believe me, they aren't all saints."

"How far away you think that is?" Pecorino asked.

"I think we'll be there in another week," Clay said. "Ten days at the most."

Pecorino turned and started back down the trail.

"Where you goin'?" Tobin called.

"To get these mules moving," Pecorino replied. "It may be ten more days before we make it to Salt Lake City, but I don't plan to spend one damn day more on this here mountain."

Elizabeth was in the relative warmth of the barn, sitting on a small, three-legged stool with her head resting on a cow's flank. Streams of milk squirted into the bucket as her hands pulled rhythmically at the animal's teats. She had been raised on a farm, and this was an old, familiar chore that brought back memories that had lain dormant for the past year.

Because of her farming background, Elizabeth was able to move quickly and easily into the Sargent household, helping Mary with her chores: washing clothes, scrubbing floors, baking, and even tending to the baby. Of all her tasks, though, she liked milking the cow the best. Here, in the silence of the barn, with only the cows for company, she could bring some peace and order back to her life, and reflect over all that had happened to her.

"Elizabeth? Elizabeth, are you in here?" Sara called.

"Moo!" Elizabeth said in reply. Then, in a singsong voice she said, "Elizabeth isn't in here. There's nobody in here but us cows."

Sara laughed. "You are, too, in here," she said. "Cows can't talk."

"Sure they can talk. They say 'moo,' " Elizabeth replied.

Laughing again, Sara skipped into the barn.

"Did you feed the chickens?" Elizabeth asked.

"Yes."

"Ah, good for you."

"Elizabeth, what was it like with the Indians?"

"It wasn't like anything," Elizabeth said.

"But weren't you scared all the time?"

"I was, in the beginning. But I got used to living with them."

"I don't think I could ever get used to living with savages."

"Not all of them are savages. There are some good Indians and there are some bad Indians."

"Papa says the only good Indians are dead Indians," Sara said. "And I think he's right."

"Why would you think that?"

"Because they are so cruel. They murder women and children and scalp them. Besides, they aren't like white people. They don't have feelings like we do."

Elizabeth thought of the attack on Standing Bear's village, and the savage butchery of women and children. She remembered the tears of grief of the Indians, and the terrible anguish of those who mourned their loved ones.

"They have feelings," she said without further explanation.

"Did you have any Indian friends?"

"Yes, I had many."

"Did you know any little Indian girls my age?"

Elizabeth closed her eyes. In her mind she could see the little arm sticking out from under the brightly colored blanket, with a bracelet made of blond hair tied around the wrist.

"Yes. I knew a little girl just like you."

"What was her name?"

"White Feather."

"White Feather?" Sara laughed. "That's a funny name, isn't it?"

"Yes."

"Was she a very special friend?"

"Yes," Elizabeth said. "She was." Finished milking, Elizabeth stood up and picked up the bucket. "I think we had better get the milk in, don't you?" She started toward the barn door, then realized that Sara was still standing behind her. She turned toward her. "Aren't you coming?"

"Elizabeth, am I your special friend too?" Sara asked.

Elizabeth smiled, and held her hand out toward Sara. "Of course you are," she said warmly.

Smiling broadly, Sara ran toward her. Hand in hand, they walked from the barn to the house.

Salt Lake City

Colonel Red Talbot, resplendent in his Righteous Militia uniform of blue and gold, looked down at the plate that had just been placed in front of him. Filled with roast beef, mashed potatoes covered with gravy, peas, and rolls, it was a more-than-sumptuous fare.

"I have to say one thing about you Mormons," Talbot said as he took his knife and fork and began cutting a piece of the thick slab of meat, "you do know how to eat."

"Yes, the Lord believes that a full stomach is the receptacle for a faithful soul," Richard Hahs replied. Hahs was a Mormon businessman.

Their table was next to a window, and when Talbot heard a rumbling sound, he looked out onto the incredibly broad street that was typical of the boulevards of this planned community of thirty-thousand-plus people. An oversized oxcart, pulled by twenty oxen, lumbered slowly up the middle of the street. The cargo was composed of only one block of granite, but it was huge, and weighed over five tons.

"Look at that," Talbot said. "All that work for only one brick."

Hahs chuckled. "Yes, I suppose you could call those granite blocks bricks. They are precut and numbered at the quarry, which is twenty miles away, then brought into town and put into place."

Looking up the street, Talbot could see the scaffolding that formed the framework around what the Mormons were calling their Tabernacle.

"At this rate, it's going to take forever to get that thing built," Talbot suggested.

"Not forever. But we estimate it will be between forty and fifty years," Hahs replied.

"Forty and fifty *years*? That's ridiculous," Talbot said. "Why would anyone work so hard, and spend so much money to build something that half of them won't even live to see completed?"

"It's a testament to our faith," Hahs replied. "And if you are going to do business with us, then you must understand—and appreciate—the faith that drives us."

"I can do that, all right, but I have a lot more faith in money."

"Money isn't everything, Colonel Talbot."

"Perhaps not, but a few dollars to the right people did get me an appointment with the territorial governor tomorrow."

"You're talking about Alfred Cumming?"

"Yes."

Hahs laughed.

"What is it? What are you laughing about?"

"Cumming is the territorial governor appointed by the federal government. But the only one here who has any real power is President Brigham Young."

"President? Like in President of the country?"

"No. He is the president of our church and, here, the church has all the power. Therefore, President Young is the most powerful person here."

"All right, how do I get to see him?"

"I could arrange a meeting," Hahs said.

"Good, good. Do it."

"Remember what I said about faith."

"Yeah, all right. If that's what it takes, I'll become a Mormon."

"It'll take that," Hahs said. "And one hundred dollars."

"What?"

"I believe you did say you had faith in money?"

"Yes, I did say that. But, what about this religious faith you were talking about?"

"When two strong faiths, such as your faith and mine, come together, the results are much more certain," Hahs said. "There is no tenet against money in the Mormon religion."

The next morning in the company of Richard Hahs, Talbot approached Beehive House, President Brigham Young's official residence. As they passed through the main gate, which was crowned with an enormous wooden eagle, Talbot saw several children playing.

"What are all these kids doing here? Is this a schoolhouse?"

Hahs laughed. "These are President Young's children," he said.

"All of 'em? How many does he have?"

"He has twenty-seven wives and fifty-six children."

"Twenty-seven wives?"

"Our men can have more than one wife," Hahs explained.

Talbot smiled. "The more I hear about this religion, the more I like it."

"I assure you, sir, taking additional wives is a testament of faith, not an exercise in salaciousness."

They were invited inside Brigham Young's residence, then Talbot was taken to another room to meet with the man himself. He had heard all about Brigham Young, for he was a man who was well known throughout the country. Physically, Brigham Young didn't cut that impressive an appearance. He was rather ordinary-looking, but even someone as jaded as Talbot felt a slight sense of awe at being in his presence.

"Colonel Talbot, I am told you wish to join us," Young said.

"Yes," Talbot answered.

"Why?"

"Uh"—Talbot thought hard, trying to come

up with the answer that would satisfy Brigham Young—"I got religion," he said.

Young's eyes narrowed. "In other words, you see some opportunity to conduct business with us," he suggested.

"Yes. That too," Talbot said.

"I see." Young stroked his chin for a moment. "I have been told about your most recent military experience. You had a confrontation with the Indians, did you not?"

"I did," Talbot answered. "You see, I'm the colonel in command of the Righteous Militia and we . . ."

Young held up his hand to interrupt him. "I am not aware that we have an organization called the Righteous Militia," he said. "And, while I am no longer the territorial governor, Governor Cumming does a good job of keeping me informed about things. I'm sure he would have told me if such a militia unit had been created."

"No, uh, Your Honor, the Righteous Militia, that's something I put together myself."

"I see. Then, you aren't actually a colonel, are you?"

This wasn't going the way Talbot had intended. He was supposed to be able to take advantage of his great victory over the Indians.

"The Righteous Militia is a private military organization, and I am the colonel of that organization," Talbot explained. "We have no federal or territorial support."

"Then that probably explains why you didn't have the right information for your attack."

"I beg your pardon? The right information about what?"

"The Indians who attacked the Cooper ranch were Shoshoni. Yet I am told you attacked a village of Ute Indians," Brigham Young said. "And that you killed quite a few of them. Why was that? As far as I know, the Ute have never taken up arms against us."

Talbot cleared his throat as he searched for something to say. Then he remembered the young woman they had captured, just before the attack. What was it she told them? Oh, yes, that there were Cheyenne in the camp.

"There may have been some Ute in the village," Talbot said. "But most of them were Cheyenne, and that is who we were after. Cheyenne, Shoshoni, Crow, they're all one and the same when it comes to making mischief for the whites."

Young nodded, for his people had, indeed, experienced difficulty with these warring tribes in the past. "I was not aware that there were Cheyenne involved. That being the case, you certainly have my support, and I encourage you to continue the good work. Now, what do you need from me?"

Talbot looked at Brigham Young with the most sincere look he could muster.

"President Young, right now I need only one thing from you. And that is acceptance in your church, so that I may turn away from my sinful ways."

"We are, and always will be, a haven for those sinners who do truly intend to walk a new path. Welcome, brother," Young said.

Chapter 18

When Mary announced that they were going into Salt Lake City the next day, Elizabeth was surprised at how excited she was at the prospect. It had been almost a year since she had last been in any town. She remembered the shopping trip she and her mother had taken into Sedalia, as they passed through Missouri so long ago.

Her father and brother had gone into Sedalia too, but they took care of men-type things; visiting the wagon yard, going to the tannery, and doing whatever else men did when they went to town.

She remembered that she and her mother had had a wonderful time. They had looked at material for dresses, at ribbons and hats, and at beautiful blooming flowers. They had brought several packets of seeds, and had planned the garden they would have when they reached Oregon. As Elizabeth thought about those flower seeds now, she felt a profound sense of melancholy sweep over her.

There had been a dance that night, a farmers'

social, they called it. Elizabeth was surprised when her mother and father went as well. Her mother and father had danced nearly every dance. She could remember the look of pure joy on her mother's face. That wasn't an expression her mother often had, for, as most farmers' wives, she led a hard life.

There was a young man at the dance. His name was Gordon, and he had danced several times with Elizabeth. There was a farm for sale next to that of Gordon's father's, and Gordon's father tried to talk Elizabeth's father into buying it.

It would have been wonderful, settling there in Missouri, near a town like Sedalia, close to people like Gordon and his family. But as Elizabeth's family had pointed out, they were going to Oregon because one could still homestead there. They didn't have enough money to buy land and have enough left over to start farming. They had no choice, Elizabeth's father had explained. They had to go on.

They had no choice, yet now they are dead. Her father, her mother, her brother. All dead.

Well, she wouldn't think about that now. That was all behind her, and there was nothing she could do to change it. She could only look ahead. And tomorrow she was going into town.

There would also be another important landmark for her tomorrow. She would be wearing a new dress, her own dress that she had made, just for her. So far, Mary had been very generous in sharing her clothes with Elizabeth, but the prospect of going into town . . . and wearing a dress of her own . . . was like Christmas and her birthday and the Fourth of July, all rolled into one. In fact, for Elizabeth, it really was like a celebration of Christmas and her birthday, for, while with the Indians, she had completely lost track of time and during her stay with them, both events had occurred, unnoticed by her.

Elizabeth was frying chicken to pack in their lunch tomorrow, while Mary bathed little Timmy. Becky, Billy, and Sara were so excited about going into town that it was difficult to get them settled down and into bed.

"I've fried the chicken and baked the bread," Elizabeth said when Mary came into the kitchen after saying her final good nights to the children.

"Oh, and it smells so good, too."

"You mean the smell isn't bothering you?"

"No, of course not. It smells delicious. Why should it bother me?"

"I don't know," Elizabeth said. "Ordinarily the smell of baking bread and frying chicken smells good to me, too, but, for some strange reason, it's making me nauseous."

"Oh, dear. Maybe you are coming down with something," Mary suggested.

"I don't know—I hope not. I'm generally as healthy as a horse. Don't know why I'm feeling so woozy now. I even opened the door to let in some fresh air, but it was so cold outside that I nearly froze to death, so I closed it."

"Elizabeth. You have been such a help. What a wonderful sister you are going to make."

This was not the first time Mary had referred to Elizabeth as her sister. But she didn't think anything about it. She could remember the way it was in her own church back in Illinois, with people referring to each other as "brothers or sisters in Christ." She assumed that's what Mormons did as well, though they did seem to take it a little further than Methodists did.

"What is Salt Lake City like?" Elizabeth asked.

"Oh," Mary said, folding her arms across her chest as if she were embracing herself, "it is beautiful! President Young has vowed to make it God's city on earth, and it is nearly so now. It will be when the Tabernacle is completed."

"How long will it take us to get into town?" Elizabeth asked.

"It's a goodly way. It will take all of the daylight hours," Mary explained. "We'll eat breakfast before we leave, have a picnic lunch on the road and then take our supper at the Lamberts' house. Matilda Lambert is my cousin. That's also where we will sleep tomorrow night."

"Oh, but I'm a stranger," Elizabeth said. "I can't impose on your family like that."

"Nonsense, you aren't a stranger. And you aren't imposing. You are already a part of our family, and will be even more so after we have gone into town."

"You mean like your sister?"

"Of course, like my sister. Would you like to

take your bath now? I'll put some water on to heat if you would like."

"Oh, yes!" Elizabeth said eagerly. "I would love to take a bath."

Half an hour later, Elizabeth slipped out of her dress and undergarments. Over in the corner of the kitchen sat a large tub, filled with steaming water. A banked fire in the woodstove radiated warmth throughout the room so that, even though she was nude, she wasn't cold.

Elizabeth caught her reflection in the kitchen window. Because it was dark outside and brightly lit inside, the window reflection was as clear as if it had been a mirror. As she studied her image, she saw a slight bulge in her stomach. She put her hand there and pressed. Odd, she thought, how her fortunes had changed so. Not too long ago she was literally facing the prospect of starving to death. Now she was eating so much that she was beginning to get fat. If she didn't watch it, she would wind up looking like Moon Cow Woman. Elizabeth giggled quietly at that prospect, then she walked over to the tub and slipped down into the water.

The water felt so good that she made the bath last as long as she could. She bathed herself with a sliver cut from the large bar of fragrant lye soap that sat on the windowsill above the kitchen counter. Then she bathed herself a second time, leaning back in the tub, stretching her legs and pointing her toes toward the ceiling.

Then she washed her hair, leaning forward to

dip her head into the water. She soaped it, rinsed, then repeated the process.

Not until the water changed from hot to warm to tepid, and then began to actually turn cool, did she step out of the tub. She started toweling her hair before she dried her body. Then, with her long blond hair as dry as she could get it, she looked toward the window one more time to check her reflection.

That was when she saw him.

He was standing just inside the kitchen door, staring at her with eyes that were unblinking and deep in thought. She gasped, but she didn't scream. If nothing else, her exposure to the Indians over the last year had taken away any sense of false modesty.

"Mr. Sargent, what are you doing here?" she asked, calmly.

"It's all right, my dear. Tomorrow we will be married," Fred said.

"Married?"

He walked over to her and put his hands on her breasts. "You have good breasts for making milk." He moved his hands down to the flare of her hips. "And wide hips. The babies will have no problem being born."

"You talk as if you are buying a cow," Elizabeth said.

"That's exactly what I told him," Mary said, coming into the kitchen then. She was carrying a large towel and she went straight to Elizabeth and began to dry her. "I told him, Elizabeth is a beautiful, romantic young woman. She should be courted like a young woman, not looked at as if one were buying livestock."

"So this is what you have been talking about when you kept referring to me as your sister," Elizabeth said, suddenly understanding.

"Why yes, of course, dear. What did you think it was? Once you have married us, you will be Fred's wife, and my sister. I know it might be difficult for you, a gentile, to understand this. But to us it is a very beautiful thing."

Elizabeth thought of Moon Cow Woman, Willow Branch, and Morning Flower. She had come to accept the fact that they were her sisters. She never expected the same thing to happen to her once she returned to the white world but, here she was, about to be forced into another marriage.

The thought of it made her laugh.

"What is it, Elizabeth? Why are you laughing?"

"No reason," she said, laughing even harder. "No reason that you would understand."

Elizabeth felt ill when she awoke the next morning, but she said nothing about it because she didn't want to do anything that would postpone the trip into town.

Her "time of the month" had started during the night, and she told Mary that she was having a little heavier flow than normal. Mary assured her that this was the cause of her nausea and discomfort, and that it would all pass, soon enough. Elizabeth agreed, so before daylight the next morning, the little group started into Salt Lake City.

When they stopped for lunch, Elizabeth stayed in the wagon and ate nothing, even though the others complimented her on how good her fried chicken was. By the time they reached Salt Lake City, Elizabeth was complaining of a general weakness, a severe backache, and something she could only describe as "bearing down feelings."

Once John and Matilda Lambert made them welcome in their home, Matilda sent Elizabeth to bed. She gave Elizabeth a tablespoon of molasses with one ounce of curative ammonia, but it didn't help. The next morning, she tried sulphate of magnesia and cinnamon water. When that also failed to alleviate the pain or slow the flow, they sent for Dr. Cooley.

The Sargents and the Lamberts waited in the parlor as the doctor made his examination. After a long while, the doctor came back down the stairs with a rather rueful expression on his face.

"Mr. Sargent, I'm afraid I have some rather distressing news for you," he said.

"What is it?" Fred asked. "Dr. Cooley, her condition isn't serious? You aren't telling us she is about to die?"

"No, no, nothing like that," Dr. Cooley said quickly.

"Oh, thank goodness," Mary said. "You had us frightened for a moment."

"Elizabeth is fine," the doctor said. He cleared

his throat and took a deep breath before continuing. "But I'm afraid she has lost the baby."

"She what?" Fred gasped. "Did you say she lost the *baby*?"

"I'm afraid so," Dr. Cooley said. He looked at the expression of shock on Fred's and Mary's faces. "Mr. Sargent, you didn't know about her pregnancy?"

"No."

"I see. Well, don't worry, Mr. Sargent, I see no reason why she won't be able to have more children. And, as I understand you will be marrying her tonight, I'm sure that is good news for you." Dr. Cooley took a bottle from his bag and handed it to Fred. "Give her a dose of this once a day, and she should recover quite nicely."

"I have no intention of marrying her now, Dr. Cooley," Fred said. "And, as to how she gets the medicine, it is her worry, and none of mine. Come, Mary, we must get back to the farm."

"Fred, we can't just leave Elizabeth here like this," Mary said.

"She nearly gave birth to an Indian's bastard child," Fred said. "Do you really want a woman like that in our house? Around our children?"

"She was a captive of the Indians," Mary tried to explain. "How could she have prevented what happened to her?"

"She could have shot herself, as any decent woman would," Fred said.

"Wait a minute," John Lambert said. "You aren't leaving her here in my house."

"She has to stay somewhere, Mr. Lambert," Dr. Cooley said.

"Well, it can't be with me. I have children too. I don't want them exposed to such immorality."

Dr. Cooley sighed. "Very well, Mr. Sargent, if you will help me get her into my buckboard, I'll take her to my office and keep her there until she is fully recovered."

"I hope, Doctor, that you aren't expecting me to pay you for that," Fred said. "As I have not yet married this woman, and as the child she lost was not mine, I feel no obligation toward her."

"Would you have me turn her out into the street?" Dr. Cooley asked, growing red in the face.

"Whatever you do to her is your own concern," Fred said. "Come, Mary. We must get started if we are to make it home today."

Mary looked at Dr. Cooley with a look of helplessness on her face. "Dr. Cooley, regardless of how my husband feels now, I do believe Elizabeth is a good girl. Please, find some way to take care of her."

"I'll do what I can," Dr. Cooley promised, and watched angrily as Fred took his wife by the hand and led her quickly out of the room.

One week later

When he learned that three wagons of freight were approaching the city, Talbot persuaded Richard Hahs to call a meeting of the merchants, to appoint him as exclusive broker for whatever the gentiles had to sell. Upon promise of a cut of Talbot's commission, Hahs agreed, and the merchants gathered in a warehouse to discuss the situation.

"Why should we appoint you our agent?" one of the merchants questioned.

"Because I can deal with the gentiles," Talbot answered. "And I can do so better than most of you, seein' as how it ain't been too long since I was one of them myself."

"But, if you are our broker, then you will expect a percentage."

"Of course I will," Talbot admitted. "Would you hold it against me for tryin' to earn a honest dollar?"

"I for one, don't begrudge it," Hahs said, trying to win the others over. "I believe in paying what is fair."

"Ah, but that is the problem," one of the other merchants said, holding up his finger. "You see, these gentiles have come a long way, bringing wagons filled with goods that are very difficult for us to obtain. Because of that, the prices they ask will be very dear . . . as they should be. Having an agent means only that we will wind up paying even more than the already inflated prices we must pay."

"That is true," one of the others said.

"Yes, I agree," still another added. "I very much want the goods they are hauling for my store. And I am willing to pay the price for them. But why should I have to pay their price plus the fee of a negotiator?"

"Well now, just hold on there," Talbot said, holding up his hands in a call for quiet. "You men are thinkin' that these freighters have you over a barrel, ain't you? You're thinkin' they brought them wagons all the way out here and they're goin' to sell to the highest bidder. Ain't that what you're thinkin'?"

"Yes."

"That is true," another said.

"Of course, that is the way of it," still another added.

Talbot chuckled, and shook his head. "Now, suppose this. Suppose there ain't no highest bidder?"

"What do you mean?"

"Suppose you make me your broker and I'm the only one that can deal with 'em. That means there'd only be one bidder. And iffen there's only one bidder, then the shoe's on the other foot. They won't have you over a barrel, you'll have them over one instead."

"How so?"

"Well, now, think about it," Talbot said. "They have brought their goods out here by wagon . . . over mountain and desert, and who knows what all. You don't really think they want to go back empty-handed, do you?"

There was a buzz of conversation among the merchants as they discussed Talbot's remarks.

"Wait a minute—are you saying we won't

have to pay a premium price?" one of the merchants asked.

"I'm sayin' they'll be forced to take anything I offer, or take their goods back."

"I say yes, let's do it!" Hahs shouted. His shout was met with the enthusiastic support of many other merchants, though one of the merchants—Lester Thurman, the owner of a millinery establishment—asked permission to speak.

"Gentlemen, there is probably something to what Mr. Talbot is saying," Thurman suggested. "He may, indeed, be able to save us some money, maybe even a lot of it. But is it worth it to our souls?"

"Your souls?" Talbot asked. "What's your souls got to do with it?"

Thurman glared at Talbot for a moment before he continued. "We have the moral obligation to see to it that these men who have braved the elements to bring goods to us be treated fairly."

"All right, I can understand that," Hahs said. "But what, exactly, do you mean by fairly?"

"I say that we establish a respectable price, one that takes into account the right these men have to make a profit, and we pay that."

"And, what do you think a fair price would be?" Hahs asked.

"As a matter of routine, we have been paying from five to ten times the eastern market price for goods that have been freighted in to us. I say we ask to see their invoices, then agree to pay six times the invoice price. That way, they will make a decent profit, and we will get it for lower than we might reasonably have expected to pay."

"Six times the invoice price?" Hahs replied. "Why should we do that? You heard what Talbot said. If we all stick together, we can get our goods much cheaper."

"No, Mr. Hahs, I think Mr. Thurman is right," Talbot said. "Six times seems a fair enough price to me. If you make me your agent, that's what I will get for you."

"Very well, then. With that assurance, you have my support," Thurman said.

"Mine too," another pitched in. Soon, all agreed, and Talbot left the meeting with a broker's commission in his hand.

"Why did you agree to pay six times the invoice price?" Hahs demanded of Talbot after the meeting broke up. "You can get it much cheaper than that. Like you said, they have no other place to go with their goods. Now that they are here, they have to sell, no matter what we offer them."

"That's right," Talbot said. He smiled. "It's also a way to make a lot of money."

"How?"

"I am goin' to buy the whole load, ever'thing they've got. But I ain't buyin' it for the merchants, I'm buyin' it for my ownself," Talbot said. "I'll get it for as low as I can."

"That's a brilliant idea," Hahs said. "Then, you sell it to the merchants for six times the invoice value."

Talbot shook his head. "Unh-uh," he said. "Then I'll sell it to 'em for whatever I can get for it, and believe me, it'll be a lot more than six times the invoice price."

Hahs's eyes narrowed. "Why are you telling me this? I'm one of the local merchants, remember?"

"I'm tellin' you this 'cause I need you. I don't have enough money to make the deal on my own. You come up with the money I'll need to buy the merchandise, then we'll split the profit, fifty-fifty."

Chapter 19

As the wagons rolled into town, Parker looked at the city with his eyes wide in wonder. Dominating the entire town was a huge building under construction, surrounded with scaffolding busy with workers. He was also impressed by the width and cleanliness of the streets, as well as the lack of saloons. None of the freighters had seen Salt Lake City before, and all were as enthralled by what they were seeing as Parker was.

The citizens of Salt Lake City seemed as fully interested in them as they were in the city. The railroad had not yet reached Salt Lake City, and the arrival of three wagons of manufactured goods from the East was always an exciting event. Even as Parker and the others were gawking at the sights of the city, they were aware that the sidewalks were filling with those who gawked at them.

"Parker, I've got an idea," Clay said.

Out of the corner of his eye, Parker saw a young woman walking down the sidewalk. Unlike the others, she seemed totally uninterested in the arriving wagons. Instead she seemed bent upon some errand. He only saw her for a brief moment, but there was something about her that caught his attention. He twisted in his saddle for a better look, but she had already disappeared behind the door.

"Parker?"

"I'm sorry," Parker said, turning back. "What did you say?"

"What is it, did you see something?"

"I'm not sure," Parker said. "You said something about an idea?"

"Yes. Let's find a place in the street where we can park the wagons, then off-load enough goods that all of it will show. I think if we spread the merchandise around a little . . . let the people get a good look at it, we might whet their appetites."

"Good idea," Parker agreed.

"Good afternoon, Miss Stanley," the pharmacist said when Elizabeth stepped into the apothecary. "What can I do for you this afternoon?"

"Dr. Cooley has made out a list of medicines he wants me to pick up for him," Elizabeth said, handing a sheet of paper to the druggist.

"Very well," the druggist said, taking his pestle and mortar down from the shelf as he looked at the list. "It'll take about half an hour. Do you want to come back, or wait?"

"I'll wait," Elizabeth said. "He wants me to bring it to him as quickly as I can."

"How is it working out . . . you working for Dr. Cooley?"

"I'm obliged to him for giving me a job," Elizabeth said. She walked over to the window and looked out at the street. The last of the three newly arrived wagons was passing by in front of the drugstore at that moment. "There seems to be a lot of excitement in town today," she said.

"Oh, yes. There always is excitement when fresh merchandise arrives from outside. President Young has managed to build quite a community here. We can supply our own food, clothing, and building material. But there are still things that make life pleasant that we can only get from back East."

Clay, Parker, Jason, Tobin, and Pecorino backed the three wagons into a position so that they formed three spokes of a wheel. Then they began unloading the wagons and spreading out their goods fanlike, on the ground. It had the desired effect, for soon there were crowds of people drawn to the scene.

"What is this?" one man asked, pointing to an item.

"That's a washing machine," Clay explained. "You open the top up here, add soap, water, and the clothes you want to wash. Then you close the top and start turning this crank. That causes a paddle inside to agitate the water, and the dirt comes right off the clothes. After that, you take the clothes out and run them through these rollers to ring them out. It's ten times faster, and ten times easier than a scrub board."

"Well, what will they think of next?"

Someone pushed through the crowd with an air of self-importance. He stood there for a moment, with his hands on his hips, looking at the display.

"Something I can do for you, mister?" Clay asked.

"My name is Richard Hahs. May I inquire as to who is leading this party?"

"I'm Clay Springer. I'm in charge."

"Mr. Springer, I wonder if you would care to come meet with our broker?"

"Your broker?" Clay asked in surprise.

"Yes. We—that is, the merchants of the city—have decided to have our dealings handled exclusively by one broker. That will greatly simplify things, don't you think?"

"That remains to be seen," Clay said. "Where is your broker?"

"He's standing right over there, away from the crowd," Hahs said. "He thought it might be better if you were able to negotiate without the interference of all the people who are slathering over your load."

"All right, tell him I'll be over directly," Clay said.

Hahs walked way, and Clay went over to tell Parker that he would be negotiating for them through a broker.

"A broker? What does that mean?" Parker asked.

"I think it means they are going to try and take the bidding away," Clay said. "It's a way of getting the goods cheaper."

"Oh. That's not good, is it?" Parker asked.

"It depends. If it means they want to pay a fair price without haggling, then it's just as well. It will save us all a lot of time. But if it means they are going to try and steal the merchandise . . ." He let the thought hang.

"What if they do try that? What can we do about it?"

"Oh, Martha, look at that Dutch oven! We must make Henry buy that for us," a woman gushed.

Clay nodded toward the people who were examining the merchandise. "We don't have any worry," he said. "Look at the way they are going through all this. If we can't make a deal with the merchants, we'll go around them and sell directly to the people."

"Good idea," Parker said.

Clay watched Parker return to the merchandise, then he followed Hahs to meet with the broker. The broker was a big man with red hair and a neatly trimmed beard. He was wearing a uniform of some sort, though Clay had never seen one quite like it.

"Are you the broker?" Clay asked.

"Yes. Talbot's the name. Colonel Talbot."

"Colonel Talbot?" Clay pointed to the uniform. "I've done some time in the army," he said. "But I have to confess, I've never seen a uniform quite like that."

"No, sir, I don't reckon you have," Talbot said. "Seein' as I designed this here uniform my ownself. I'm a colonel in the Righteous Militia."

"The Righteous Militia?"

"We're sort of a private army, so's to speak," Talbot said. "When the Indians give us trouble and there ain't no federal army around to help, why, we take care of things ourselves. And who might you be?"

"I'm Clay Springer."

"You're speakin' for the merchandise?"

"Yes. I have a partner, but I can speak for us both. Now, I'll ask you the same thing. Are you speaking for the merchants?"

"Yes. And I'm prepared to offer you five thousand dollars for the entire load."

Clay stared at Talbot for a second, then turned and walked away without saying a word.

"Hold on there, Mr. Springer!" Talbot called after him. "You aren't even going to make a counter offer?"

Clay stopped, then looked sharply back at Talbot. "You didn't come here to deal, you came here to steal," he said. "And I'm not going to have anything to do with it." Again, he turned and walked away.

"What choice do you have?" Talbot called after him. "I told you, I'm the broker. I'm the only one here that's going to make you any kind of an offer. None of the merchants are going to talk to you."

"The merchants are out of it," Clay said. "I'm going to sell directly to the people."

"Talbot!" Hahs said quickly. "You can't let him do that! The merchants will hang us!"

Talbot followed Clay all the way over to the wagons. "Mister, I don't know how folks do business where you come from, but here we do a little honest bargaining."

"Honest?" Clay said. "There's nothing honest about it."

"All right, all right, I'll admit, maybe I did start the bidding too low. I'm willin' to give it another . . ."

"You!" Parker shouted, seeing Talbot for the first time. "You're the son of a bitch who killed my parents!"

Talbot looked over at Parker as one might look at a harassing cur dog.

"You're crazy, boy. I've never seen you before in my life," Talbot said by way of dismissal.

"You're the one! You think I could ever forget you? You were with the Indians when they attacked our wagon."

Talbot stared directly at Parker. It was obvious this cur wasn't going to just go away with a swift kick.

"Boy, I say you're lyin'," he said. "But even if you wasn't lyin', even if you was tellin' the truth, there wouldn't be nothin' you could do about it. That happened back in Kansas. We're in Utah now."

"How do you know it happened in Kansas?" Clay asked pointedly. "The boy didn't say anything about Kansas."

"Sure he did. He . . ." Talbot started, then, midway through his sentence, his hand suddenly dipped toward his gun.

"He's going for his gun!" Pecorino shouted, but his warning wasn't necessary. Parker was ready for him, and his own pistol was out and booming before Talbot could even bring his gun level. A stain of red spread across Talbot's chest. He wore a surprised look on his face, shocked by the fact that the boy he had left for dead out on the Kansas prairie had come back to kill him. He gurgled a curse as the blood rose in his throat, then dribbled from the corners of his mouth, matting his beard. He fell backward, his heavy body sending a puff of dust as he hit the street. His arms flopped out to either side of him, the unfired gun dangling from a crooked but stilled finger. It had all happened so quickly that the first indication any of those on the outside edge of the crowd got was the booming sound of Parker's gun.

Parker stood there for a long moment, the gun still in his hand, smoke curling up from the end of the barrel. He looked at Talbot's still form lying on the dirt street.

Talbot wasn't the first man he had killed. He may have killed, or at least participated in the killing of Arnold Fenton, when the outlaws hit the wagons. And he certainly had killed some Indians when they were attacked on the trail. But this was the first man he had ever killed face-to-face, and Parker wasn't enjoying the sensation he was feeling right now.

"Drop your gun, boy," a voice said firmly.

Parker looked toward the sound of the voice and saw a man holding a gun pointed at him. The man was wearing a badge, and held a cocked pistol. "Drop the gun now!" he said again, this time with more emphasis.

"Sheriff, Talbot drew first," Clay said.

The sheriff looked around. "Can anyone here vouch for that?"

"Yeah, I can. I seen it," Pecorino said.

"Me too," Tobin added.

"So did I," Jason said.

"You all came in together, didn't you?" the sheriff asked.

"Yes, but that doesn't mean we aren't telling the truth," Clay said.

"What about any of you folks?" the sheriff asked. "Any of you see what happened?"

The local citizens looked at each other and shrugged. Though none of them could validate Clay's claim that Talbot drew first, neither did any of them make the accusation that it was the other way around.

"What is going on here?" another voice asked. This voice was familiar to all of the citizens, and they turned toward him, silent in respect.

"President Young, evidently these gentiles had an altercation with Colonel Talbot. And this boy shot him."

"Are you Brigham Young?" Clay asked.

"I am."

Clay reached for his inside pocket and, as he did so, half a dozen guns were cocked. Quickly,

Clay pulled his hand away, empty. "I have a letter for you," he said.

"Who is the letter from?"

"It's from Colonel Alexander Doniphan," he said.

Young held out his hand. "Let me see the letter."

Slowly, Clay withdrew the letter, then handed it to Brigham Young. Young pulled a pair of glasses out from his vest pocket and put them on, hooking them over each ear, one at a time. He read the letter, then nodded.

"Colonel Doniphan was a friend to us, when we sorely needed a friend," he told the others. "He vouches for Mr. Springer, and asks that we deal with him fairly."

"Perhaps that is what this is all about, President Young," one of the merchants suggested.

"What do you mean, Mr. Thurman?" Young asked.

"As merchants, we authorized Colonel Talbot to act as our broker." Thurman looked at Clay. "But maybe you didn't consider an offer of six times your invoice price to be fair."

"Six times our invoice price?" Clay replied. "Is that the offer you told him to make?"

"It is," Thurman said, and several others around him nodded in agreement.

Clay shook his head. "I would have gladly accepted that offer," he said. "The offer Talbot tendered was five thousand dollars for the entire load. That's less than I paid for it back in Missouri."

"That may be, but that's still no reason to kill him," the sheriff said.

"That's not why I killed him," Parker said. "Our association goes back long before now. Anyway, he drew first."

"I know you say he drew first. But other than the word of your own friends, there is no way we can prove that. Even if what you say is true, that still leaves the question as to why? Why would he draw on you, a mere boy?"

"Because I recognized him as the one who killed my mother and father," Parker said.

"Young man, are you making the accusation that this man killed your mother and father?" Brigham Young asked.

"Yes I am."

"How? Where?" Young asked.

"In Kansas. My mother, father, sister and I were on our way to Oregon. We were attacked by Indians, and he was with them," Parker said, pointing to Talbot's body.

"Oh, how awful," a woman in the crowd said.

"Talbot was riding with the Indians?" another asked.

The sheriff held up his hand to silence the now buzzing crowd. "This leaves us right where we started," he said. "Talbot isn't here to dispute you. You can say that this man killed your parents, but you can't prove it."

"I can prove it," a woman's voice said from the crowd.

"Elizabeth?" Parker recognized her voice immediately. He looked around in astonishment, craning his neck over the crowd.

"Parker!"

A young woman dashed out of the mob and embraced Parker. A murmur of surprise and curiosity rippled through the crowd.

"That was you! I thought I saw you when we rode in, but I couldn't believe it. Clay! Clay, she's alive! Elizabeth is alive!" Parker shouted excitedly.

"I can see that," Clay said, smiling happily at his friend. Clay's smile was mirrored in the faces of Parker's other friends as well.

"You're the girl that's workin' for Dr. Cooley, aren't you?" the sheriff asked.

"Yes."

"What's your relationship to this boy?"

"He's my brother. I thought he was dead. I thought he was killed when Talbot murdered our parents."

"And I was afraid she was dead," Parker said. "When Talbot and the Indians took off with her, I thought I would never see her again."

"She *was* took by the Indians. I heard that from the Lamberts," someone in the crowd said. "You know, she was found by the Sargents, and they brought her into town."

"Miss Stanley," Brigham Young said as he turned to her.

"Yes, sir?" Elizabeth replied.

"You say you can prove that Colonel Talbot was with the Indians when your parents were killed?"

"Yes, sir."

"How can you prove that?"

"Does Talbot have a gold watch on him?"

The sheriff nodded at one of the men closest to Talbot's body, who then bent over and started going through Talbot's pockets. He took out a watch and held it up. Again, there was a murmuring response from the crowd.

"Look there, he does have a watch!"

"And it's gold."

"Look on the inside cover," Elizabeth said. "It says, Elizabeth Gaye Stanley, 10–9–48, and Parker John Stanley, 6–15–52. That's my birthday, and my brother's birthday. Pa had his watch engraved on each occasion."

"What does it say, Earl?" the sheriff asked.

"Just like the girl says," Earl replied.

"Sheriff, I think that is sufficient proof," Brigham Young said. "This case is closed." He looked over at Talbot. "Get the body of this sinner out of here, and let's get on with the business of trading with our guests."

Epilogue

"Come on, Jason," Pecorino called to him. "California's a long way from here." Tobin and Pecorino were mounted on fresh horses, bought with their share of the money. Jason was standing beside his, talking to Parker, who had come to see them off.

"Yeah, I'm coming, just a minute," Jason said. He turned back to Parker. "You sure you won't come with us? We make a pretty good team."

"We do make a good team," Parker said. "But, I've found my sister now, and we're all the family either one of us have. I think we'll stay together for a while."

"I can understand that," Jason said.

"Jason, you comin', or what?" Tobin asked.

"I'm coming," Jason said. He shook Parker's hand. "It's nice knowing you, Parker," he said. Jason swung into the saddle.

"It's been nice knowing you too," Parker said. He looked at the other two. "All of you." He recalled what Penny had said to him when he had left her back in Pueblo. "I hope the three of you have a good rest of your lives."

* * *

Having sold the mules and wagons at a profit, Parker and Clay would be taking Thursday's stagecoach back to Missouri. That was still two days away, which gave Elizabeth time to say her good-byes and make arrangements to go back with them.

For today, though, Elizabeth packed a picnic lunch for them and, borrowing Dr. Cooley's buckboard, the three drove out to the Great Salt Lake. During the trip out to the lake, Clay and Parker were telling Elizabeth about the men who had made the wagon trip with them.

"They were good men, all of them," Parker said.

"That's the truth," Clay agreed. "We couldn't have made it with lesser men." He turned in his seat to look back at Parker, who was riding behind himself and Elizabeth. "And I would have never made it with a lesser partner."

"Clay, stop here," Parker said a few minutes later, when the buckboard reached the edge of the lake.

Clay stopped the team and set the brake.

"I'll just be a few minutes," Parker said. He hopped down, then reached under the seat to get a hat.

"Where in the world did you get that?" Elizabeth said, seeing it for the first time. "What an awful beat-up hat that is."

"You're wrong, Elizabeth," Parker replied. "This is a fine hat. This is as fine a hat as I've ever seen."

"You have to be teasing."

"No, I'm not teasing, am I, Clay?"

"That sure is a great hat," Clay said knowingly.

With the hat in his hand, Parker walked down to the edge of the Great Salt Lake. He stood there for a long moment, looking out over the lake. Then he looked at the hat.

"What's he doing? Now he's talking to that hat!" Elizabeth said.

"He's not talking to a hat."

"Of course he is. I can see him."

"No. What you see is Parker saying good-bye to Marcus Pearson, an old friend," Clay said.

"Well, Marcus, here is the Great Salt Lake," Parker was saying aloud. "I can't see you, but somehow I've got a feeling that you are right here, with us."

Parker threw the hat out over the lake. It sailed for several feet before landing on the surface of the water. There, it floated high and serene. The lake was just like Marcus said it would be.